Philip turned around then, his expression inscrutable. He spoke as he strolled toward her. "You have told me how to behave when we are in public, when we have guests. But what about when we are alone, Charlotte?"

He was getting close, far too close.

"How should I behave then? Or should I behave at all?"

Her instincts told her to leave, to sashay away, to use the movements of her body to distract him from whatever devious purpose he intended.

"Would a good husband touch you like this?" Philip raised his arm, cupped her cheek tenderly in the palm of his hand.

"Or perhaps like this?" He laid his other hand at the small of her back. Charlotte wasn't certain whether he used it to pull her toward him or to keep her still as he stepped closer to her, but suddenly she had no space to breathe, to move. He was there, everywhere, surrounding her.

# Seducing the Duchess

## ASHLEY MARCH

A SIGNET ECLIPSE BOOK

SIGNET ECLIPSE
Published by New American Library, a division of
Penguin Group (USA) Inc., 375 Hudson Street,
New York, New York 10014, USA
Penguin Group (Canada), 90 Eglinton Avenue East, Suite 700, Toronto,
Ontario M4P 2Y3, Canada (a division of Pearson Penguin Canada Inc.)
Penguin Books Ltd., 80 Strand, London WC2R 0RL, England
Penguin Ireland, 25 St. Stephen's Green, Dublin 2,
Ireland (a division of Penguin Books Ltd.)
Penguin Group (Australia), 250 Camberwell Road, Camberwell, Victoria 3124,
Australia (a division of Pearson Australia Group Pty. Ltd.)
Penguin Books India Pvt. Ltd., 11 Community Centre, Panchsheel Park,
New Delhi - 110 017, India
Penguin Group (NZ), 67 Apollo Drive, Rosedale, North Shore 0632,
New Zealand (a division of Pearson New Zealand Ltd.)
Penguin Books (South Africa) (Pty.) Ltd., 24 Sturdee Avenue,
Rosebank, Johannesburg 2196, South Africa

Penguin Books Ltd., Registered Offices:
80 Strand, London WC2R 0RL, England

First published by Signet Eclipse, an imprint of New American Library,
a division of Penguin Group (USA) Inc.

First Printing, October 2010
10   9   8   7   6   5   4   3   2   1

PUBLISHER'S NOTE
This is a work of fiction. Names, characters, places, and incidents either are the
product of the author's imagination or are used fictitiously, and any resemblance
to actual persons, living or dead, business establishments, events, or locales is
entirely coincidental.
    The publisher does not have any control over and does not assume any re-
sponsibility for author or third-party Web sites or their content.

To my mother, who never doubted my success or ability, whom I could always trust for her unfailing support and love. I miss you every single moment.

Alisa Tate, 1960–2010

## ACKNOWLEDGMENTS

I am fortunate not only to become a published author, but to have had two fantastic agents to guide my every step. Stephanie, thank you for being the first reader to fall in love with Philip. And to Alanna, thank you for your enthusiasm when I needed you most.

Also, to my wonderful editors Laura Cifelli and Jesse Feldman. Thank you for your unending patience and kindness, and for transforming Philip into an even better hero.

To Kat and Anna, my fabulous critique partners. I could never have done this without you! Thank you for reading . . . and rereading . . . and rereading. . . .

Finally, to my husband, Luke. For the cleaning and the cooking, for getting up with the baby at four a.m. so I can sleep in, for your many sacrifices and love and support. You bless me every day. 143.

# Chapter 1

She was exquisite, a sin to be indulged in and never repented.

The sound of her laughter, rich and full, a siren's song, caught at his soul. It lured him to the edge of his seat until his nose was nearly pressed against the carriage window.

She did not walk like a lady; she didn't walk like any other woman he had ever known. Every move was calculated to draw masculine eyes to the voluptuous lines of her body—the taunting sway of her hips, the subtle arch of her spine, the inviting tilt of her head. Even the moon desired to be her lover, its long fingers caressing her face and throat in admiring regard before she disappeared into the gambling den.

She was stunning. A beautiful harlot.

Six months he'd spent wooing her. Invitations to the theater, the opera . . . giving his undivided attention in the hopes she would at last turn her affections toward him.

He'd tried to ignore the other men, knowing that soon he would be the one she graced with her smiles, the one she would return home with each night. He'd waited patiently, desperately. Even this night, he'd followed her across London, watching her flit from one social engagement to the next, on the arm of a different man each time . . .

But no longer.

Philip stared at the building's entrance, his heart speeding foolishly.

Straightening, he opened the door and stepped from the carriage.

No sooner had he passed through the foyer of the gambling den than he spotted her, perched on the lap of some rotund, fortunate bastard, her half-naked bosom exposed to his leering gaze. One gloved arm was looped around his neck, a purchase for balance as she leaned forward over the table, the spin of dice cast from her hands in a cheery clatter.

As Philip strolled toward her, he lifted his hands to his cravat, slowly, single-mindedly, untying the careful knot his valet had perfected earlier in the evening.

The cravat fell apart easily in his fingers, and he dragged it loose, the mangled cloth dangling from his fingertips.

"Good evening, gentlemen."

Immediately the gaiety at the small table ceased. Upon spying their new guest, a few of the men scraped their chairs backward, their eyes darting nervously between Philip and the woman.

For too long he'd allowed them to believe that her actions and the company she kept didn't matter to him. Now he was prepared to create a scandal in front of everyone for his message to be undeniably clear: despite her past lovers, she would soon belong to him alone.

The man whose lap she occupied met his eyes and then quickly glanced away, his tongue creeping forth to wet his lips. Philip couldn't blame his indecision; if she had been sitting upon his lap, he would have been loath to give her up as well.

Philip nodded to him. "You, there. What is your name?"

The man's eyes bulged out of their sockets. "Lord Denby, Your Grace. My name is D-Denby."

Philip nodded. "Very good. Denby, my dear fellow, I believe you have something which belongs to me."

A bead of sweat popped out on the man's forehead. "Y-Your Grace?"

The woman, who thus far had only watched the proceedings with an amused smile, narrowed her eyes at Philip and tightened her grip on Denby's neck. "He means *me*, Lord Denby."

"Oh." The man started, and with trembling fingers grasped her arm, frantically trying to push her away. His breath came in short gasps, and he looked at Philip with a plea in his eyes. "She won't come loose, Your Grace."

"Oh, Denby, you coward," she murmured. With a toss of her head, she detached herself from him and rose gracefully from his lap. She stared up at Philip for a long moment, her bright blue eyes daring, mocking.

When she attempted to brush past him, he caught her arm easily in his hand.

The entire room hushed. Philip could feel the heat of a hundred eyes scrutinizing his every movement.

Tomorrow morning this would be in the scandal sheets, upon everyone's lips. Even if he wished it, there was no going back now. He had made his decision.

Her chin had lifted when he halted her departure, and he smiled down at her, a quick flash of teeth. Her sharp indrawn breath gave him no small measure of satisfaction; she was not as immune to him as she would have him believe.

"Lord Denby," he said, his eyes still focused on her sweet, temptress face.

"Yes, Your Grace?"

Philip maneuvered her until she stood between them. "Be a good fellow and hold on to her for a moment, would you? Don't let her escape."

"Er, yes, Your Grace." Denby settled his thick, ring-laden fingers on her shoulders.

"What is the meaning of this?" she demanded, twisting in his grip, her eyes furious, darkening from sapphire to the dusky haze of twilight.

Philip ignored her struggles. He drew her arms together with one hand and draped his cravat over her wrists with the other. Then, quickly so she didn't have a chance to resist, he knotted the material and gave it a tug.

Perfect.

"Very good. You may release her now, Lord Denby."

"What are you doing, Philip? This is ridiculous. Untie me at once!"

It had been a very long time since she had said his name. Even though it fell like a curse from her lips, it was good to hear it all the same.

Philip grasped her upper arm again and looked around the room. Trollops and whores, rakes and scoundrels gaped at him, openmouthed. He nodded to them, ever aware of the sinuous heat seeping from her skin—a twisting, vagrant fire now burning past his gloves to the flesh of his palm.

The woman tried to jerk away, but Philip held her tightly. He would never let her go again. "Release me, you arrogant son of a—"

Philip clapped his hand over her mouth. With a shake of his head, he withdrew a linen kerchief from his pocket. "I had hoped this wouldn't be necessary, but you force my hand, dearest."

She tried to sink her teeth into the flesh of his palm, but fortunately he withdrew it in time. He was certain she'd meant to draw blood. While she sputtered more curses, he proceeded to wrap the cloth around her head, careful only to muffle and not gag her. He tied it at the back of her head, his fingers lingering on the silken tresses of her upswept hair. The sable locks gleamed beneath the dim, smoky lights, tempting his restraint, provoking memories of a time when his hands had tangled freely in her hair. When she had sought his touch, his embrace—

Philip wasn't fast enough to block her kick, her foot connecting painfully with his lower shin.

He crushed her against him, her back to his front, his hands clasped together beneath the delicious swell of her breasts. He tried to move her toward the door, but she hung like a dead weight in his arms. Only when he dragged her did she begin to writhe against him, her body pitching against his.

His audience had apparently recovered from their stupor, for their voices rose in a fevered crescendo as he neared the exit. But the noise was only an indistinct rumble in the background as he focused on her attempts at freedom.

Her elbow managed a sharp blow to his ribs. Philip grunted, then hoisted her over his shoulder and carried her out the door. Her gag was loose enough that her curses brutalized his ears, but Philip continued on with grim determination. She struck his back with her bound fists at every step, but he didn't stop until he stood in front of his carriage.

The groom opened the door.

"Here we are."

She shrieked as he dragged her down and shoved her headfirst through the entrance, his hands helping as they pushed against her bottom.

"Damn you, Philip!"

He climbed in after her, careful to avoid stepping on

her skirts or any scattered appendages. Leaning down, he grabbed her by the elbows and assisted her to a seated position.

The door closed, the carriage shifting as the coachman and groom took their places. The sharp crack of the whip rent the air, and they were off.

Philip allowed a brief sigh of victory.

He'd done it. He had kidnapped his wife.

# Chapter 2

Charlotte took a deep breath, but it did nothing to stop her fists from shaking or her knuckles from knocking together in her lap. He had bound her. She inhaled the masculine scent of his handkerchief, draped loosely across her mouth. He had bound *and* gagged her.

"I hate you, you know," she mumbled, the angry thrum of her blood beating a furious tattoo in her temple. After three years of almost completely ignoring her, tonight he had intentionally and ruthlessly humiliated her.

"Yes, I know. You are always so accommodating as to remind me, lest I forget."

Charlotte considered him carefully. His response was uttered in the same stiff, mocking tone he always adopted with her. Despite this, she could come to only one conclusion: the man sitting across from her was not her husband, the Duke of Rutherford. He was a stranger.

For one, her husband made it a habit to never seek her out. If not for the despicable habit he'd acquired in the past few months of escorting her to the theater or the opera, Charlotte doubted he ever thought about her existence.

He certainly didn't care how much she disliked—no, absolutely *loathed*—the theater and the opera.

But secondly—and most importantly—her husband hated scandals, and especially the people who created them. This, of course, was the primary reason she made her own actions as shocking and outrageous as possible.

It was why she'd become a whore, refusing to relinquish the hope that she would one day break him . . . Only she'd never thought he would abduct her and make a scandal of them both.

As he leaned forward to peer out the curtained window, Charlotte studied his profile. Despite his uncharacteristic display, he did not appear any different externally.

He looked as cold as ever, more marble than man. The carved line of his jaw, the firm sculpture of his mouth—not even a strand of black hair dared to stray from its place.

The violent sway of the carriage as the coachman urged the horses faster and faster did not seem to unnerve him. She, on the other hand, was close to lurching forward into the chasm of space between them.

He turned to face her, and she started with the realization that she'd been staring at him for quite a while. And he must have known she was; Philip somehow always seemed to know everything.

"Shall I remove the handkerchief?"

His polite tone and small smile made Charlotte narrow her eyes in suspicion.

She knew this tilt of his lips at five degrees indicated humor, whereas an exaggeration at forty degrees revealed his condescension and indulgence. Over the past three years she had become rather adept at reading his every expression, picking apart his every utterance to find the meaning behind the screen of words.

And it was important to distinguish the two lip movements, if for no other reason than that he very rarely allowed any trace of genuine emotion to escape through his carefully guarded stoicism. She had witnessed his ducal mask slip on only two other occasions, and both times something had gone dismally awry.

Shifting uneasily in her seat, she attempted to decipher the devious thought which had provoked that singularly frightful curve of his lips. He could be smiling simply because he was pleased with himself—the ass—or because he enjoyed the sight of her all trussed and trundled up like a Christmas Day goose. Or, she reflected hopefully, he could be smiling because he was considering sending her to another country, after which he could go about finding a new wife, a better wife. She would like to go to another country, far away from him, where memories could not taint each day.

"Ah, yes." His slight smile disappeared, his lips folding into a neat, tightly formed line. "I had forgotten for a moment that I am the spawn of Satan. Of course you don't wish to speak with me."

"There's nothing to say that hasn't already been said between us. Or are you at last willing to petition for a divorce?" Her words were muffled as the linen cloth rubbed over her lips, but she could tell by the way he stared at her, his gaze unreadable, that he understood the words. She was well accustomed to his lack of expression, this defense of his.

It always made her want to shake him until a shadow of humanity slipped through his facade—anything but this emotionless detachment. However, since he had tied her hands together so cleverly with his cravat, she could only swallow her exasperation.

She hated dukes, the whole stupid, stubborn lot of them, but Philip in particular.

The carriage veered around a corner too sharply,

sending Charlotte tumbling forward. She screamed, certain that her head was going to catch her fall before she could maneuver her elbows beneath her.

And then she cursed, because rather than either her head or her elbows hitting the floor, her husband caught her.

His hands steadied her shoulders, his breath fanning over her hair. Charlotte looked up. "Why is Fitzjames driving so bloody fast?"

In the pale moonlight streaming through the window, she could see his silver eyes flicker. Charlotte lifted a defiant brow. Along with her flirtations and coquetry, she had refined her rather spectacular flair for profanity.

*Take that, your dukeliness.*

But Philip only drew her up to sit beside him, his thigh uncomfortably close to hers. Charlotte sucked in a breath when he reached behind her head and untied his handkerchief. Then he leaned back to sit as straight and rigid as before while he tucked the linen cloth into his pocket.

"There. Now you may chatter away as you like."

"Sod off."

"Very clever, my dear. Your improvement of mind and vocabulary is impressive, as always."

Charlotte scowled. She hated when he used that particular condescending tone. Though she tried, she could never quite match it. Instead she settled for shoving her shoulder against him. "At least move over, then." His nearness was vastly annoying; the heat radiating from his body made her all too aware of him. It had taken her a long time to convince herself she was no longer attracted to him, and she wasn't willing to give up her hard-won indifference so easily.

Of course, she could have clambered to the other seat, but she didn't want to face backward. If Philip insisted on being rude and not giving her the forward-facing seat, then he would just have to share it.

But at a distance.

He swiveled his head and looked down his nose at her with those silver moonlight eyes that made her think of angels and demons and soft, quiet rain. "You might discover that if you exercise your manners and ask nicely, I will accede to your wish without the use of physical force."

Charlotte leaned away, her fingers curling into her palms. "Would you mind terribly, Your Grace, if you scooted your ass over a few inches? Perhaps a foot?" Tilting her head, she batted her eyelashes at him.

His lips quirked to a ten-degree angle. Egad, the man was practically grinning.

"Very nice attempt, sweetheart. But you forgot to say please."

She bared her teeth. "Very well. *Please* move your rotten, snobbish, narcissistic ass over to the other side."

He regarded her for a long, silent moment, then: "Perhaps I shouldn't have removed the kerchief after all."

Really, it was too much. Charlotte lunged at him.

Philip almost laughed. Almost. But he was too busy defending himself from the hellion who rammed her bound fists at his ribs to give in to the urge.

It was incredible. He hadn't felt this alive in . . . well, since before they had married, when he was still courting her, wooing her, trying to seduce her.

He winced as her elbow caught his midsection, her body twisting and contorting in curious ways while she attempted to do him injury.

Philip wrapped one arm around her waist and the other around her chest. Amazingly, she had somehow come to be sitting on his lap.

Perhaps not sitting, exactly. Sprawled would be a much more accurate description: her head laid against his shoulder, tipped back so she could glare at him; her legs were parted over his knee, her slippered feet scrambling to find some way to propel herself out of his hold.

He knew he should let her go. He knew she hated being restrained, hated being controlled. But her body was soft, and the light scent of jasmine rose to his nostrils. She was everything he'd never known he'd wanted, and she was in his arms.

"Philip?"

His gullible heart leaped. If he hadn't known better, he would have thought by the way she said his name—breathy, with a touch of adoration, as if he were the only man in her world—that she actually enjoyed his embrace.

But he did know better. Philip subdued his recalcitrant heart. "Yes?"

"If you do not release me at once, I vow that at the first opportunity I shall incapacitate you, and any hope you have of ever reproducing will be lost."

Philip carefully set her away from him. "I had forgotten how charming and pleasant you can be."

"Only with you, dear husband. Only with you." She thrust out her arms. "You may untie my wrists as well."

"I don't suppose you would say please."

"I don't suppose you really care that much for a son."

Philip cleared his throat, swallowing his laughter. "I will allow you to use that threat only so often. Once we are out of the confines of this carriage, I will be better able to protect myself."

Her eyes narrowed, a thin smile tilting her lips. "You may try."

His hands closed around her wrists, so delicate, so fragile beneath his fingers. He remembered how smooth, like satin heat, her skin had once felt beneath his touch. Then there had been no gloves to encumber him; it had been only his flesh against hers. Philip traced a long, lingering trail over her wrists with his thumbs.

Charlotte made a noise in her throat, and he glanced up. Her expression was inscrutable. "Just untie the damned cravat," she ordered him.

Philip's fingers stilled. An eternity had passed since that night, three years ago. Though only thin scraps of cloth, their gloves were yet another impenetrable veil between them, a reminder that the only thing they shared now was the past.

It took him only a moment to loosen the binding. As soon as she was free, Charlotte slid away from him.

Philip turned his head as he tucked the cloth in his pocket, alongside the handkerchief.

"Why did you abduct me?"

Staring at the window, he watched Charlotte's reflection as the moon chased the carriage through the standing shadows of the trees.

He drew in a deep breath. "Your actions do not become a lady of your station. The Duchess of Rutherford, a halfpenny whore."

"Ah. I've embarrassed you. I've embarrassed the Rutherford name. What a shame. But then, you knew I wasn't a lady when you married me. You chose me, Philip. Or have you forgotten?"

"I made a mistake." It was, possibly, the first time in his entire life—certainly the first he could remember—that he'd uttered those words.

Charlotte laughed—a throaty, full-bodied sound, so rich and warm he wanted to laugh, too. He turned to face her, and was taken aback by the bleakness in her eyes.

"A mistake." Her smile taunted him. He knew what she was thinking: if he had granted her request for a divorce when she first asked, she wouldn't have wasted three years of her life as his duchess. "But why now, Philip? You never gave a damn in the past about what I did, who I lifted my skirts for."

He stiffened.

"Damn you, Philip! Answer me!"

She blinked, once, twice, before jerking her head to look out her side of the carriage—but not before he saw the sheen of unshed tears glistening brightly in her eyes.

"It's simple, my dear," he drawled. "You have become a liability. I will return you to Ruthven Manor, where you will no longer be able to feed the rumor mills."

Her head was turned away from him, but Philip clearly heard the sound she made at his pronouncement.

She snorted.

At him.

A duke.

He didn't know why he should be so surprised. She'd already cursed at him, laughed at him—hell, she'd even attacked him. And she was the only person he knew who didn't pander to or fawn over him.

If it had been anyone else, he would not have tolerated the insolence. But he had long since learned that Charlotte did not quaver at his coldest glare, nor did she fear his cutting tone.

Her expression was scornful as she turned to him. "Do not think that abandoning me in the countryside will solve your problems."

She leaned toward him, a seductive pout on her lips. Philip forgot to breathe as her gloved hand lifted and she trailed a finger along his jaw. He could not remember the last time she had touched him like this—a voluntary, intimate gesture.

Her breath fell softly against his skin as she murmured, "Until you grant my request, I am determined to do everything I can to make your life a living hell." Her finger paused, then bounced off the tip of his nose at precisely the same time she said, "Your Grace."

Growling, Philip caught the offending appendage before she could draw her hand away. "You have become quite accomplished, haven't you? Who could have known that the charming little squire's daughter would become so successful as a mistress to the masses?"

She tried to tug her hand away, but he held firm, turning it over in his grasp until her palm faced upward.

Philip looked into her eyes. "Do you want me to release you?"

"Yes."

He used his other hand to stroke her palm, his index finger tracing paths inward and outward, always returning to the center, like the rays of the sun. "And yet you allow other men to touch you."

Philip skimmed his fingers upward, over her wrist, along the inside of her elbow, until he reached the edge of her glove. "To undress you."

He pinched the fabric between his fingers and pulled, dragging her glove downward. It was a prolonged torture, a delicious torment as inch by inch more of her skin was revealed. She might put her more generous endowments on display for other men to admire, but this—this flesh of her arm, gleaming so white and pale in the black night—this intimacy belonged to him.

No matter how many men she had taken as lovers, no matter how many had seen her nude in the past, he vowed no other would ever again have the privilege to view her thus.

Philip exhaled—a long, shuddering breath—as the glove rolled past her wrist and over her hand, finally falling away from her fingertips.

He drew her hand to his mouth, pressing his lips to the center of her palm. "To kiss you."

She said nothing. But he felt her tremble, and his own hand was none too steady as he kissed her again.

"To—"

The door to the carriage opened. "We've arrived, Your Grace."

Philip blinked at Gilpin, the groom. He hadn't even realized they'd stopped, so entranced had he become.

Charlotte hastily withdrew her hand from his. "Where are we?" she asked the groom. Her profile was serene, her voice calm. Philip wondered if he had imagined the trembling.

"Old Fane's Crossing, Your Grace."

She turned to him. "My glove, Philip."

He bent his head, searching the shadows. "I sent Fallon ahead to arrange for rooms. Supper will be waiting, and baths will be prepared soon afterward. Your maid is—"

Philip glanced up as the carriage shifted.

She was gone.

# Chapter 3

Philip shoved through the door to the inn. The sounds of raucous laughter and whistling immediately assaulted his ears.

He should have chained her and swallowed the damned key.

The public room smelled dark and dank, of stale beer and old blood, the dim lights serving only to accentuate the atmosphere of vulgarity and ruthlessness. Philip swept the room with a glower and tensed when he spied Charlotte standing on a table in the middle of the room. She was in the process of peeling off her other glove.

Her eyes sparked as she watched him approach, her smile slow and taunting.

One of the men at the table, a young pup who appeared to be fresh out of university, stretched a hand toward her ankle. He howled in pain as Philip wrenched his fingers and threw him to the ground.

Philip's blood pounded in his veins, hot and heavy, as he stared down at the man he had leveled. He usually carried out his battles with wit and the sharp blade of his tongue, but God, it felt good to be uncivilized, if only for a few minutes.

Something fell on his head, and Philip ignored the crowd's heckling as he reached to draw it away. He glanced at the long ivory kid glove hanging from his fingertips, then up at Charlotte.

Her skin was bare from her hands to her shoulders, and she glared at him in challenge as she lifted her arms to the crowd. "What do you say, gentlemen? Do you want to see more?"

A chorus of slurred voices rose in encouragement, and she lowered her eyes once again to his as she began to pluck the pins from her hair.

As each pin fell with a defiant *ping* before him, and every lock of her sable brown hair curled seductively around her shoulders, a black, growing rage built inside Philip. It hummed in his blood, pulsed at his temples, curved his mouth into a cruel sneer.

He leaned forward and flattened his palms over the wood of the table, its surface splintered and rough beneath his hands.

The table tipped, and Charlotte cried out and went tumbling to her knees, her fingers white at the knuckles as she fought for balance.

Philip pushed harder, sending the other occupants at the table scattering and forcing her to slide into the brace of his arms.

She fought to escape him, the sweet smell of jasmine rising to his nostrils as her hair brushed against his jaw. And if he tilted his head at just the right angle, he could glimpse the edges of her dark pink nipples when she arched her back in an effort to twist away from him.

As Philip admired the delightful view she presented, he revised his earlier thought: it felt *damned bloody good* to be uncivilized.

He tucked her against his chest, careful to dodge

the wild flailing of her arms and legs. Drunken shouts from the other patrons demanded he release her, but he ignored them and headed toward the innkeeper, a surly, red-bearded man wearing a cloth wrapped around his waist. The man scratched at his beard as Philip neared.

"The Duke of Rutherford. I believe my man arranged for a few rooms."

The innkeeper's torso jerked forward, an unaccustomed bow. Philip turned his chin aside to avoid Charlotte's thrashing head. The innkeeper stared. "Two floors up, sixth door on the left. The servants' rooms are across the hall, Your Grace."

Philip swung around and carried her up the stairs, down the corridor, and into his rented room.

He kicked the door closed, his chest heaving with the effort to restrain her. She had never ceased struggling, and his cheeks stung where her hair whipped across his face, her knees and elbows landing with splendid accuracy against the pit of his stomach and across his lower ribs.

Before she could manage to incapacitate him with a thrust to his groin, Philip strode forward and tossed her onto the bed.

For a moment, he couldn't move. For a moment, he forgot he was the ninth Duke of Rutherford, cold and disciplined and born to uphold the honor of his forefathers—a man trained since childhood to resist his baser instincts, to resist the call of temptation.

Her arms were propped behind her back, holding herself up, her knees bent as if prepared to launch herself at him again, her skirts fallen to her thighs and revealing a pair of luscious, slimly curved legs encased in scarlet-trimmed stockings. Her eyes sparked blue fire as she looked at him—*dared* him to do what every sex-starved muscle in his body demanded—to throw himself

on top of her and soothe his anger and jealousy between
her spread thighs.

Hell, even his oxygen-deprived brain argued that he
had already gone down an irreversible path tonight by
kidnapping her and using his fists like a commoner to
knock down his competition.

Why shouldn't he finish the evening out like a king,
feasting upon the smooth, elegant curves of her body,
slaking the lust he'd kept imprisoned inside for so
long?

But it was the knowledge that she wanted him to do
it, to prove himself to be no better than the hundreds of
other men who hungered for her—it was this that stayed
him, that stiffened his resolve to wait. Unlike the others,
he was the only one who had ever claimed her heart . . .
and he would be the only one ever to do so again.

Charlotte's arms ached from holding the alluring position she'd immediately moved into when Philip threw
her on the bed.

At times, her body was the only defense she could use,
hers to manipulate into attracting men, to have them do
exactly as she wanted. She knew how to use her lips, her
eyes, the touch of her hand to full advantage—she could
invite men closer or repel them with a single look, without her heart ever having to become involved.

Her beauty assured that, if she desired it, she would
never have to be alone again. Yet despite her dozens of
admirers, none had ever been able to soothe the ache of
loneliness that she woke to each morning and escaped
from as she fell asleep each evening.

Charlotte swallowed the jagged lump of disappointment as Philip's eyes shuttered once again, hiding the
flare of desire she'd witnessed for the space of a heartbeat. He was the only man who'd ever been able to see

through her pretense, the only one to throw her beauty and her vanity back in her face.

But Charlotte had learned much over the years. She had watched him, studied him, tried to understand what had first drawn her to him. And she had discovered that just as she used a provocative pout or a husky softening of her voice, he employed patience and persistence to have his own way.

And, by God, it was time she showed him she was not the powerless little fool she had been when he had seduced and married her.

Charlotte turned her head to the side, tilted her neck, pasted an inviting smile on her lips, and looked at him through her lashes.

Hmm. Nothing. He betrayed not even a flicker of interest as he stared at her.

Sliding her legs along the bed, she moved slowly, silkily—the fluid motion meant to call attention to the lines of her body, sleek and feminine. As she rose to her feet, his expression grew darker, more intense, and for a frightening moment Charlotte felt as if he could see right into her soul.

She lowered her eyes to the opening of his shirt, the warm tone of his skin sprinkled with black hair. Electricity slid along her arms as she moved toward him, and though neither of them said anything, the tension radiating from his body told her he was not as unaffected as he appeared.

Her bare hand, free of the restricting propriety of her glove, touched his coat, her palm resting above his heart for a long, breathless moment. His silver eyes burned into her, his mouth relaxed, his chin firm—no movement at all except the steady pounding of his heart beneath her hand.

She circled him—their only point of contact the pads

of her fingertips across his chest, the tense muscles of his shoulder, his back, his other shoulder.

And still he did not move.

He was a statue, immobile, apparently unconcerned by her careful caress. And yet, as she placed her palm once more over his chest, she could feel his heart thrumming at a frantic pace.

A sweet song of victory coursed through her veins, and Charlotte curved her lips in a sultry smile as she slid her hands up, wrapped them around his neck. She pressed her body along the full length of his, her breasts rubbed to erect points across the fine wool of his waistcoat.

It had taken her three years, but she had finally won this battle. Now he was the one to be seduced, his emotions the ones to be toyed with, his heart the one to be—

"Enough."

His fingers bit into her wrists as he pried her arms from around his neck, his grip harsh and punishing when he thrust her away from him.

Charlotte frowned, suddenly uncertain. She recoiled at the pale gleam of disgust shining in his eyes as they raked over her, his mouth curled in disdain at the temptation she had offered him.

His voice rolled over her like a crack of thunder, breaking apart her illusion of confidence. "Did you expect me to react like all the others? Did you think I would throw you to the floor or bend you over the bed and rut you like an animal?" He strode forward and clasped her shoulders, his grip heavy with condemnation as he shook her. "You will not act the whore with me, Charlotte. Do you understand?"

He shook her again, roaring as he repeated the question, "Do you understand?"

After a frozen moment of silence, Charlotte tilted her head back, tipping her mouth at the corners. "Old habits, you know. I don't suppose I know how to act any other way—other than as a *whore*." She brought her hand to his jaw, leaned in close, her lips a breath away from his skin. "Does it offend you? I'm dreadfully sorry. Perhaps you should cast me aside and find a new wife."

He slashed her a dark look, his eyes the color of a storm cloud, brewing with violence and wrath, before he brushed her off and stalked away to the other side of the room.

Charlotte sat on the bed and slipped off her shoes. She stared at her fingers, their slight trembling, and clenched her hands into fists to still the movement. "God knows you've put up with me long enough. You should be close to gaining your sainthood now, Philip. And you deserve a good wife, a good duchess, someone who is as stiff and cold as you are."

She tucked her hair behind her ear so she could watch him out of the corner of her eye. Propping one leg up on the coverlet, she pulled her dress and petticoats over her knee and reached to untie her garter. "Someone who will accommodate you in bed, who won't cry when you leave her to go to your mistress, someone who doesn't welcome other men as her lovers."

His back had been turned to her, but at her last word he pivoted on his heel, a thoughtful expression creasing his brow as he strolled toward the bed. "Hmm. That does sound rather appealing."

Charlotte angled her body toward him so he could see as she drew her stocking down her leg. "Indeed. Don't forget that she could be someone that the *ton* respects as well. Perhaps the daughter of a marquess or earl, even."

Philip paused as he removed his boots. "Do you think she would read the *Times* to me at breakfast?"

Her fingers froze in midair, her other stocking suspended above the floor. It was the first time he'd ever actively acknowledged her suggestion that he marry someone else. "Perhaps."

She saw him nod as he lay down on top of the bed, fully clothed, his arms crossed behind his head as a pillow. Charlotte frowned at him. "Are you planning to sleep like that?"

He glanced at her, his brows knit in consternation. "You mean you aren't going to undress me?"

"You have a valet. Summon him."

"Do you think she would?"

"Who?"

"My ideal wife." A roguish grin crossed his lips, and Charlotte sucked in a breath at the sight of it.

It transformed his face—gone was the ducal veneer, the aristocratic posing and the duty-bound polish. In its place was a man who could melt a woman's heart with one glance of his liquid-silver eyes, who could have her quivering and helpless in his arms just because he said her name in that dark, velvet-edged voice of his.

Charlotte straightened. She was no longer that woman. "Probably not," she said crisply, and turned away, all of her intentions to continue taunting him as she removed her clothing forgotten.

"Oh," he said. The bed groaned as he moved to blow out the brace of candles nearby. "Well, then, since I cannot have an ideal wife, I suppose I shall just keep you."

Charlotte flopped onto her back and stared up at the ceiling—a black void of nothingness high above her head. "Me."

The bed frame creaked again as he lay down beside her. "Yes, you."

"A strumpet."

A heartbeat of silence, and then: "I prefer to think of you as a sheep."

Charlotte choked as she inhaled. She twisted her neck to look at him, but all she could see were the stark angles of his profile, and she focused on the aquiline jut of his nose. "A sheep?"

"Yes, a metaphor for a woman led astray. A woman who, by the kind and gentle reprimand of her noble husband, might be brought back to the straight and narrow path."

She huffed. "If I am a sheep in your metaphor, then you must be—"

"God," he finished, his voice smug. And although she could not see it, she knew he was smirking.

Charlotte crossed her arms over her chest—which was ridiculous, really, because not only could he not see her affronted expression in the darkness, but she was also lying down.

"I presume by your silence you do not agree with my deified role?"

"I think I'd rather go to hell than have you rescue me," she said, then turned her back to him.

Charlotte was all too aware that he lay not half a foot from her. If she reached out her arm, she would be able to touch him. And it was entirely possible that sometime during the night the space between them might diminish, and she might wake up in the morning with his leg thrown over hers, or her head pillowed on his chest.

There was a reason Charlotte had not shared a bed with a man for three years. It was far too intimate.

It only then occurred to her that they were sleeping in the same room—so caught up had she become in teasing and testing him that she hadn't even inquired why she didn't have a separate chamber. She could only assume he did not trust her to leave his sight.

A quiet snore rumbled from Philip's direction. Breathing a small sigh, Charlotte tucked her elbow beneath her head and counted as each second passed.

After five minutes, she lifted herself inch by inch off the bed—first her head, then her arms, her torso, swinging her legs to the floor—until finally she stood, triumphant, her hands on her hips as she stared down at his sleeping form.

Tiptoeing over to the door, Charlotte grasped the doorknob in her hand and—

Nothing. It wouldn't turn.

She bent down to peer through the keyhole, to see if someone had locked the door from the hallway, and—

She gasped as his hands wrapped around her elbows and pulled her upward. His breath ruffled her hair as he whispered in her ear, "Did you honestly think I would give you the chance to escape?"

"I was going to find my room."

His thumbs caressed the sensitive skin on the inside of her arms. "You do not have a room. Come, Charlotte." He trailed his fingers down to her hand, turning her around. "We are husband and wife. We do not need two rooms, do we?"

She shivered at his unwelcome touch. "You bastard."

His soft chuckle was as deep and dark as the devil himself. "It's been quite a long time since I've heard that word from your lips, my dear."

She ripped her hands from his hold. "You were never around to hear me say it. If you had been, you would have heard that and much, much more."

"Forgive me. The thought of searching every home in London to find my wayward wife did not appeal to me. Besides, I've never been too fond of an overcrowded bed. When I wish to slip between a woman's thighs, I don't want to find another man already there, having his turn."

Her palm cracked against his cheek, the sound as sharp as the pain in her chest.

Philip caught her arm when she would have dropped it to her side, and her heart drummed an accelerated staccato at the silver flash of his eyes. But he only raised her hand to his mouth, his lips brushing over her knuckles in a light caress, as if they were a gentleman and a lady meeting for the first time at a crowded London soiree.

Except they were alone, and she wore no gloves to protect her from feeling the warm strength of his hand, the firm, hot, velvet pressure of his mouth against her skin. And God help them, because they both knew he was no gentleman, and she was certainly not a lady.

"Apologies," he murmured. "That was badly done of me."

Charlotte swallowed. It was the first time he'd ever apologized to her—for anything.

But it was too late to pretend to be civil now. One moment could not undo the years of animosity and indifference. The chasm of silence and distance could never be bridged.

Not even by an apology and a kiss.

Or by revealing the truth.

Yet if he thought he had hurt her, he was mistaken. His cruel words might have crushed her spirit a long time ago, but now they only wounded her pride.

Charlotte lifted her chin and smiled. "No apologies, Your Grace. It isn't becoming to one of your station. Remember, you are a duke, after all."

Philip gritted his teeth as he watched Charlotte's dark form sashay back to the bed, the lines of her body caressed by a sliver of moonlight peeking through the curtains.

"Shall I call for your maid to help you undress?" he asked, silently berating himself for losing his temper. While he had been determined to resist the temptation she presented, her seductive touch had nearly been his undoing. It seemed the longer he was around her, the more difficult it became to maintain his composure.

Worst of all, he'd lashed out at her for it, giving her yet another reason why she should hate him.

She stilled. "Yes, please do."

A few minutes later the candles were lit again and Philip stood next to the door as Charlotte's maid unbuttoned, untied, and unhooked her layers of gown, petticoats, and corset. He had only a brief glimpse of her cotton shift before she slipped on a dressing gown.

At Charlotte's dismissal, the maid curtsied to them both and hurried out of the room.

"This is new." She turned around, her eyes narrowed. "You've begun purchasing clothes for me, Philip. How . . . strange."

He wasn't sure why his heart pounded so as she fingered the ties of her dressing gown. He had bought it for himself, not for her. He'd wanted to see if the royal blue color would match the hue of her eyes. He had thought of how lovely she would be, her rich, luxurious hair a contrast to the jeweled tone of the robe.

His imagination had not come close to doing her beauty justice.

In comparison to the sparkling sapphire brilliance of her eyes, the gown appeared faded and worn, the fabric less lustrous as her hair shone like spun silk in the candlelight.

She smoothed the material over her waist, her hips, before glancing up at him. "Thank you."

Philip pried his hands apart behind his back, but he didn't step forward. He didn't trust himself to get within a foot of her at the moment. "You like it, then?"

Charlotte nodded. "Yes. It must have cost you a fortune. I've never seen a design so simple, yet so intricate."

He swallowed. Civility. He was tempted to barge into the other room, grab the entire trunk of clothes he had brought along, and dump it out at her feet—if only to gain him five more minutes free of her contempt and hatred.

It was maddening how easily she made him forget that he was a duke, that he was not the type of man to engage in spontaneity, someone who would give in to his impulses to do everything he could to be near her, to make her happy.

If it had been the least likely, he might have considered that she was changing him. For a moment—only ten seconds, if one were to be exact—Philip was uncertain of what he should say, what he should do.

And so he stared at Charlotte, ensuring that his expression was impassive, that it gave nothing away he didn't want her to see. Eventually her small smile slipped and, lowering her arms, she returned to the bed.

Philip hesitated. "I—"

She shifted to her side, her back toward him.

He closed his mouth. He snuffed out the candles with his fingertips, but did not remove his own clothing. Sharing a bed with her was a difficult enough test to his willpower.

Lying down, he concentrated on his breathing for what seemed an interminable length of time—slow, relaxed movements of his chest, in and out, in and out—anything to keep him from dwelling on how close she was, how easy it would be to reach out his hand and stroke her hair.

An eternity later, Charlotte sighed in her sleep and twisted toward him, her arm flung out so that her fingers brushed across his ribs. His breath seized in his chest, the calmness he had strived for immediately disappearing.

It took him almost another ten minutes to resign himself to sleeping in the chair on the opposite side of the room—close enough so he could prevent her from trying to escape in the middle of the night, yet far enough away to have a chance of resisting the temptation her restless body offered.

Philip leaned his head against the back of the chair and closed his eyes, but he could not dismiss the memory of Charlotte as she'd stood in front of him earlier, her eyes promising wickedness, her palm pressed against his wildly racing heart.

As self-centered as it seemed to be now, he'd always assumed her harlot performance was all a show of bravado for his benefit, meant to make him succumb to her demands.

He knew she'd taken lovers over the years—a woman wasn't rumored to have slept with more than a dozen men without there being some truth to the accusation—but he couldn't fault her for it. After all, he'd dismissed his mistress only six months ago.

But he'd deluded himself into thinking that Charlotte did it only to spite him; it appeared that she actually enjoyed her life as a fallen woman.

She no longer possessed any of the awkward shyness she had exhibited around him at the age of nineteen, that small flaw in the midst of her vibrancy and exuberance which had made her susceptible to a duke's flattery and attention.

Charlotte was confident now. She was independent.

She didn't need him at all, and that scared the hell out of him.

# Chapter 4

"Yer Grace, Yer Grace."

Charlotte growled and batted at the hand tapping her shoulder.

"Yer Grace, please. He said we must be in the courtyard in ten minutes."

Charlotte rolled over and cracked one eyelid open. The room was awash in lavender predawn shadows. Groaning, she promptly shut it again and wondered why she'd never considered murder as an option to rid herself of her overbearing, despotic husband.

It was criminal to expect her to rise from bed this early.

Charlotte lifted an arm and waved her maid away with a flick of her wrist. The pathetically weak motion did no more than dislodge the coverlet from her shoulder, which subsequently made her grumble at the rush of cold air surging inside her warm haven.

Anne's worried footsteps paced around the side of the bed. "We've only seven minutes more, Yer Grace. He said he would be angry if we were late. Oh, please sit up. I will help you with everything else. Yer Grace? Yer Grace?"

Charlotte burrowed deeper beneath the covers. "You may tell that old fusspot to go bugger himself."

"Oh, dear."

A meager light flickered across her eyelids, and Charlotte opened her eyes once more to find the maid at the window, worrying the curtain with anxious fingers as she peeked at the courtyard below.

"He has his timepiece out."

Charlotte grunted and flung her pillow over her head.

"Five more minutes. And he's frowning something awful now."

"Hmm. How dreadful."

Although she lay inert in the bed, pretending to be entirely unconcerned with Philip's mandate or the passage of time, she could not keep her heart from beating faster with each warning the maid called out.

She had woken in the middle of the night with a fantastic retort to his callous words. It was much better than her previous comment about his station, and she was dying to have another confrontation with him now.

"Three min—" Anne cut herself off, gasping.

Charlotte jerked upward, swatting her hair out of her face. "What is it?"

Her eyes darted from the swaying curtain to the maid, who had backed up to the adjoining wall. Anne's hand palpitated against her chest, as if she were trying to help her heart restore blood to her pallid cheeks. "He's coming," she whispered.

"What? I thought he said ten minutes."

"He did. I don't know—"

Charlotte pointed to the door. "Quick! Leave before he gets here."

Anne shifted from foot to foot. "Are you certain? We still have time—"

"Now! Go, go." She waited only long enough for the maid to scurry out before she flopped back down and yanked the covers to her chin, forcing herself to take deep, measured breaths.

She closed her eyes, but they immediately popped open, as if looking at the wall in front of her could somehow help her hear the approach of his footsteps.

She doubted she would be able to hear anything above the incessant drumming of her pulse; it pounded in her ears, mocking her attempt at composure, blurring the words in her mind that she had memorized during the night. She opened her mouth, as if moving her lips could help her to grasp the phrase she needed to set him in his place once and for all.

The hinges of the door squealed as it opened, and Charlotte flinched as if he had slammed it against the wall. She squeezed her eyes tight as he neared.

Suddenly the covers were wrenched away from her. Charlotte gasped and sat up, instinctively reaching down to pull her shift over her legs. She glared at Philip, who stood at the foot of the bed, his eyebrow arched in amusement as he watched her scramble to find her dignity.

"Good morning, Duchess."

Charlotte took a deep breath and squared her shoulders—not an easy feat to accomplish when one hand was busy tugging a thin scrap of cotton over her thigh and the other was holding her up. "You are not the first ugly man."

Philip's brow lowered.

No, that didn't sound right.

"You—you are not the first man . . ."

Blast it all. Charlotte released her death grip on her shift and climbed off the bed. "You are not the first man to get ugly when denied an invitation to my bed." She poked him in the chest.

Philip wrapped his hand around her finger. "Been holding that one in, have you?"

His other hand lifted to cup her cheek, then slid beneath her jaw and around to the nape of her neck. Charlotte opened her mouth to demand that he release her, but before she could speak, he bent forward and placed a gentle, almost-tender kiss on her forehead.

His lips brushed her skin as he spoke. "Do you not realize, Charlotte? I have no need for an invitation."

"Because you are my husband and I am your property," she mumbled dully.

"No," he said, stepping away to survey her state of undress with cold regard. "Because I have no wish to warm your bed, or to have you warm mine."

Charlotte lifted her chin, determined to hide how his words stung her pride. It wasn't as if she wanted to lie with him again. She didn't. She only wanted him to desire her so she could have something to hold over him, a way to control him, so the world wouldn't seem so out of balance whenever he came close.

"That is my wish as well," she said.

"Very good. I am glad we understand one another. Although there will come a time when we will have to copulate for the sake of producing an heir, I do not foresee a need for such anytime soon."

She could think of nothing more horrifying than creating a child with him, a permanent bond he could use to hold her to him forever.

"I will never—"

He held up his hand, his eyes flashing in warning. "Never say never, my dearest. I should so hate to prove you wrong."

Charlotte bared her teeth. "I will never invite you to my bed, no matter the reason. And I would rather die than bear your child."

Philip clucked his tongue. "Such harsh words for a

woman in nothing but her nightclothes. Come now, darling. I am not tempted by your scandalous dress, and we must be on our way." He turned his back on her. "You have already exceeded your allotted ten minutes, but if you will make haste now, I shall allow you to dress without my assistance."

A slow smile tugged at her lips. She supposed he meant for his threat to send her running to the door, hollering for Anne. But the thought of having her husband, the Duke of Rutherford, the same man who behaved as if he held up the heavens with his bare hands, act as her lady's maid . . . Well, the idea was far too appealing.

Charlotte stretched and yawned. She padded over to the nearby chair and sat, waiting and watching.

It did not take long before Philip spoke again. "You are not getting dressed."

She leaned her head back against the chair and crossed her legs. "How perceptive of you."

He turned around, his gaze spearing her in her idle pose. "Very well."

No two words had ever before sent such a rush of anticipation creeping up Charlotte's spine as those did, spoken with a hint of a growl beneath his soft, cultured accent.

He left the room for only a moment, and when he returned, he carried in his arms a golden dress, its material gleaming bronze as he stepped through a splash of sunlight.

If Charlotte had been someone else, and he had been a different man, she would have thought he appeared quite dashing and handsome as he strolled toward her, his eyes lit with purpose, his mouth firm with determination.

He paused before her. She raised her leg and pointed her foot. Then she wiggled her toes. "Stockings first, please."

A burst of laughter nearly escaped her throat as he glared down at her leg, his nostrils flaring. But then he lifted his gaze and smiled at her—a quick, blinding flash of teeth, much too charming—and Charlotte straightened as warning bells rang in her ears—

"As you wish, Your Grace," he said, and dumped the dress on her head.

Charlotte felt like a china doll, awash in a sea of lace and satin, breathing in the clean, stifling, fresh smell of the fabric as she tried to find her way to a pocket of air. At last, she lurched to her feet and flung the dress aside—only to discover that Philip had never moved, and her nose was a mere inch away from his cravat.

She sniffed and looked down at his hands. They were empty. "Where are my stockings?"

He reached inside his pocket and drew forth a pair, dangling them in front of her face. "Right here, Your Grace. If it pleases you to sit down . . ."

Charlotte threw him a warning glance as she turned and plopped into the chair once again.

Philip kept his head lowered while he knelt before her, and if she hadn't known better, she would have thought she heard the low rumble of a chuckle as he reached for her foot.

He pushed her shift to her thigh with one hand and extended her leg toward him with the other. She knew he didn't intend for his touch to be so sensual, his gloved fingers sliding along the curve of her calf and down to grasp the tender skin at her ankle, but still she swallowed a gasp at the intimacy of the gesture.

No man had ever touched her thus before.

He stroked her ankle on either side with his thumbs, a slow, provocative caress, and she tensed, ready to jerk out of his hold. At the last moment, he released her, and Charlotte dared to breathe again.

He moved the stocking over her toes, his fingers gliding along her skin as he drew it ever upward. He lingered at the arch of her foot, her ankle, her calf, leaving a trail of tingling nerves wherever he touched her. As he brushed the inside of her knee, Charlotte jumped.

He raised his head, and Charlotte couldn't help but think that his mouth, his firm, lovely-looking mouth, was so very close to the juncture of her thighs . . .

"I never knew you were ticklish."

She jumped once more as his fingers flicked the sensitive skin behind her knee. "I'm not," she said. "You . . . surprised me."

"Ah." His eyes told her he knew she was lying, but he didn't try to tickle her again.

No, that would have been too kind a reprieve from the torture he inflicted on her. She had made a horrendous mistake; she should never have attempted to call his bluff and allow him to dress her.

Her amusement at seeing him play the servant's role had long since disappeared, replaced by an unexpected, unwanted reawakening of desire as she watched his hands carefully smoothing the stocking over her leg.

Charlotte bit her lip when he fastened her garter into place, the tips of his fingers brushing the inside of her thighs. His movements were exacting, solicitous, methodical even—nothing to make her think he was trying to arouse her.

Certainly he could not have known her thighs would tremble at the whisper of his breath across her skin, or that her own breath would hitch in her chest as he continued his unintentionally erotic ministrations on her other leg.

Charlotte's hands tightened on the arms of the chair. She was a fool. Here she was, barely able to keep from swooning at the pleasure of his touch, and he—

He—

She cocked her head, listening.

He was humming!

Humming, as if he were engaged in some mundane chore and only the tune in his head could keep him amused. While she was a tense, muddled mass of need and want, and—

Oh, for heaven's sake, now he was whistling?

Charlotte planted her foot on his chest and shoved.

He tumbled backward onto the floor. "What the devil—"

"Out!" She stepped over him and stalked to open the door. Unable to meet his eyes, she stared at the top of his head as she pointed to the corridor. "Get out!"

"Charlotte—"

She turned away and yelled at the top of her lungs. "Anne!"

Almost immediately the door across the way opened and a mobcap peeked through the crack. "Yes, Yer Grace?"

"Assist me at once."

"Yes, Yer Grace." The maid scurried across the hall and into the room.

A tuneless whistle pierced Charlotte's ear as she twisted around again. She gasped and glared at Philip, who had snuck up behind her. He met her glower with an even gaze.

"We do not have time for your theatrics. We are already behind. We must leave immediately—"

"Yes, yes, I know. Two minutes. I will be down in the courtyard in two minutes. Just"—she used all of her strength to push him an inch toward the corridor—"if you would . . . just . . . leave . . ."

He glanced up from where he had been peering at her fingers on his shoulder, as if they were little, annoying insects. "All you had to do was ask." He gave her a short, mocking bow, his mouth curved in a smile, then took a step backward.

Charlotte slammed the door and whirled around to face Anne, whose brown eyes had widened to an almost impossible degree.

"Quick, don't just stand there. We have two minutes." She took a deep breath. "I cannot have him barge in here, trying to dress me again."

Or next time, she just might ask him to help her undress.

"Easy, boy," Philip murmured to his stallion Argos. The horse nickered and stamped his hoof twice on the ground.

Philip felt much the same way as he glanced down to check his timepiece once again—impatient and very, very frustrated.

He could not keep his thoughts from straying to the image of Charlotte in that damned chair, her legs splayed before him in their lush, ivory splendor, the feel of her skin like satin beneath his fingers.

The memory was enough to make him hard all over again. Thank God he'd thought of something to provoke her. If he hadn't hummed and whistled like an idiot, he'd no doubt be standing behind her right now, his hands trembling as he fiddled with her laces.

He'd have gone mad. Bloody, irrevocably mad.

But he was insane to make such a threat to her in the first place. He'd known she would rebel against his authority, as she always did.

And yet he allowed her to believe he was so anxious to leave for Ruthven Manor that he lowered himself to play her lady's maid. To kneel before her, ready to button her up and lace her tight, when all he really wanted was to strip her bare until all that remained was his hands and mouth, his skin on hers, her sapphire eyes flashing beneath him as he drove into her again and again.

Philip groaned and shifted in the saddle, his groin

throbbing as he remembered how very close he had come to touching the apex of her thighs.

Argos whinnied, and Philip snapped his head up to find Charlotte strolling toward him, a wide grin gracing her lips beneath the brim of her bonnet.

Philip sucked in a breath. It had been a very long time since she had smiled at him like that, as though she were actually glad to see him.

If it'd been anyone else, he would have smiled in return. But he knew Charlotte, and she was never glad to see him; in fact, she'd slammed the door in his face not five minutes ago.

Though he loved her, he didn't trust her—at least, not when she was smiling like that.

"You're late," he said. His eyes ran over her gown the way his fisted hands couldn't.

Ironically, he'd forgotten to purchase traveling clothes for her. Ball gowns, tea dresses, pelisses, and negligees—all these he'd remembered. Modest designs for the pieces she would wear in public, to replace the usual scandalous gowns she preferred . . . and new nightgowns he alone would see to replace the ones she'd worn to her lovers' beds. It was an odd habit he'd acquired over the past few months, a substitute for not being near her, for not touching her. There was an intimacy in choosing the clothes that might one day caress and cover her skin, and even though he'd doubted she would ever wear them, he took great satisfaction in knowing she had no other choice now. He'd left her other clothes in London, and he would make certain the few articles stored at Ruthven Manor were removed as soon as possible.

Charlotte shrugged and lifted her hand to pet Argos. The blasted horse dipped his head into her touch. Was there a male of any species that could resist her?

She murmured something soft and indecipherable to

the stallion before she turned to look around. "I don't see Bryony. I assume you sent her on to the stables at Ruthven. Which horse shall I ride, then?"

It was on the tip of his tongue to tell her she would damn well ride inside the carriage, safe and tucked away so he'd be able to maintain some sense of his sanity for the rest of the way home.

But God help him, she smiled at him again.

And that open, joyful curve of her lips affected him more than her fluttering eyelashes and pouting mouth ever had.

Philip swallowed. "I—" His gaze sharpened, narrowing in on her attire. "You aren't wearing a riding habit."

She looked down, smoothing her dress. "I can tuck my skirts beneath me."

"We have no sidesaddle."

"Do not worry, Your Grace. It won't be the first time I've ridden astride." She paused. "I'm quite good at it, I'm told."

Philip growled at the blatant innuendo. "Gilpin," he called, never taking his eyes from hers.

One of the grooms on horseback trotted toward them. "Your Grace?"

"Assist Her Grace onto your gelding."

Charlotte tapped his knee, and Philip jerked, startling Argos. "Be careful, Philip. I might begin to believe you've developed a soft spot for me if you continue taking my wishes into consideration."

"I—"

But she had already turned away, laughing, and he couldn't decide whether he had been about to admit or deny her accusation.

Philip berated himself. He could not allow her to get the upper hand.

Once Gilpin had climbed up on the carriage and Charlotte was settled on the gelding, Philip signaled the coachman. The entourage began to travel the remaining four hours to Ruthven Manor.

Philip soon heard the thundering of hooves behind him as Charlotte rode up to join him at the front.

Most men would have been too intimidated by him to attempt to breach his solitude, and no woman he knew would ever have chosen a horse over the carriage, let alone agreed to ride without a sidesaddle.

He covertly studied her out of the corner of his eye. She sat tall and straight, her head held high and her hands loose on the reins, needing only to coax her mount with the barest nudge of her thighs. Her skirts . . .

Philip turned his head to fully look at her. His gaze traveled downward, to where the enticing curve of her calves was revealed by the hike of her skirts.

"Do you know I haven't returned to Warwickshire since we married?"

Philip started and glanced away. Then, realizing he was behaving like a schoolboy, he swung his head back to stare at her. "Have you not?"

"No."

Philip frowned. "Surely you must have. I travel to Ruthven at least six times a year."

She flicked her hand in the air. "Yes, but I've never gone with you. Though I'm not surprised you didn't notice my absence. In truth, I might not have known you'd left except that you took the butler with you each time."

He considered her for a long moment, the thudding of the horses' hooves and the rumble of the carriage wheels the only sound to break the silence. "You're afraid to return."

She slid him a sidelong glance, her mouth curved in a self-derisive smile. "You are mad if you believe I would ever admit such a thing to you."

"But you are," he pressed, feeling as if he'd never really known her. Never looked close enough to really see her. He swallowed past the sudden, bitter taste of guilt. "Why?"

Her smile disappeared. "When I last saw my parents, they told me to never show my face again if I married you."

Philip scoffed. "What parents wouldn't want their daughter to marry a duke? Surely I wasn't that terrible."

She gave him a disbelieving look.

"Very well," he muttered. "But it's not as if your brother died. It was only a few broken ribs."

"Yes, but he was still their son, even if they refused to recognize him as such. My father only disowned him to force him to accept his responsibilities."

Philip looked straight ahead. "Either way, Ethan deserved it."

*"Hullo," Ethan said.*

*Philip turned to the butler. "You may go, Fallon."*

*Philip waited until he disappeared, then stared at the man on his doorstep. The man whom he'd once considered his closest friend. The man who had betrayed him. A few yards behind Ethan, scuffling her toe in the grass and feigning disinterest, stood Charlotte.*

*Philip tried to close the door, but Ethan blocked it with his shoulder, pushing until the door swung wide open again and he stood at the edge of the marble entryway. "Five minutes," he said, breathing harshly. "That's all I ask."*

*"You returned," Philip said dully. "I heard she left you to rot in the middle of the countryside."*

*"You've seen her then? How is—"*

*"No, I haven't seen her," Philip bit out. Nor did he intend to. Joanna, also, had betrayed him.*

*Ethan shook his head, rubbing at the back of his neck. "Look, I came to apologize."*

"*Apologize?*" he echoed.

As if Ethan thought he could earn redemption with a few words. As if stealing off in the middle of the night with Philip's fiancée could be dismissed simply because he managed a repentant expression and a contrite tone. Did he understand nothing of respect, of honor?

Of course he didn't.

Philip clenched his hands into fists. It appeared his grandfather had been correct, after all. A squire's children were no better than the lowest of commoners, and Ethan Sheffield was nothing more than a squire's son. And he wasn't even that any longer, since he'd been disowned.

Ethan cursed. "I'm sorry, Philip. I didn't plan to do it. I never meant to—"

"You will leave my house now. And if I ever see you again, you will address me as 'Your Grace.'"

Ethan stiffened, scowling. "Don't go getting all high and dukely on me. This doesn't mean we can't—"

"Leave. I'll not say it again." Philip advanced toward him, his temple pounding. His gaze narrowed until all he saw was Ethan, once the greatest of friends, the brother he'd always longed for . . . and now a stranger.

"Goddamn it, Philip, why won't you listen to me?"

Philip swung, his fist connecting with Ethan's jaw. His head snapped to the side. Philip followed with a blow to his abdomen, then watched as Ethan's face contorted with pain.

Philip heard Charlotte scream.

He wasn't satisfied. "I trusted you," he said, stepped forward. Now there was no one he could trust.

Ethan straightened, grimacing. He held up his hands. "I won't fight you. And I will work to regain your trust."

Philip laughed and swung again, needing to hurt Ethan, to wound him as he'd been wounded. To show him that what he'd done was irreversible, and that the distance between them could never be bridged.

*This time, though, Ethan ducked, then lunged, plowing Philip to the hard marble floor.*

*They rolled, Philip beating at Ethan's ribs while Ethan fought to pin him to the ground.*

*A swirl of skirts, a whiff of jasmine. "Stop it," Charlotte shouted, her hands grasping at Philip's arms.*

*Philip grunted and shifted away where their flying fists wouldn't injure her. However, his gallantry cost him. While he thought to protect Charlotte, Ethan landed a succession of jabs to his kidney.*

*Roaring, Philip lurched out of his hold. "I thought you wouldn't fight."*

*Ethan sprang to his feet, crouching. Blood ran from his nose and a corner of his lip. "Does it make you feel better to hit me?"*

*"Yes."*

*"Then do it again."*

*"No!" Charlotte scrambled between them, arms outstretched. "Philip, please. You've done enough, haven't you? It's enough, damn it!"*

*Philip clenched his jaw. He should have expected her to side with her brother. She was just another Sheffield, no longer a friend but Ethan's ally. "Get out of the way," he snarled.*

*Ethan strode forward, wrapping his arm around Charlotte and tucking her against him. "Don't you dare threaten her. This is you and me. I'll send her away, and then we'll finish it." Ethan paused. "Do you understand?"*

*Philip stared at them, saw how they protected each other. They had always been close, friends as well as brother and sister. Doting on each other, even when they argued. In the past, he'd almost felt as if he'd become part of their family, as if he belonged. But now they looked at him as if he were a monster, the same dark brown hair framing the same bright blue eyes. As if he were the one who had betrayed them.*

*Then Charlotte tilted her head toward Ethan, her words too soft for Philip to decipher. And when Ethan looked down at her, Philip realized with sudden clarity that he'd been wrong to believe he could hurt Ethan through bruises and broken bones.*

*The perfect revenge stood before him, beautiful and innocent.*

*Charlotte.*

"I once believed I hated him," Charlotte said, so low it took Philip a moment to register her words.

"Ethan?"

"Yes, for what he did . . . and for what it did to all of us."

This, another sin he'd committed: turning Charlotte against her brother. But Philip had done much worse to gain her condemnation.

Ruining Charlotte through seduction hadn't been sufficient. He had to court her and marry her, claim her heart and her body, and then inform her of the truth: that he'd only pretended to love her as vengeance against Ethan. Then he'd cast her aside, trapped in a marriage he needed only for the sake of producing heirs.

His plan had worked well. Philip would never forget Charlotte's face the morning after their wedding when he'd told her—the joy leached from her eyes, the stark whiteness of her cheeks. Only one part had failed: Ethan had departed England, unaware of Philip's revenge.

He'd been a bastard. A foolish, idiotic bastard. And now he was paying his penance for it, for he could imagine no greater punishment than loving Charlotte while she thoroughly despised him.

Drawing his mount closer to hers, Philip attempted to peer beneath her bonnet to see her expression. "They loved each other."

"Did they?" Charlotte laughed, but this time it was

hollow, an empty echo of the joyous sound it should have been. "And I loved you."

It was not the declaration he had hoped for—that simple, single hard consonant on the end of "love" declared it to be past tense, a memory of something she had once experienced. And by the bitter tone of her voice, he knew it was not a pleasant memory.

Nevertheless, he clung to those four words as a dying man prayed for salvation, as if the hope of her love could redeem him for all the soul-blackening things he'd ever done.

After all, if she had once loved him, could he not persuade her to love him again?

"Ah, memories." Charlotte snapped the reins, urging the gelding faster. She threw him a saucy grin over her shoulder. "Speaking of which, do you remember the time I bested you in a horse race? Never mind. Of course you do. If I recall correctly, it happened every time you wagered that you would win."

Philip bent forward, his knees pressing against Argos's sides. "You were younger and smaller, less experienced. Allowing you to win was the gentlemanly thing to do."

"Yes, of course. Gentlemanly." She leaned low over her horse's mane. "Would you care to make another wager now?"

# Chapter 5

Charlotte hurried down the stairs, her fingers skimming the railing, her feet barely touching each step in her haste.

Even though she'd lost the race and the bloody wager, she couldn't submit to Philip's terms.

As she neared the front entrance, the butler, who stood as a silent sentry along the wall, moved to block her path.

"I am to inform you that you may not leave the house," Fallon said, his eyebrows drawn together like horizontal caterpillars, his mouth a thin ribbon of displeasure.

"Very well. I have been informed." Charlotte moved to circle around him, but he mirrored her movements—a left step to her right, a step back to her forward lunge.

She sighed. "I suppose His Grace also ordered you to restrain me by physical force if I attempted to do so?"

A strong arm wrapped around her waist. A deep voice murmured in her ear. "No. Fallon was only to stall you until I arrived. I will be the one to take pleasure in restraining you."

Charlotte tensed, and Philip's arm immediately fell

away. She whirled toward him. "Am I a prisoner here, then?"

She nearly stamped her foot at his impeccable appearance. God, it wasn't fair. It was impossible that he should look so attractive when it was just past the crack of dawn. She was sure her own face still held creases from her pillow.

"A prisoner?" The way he looked at her made Charlotte shiver, as if he contemplated tying her to his bed. But she knew he was only trying to intimidate her again.

He reached out and trailed a finger along her cheek, down her throat. "No, you're not a prisoner. But I can't help wondering why you are awake so early. Surely you weren't trying to escape, to renege on our wager?"

"No," Charlotte glanced away. Damn it. If only that blasted oak tree had been a foot closer to the window, then she'd never have been caught.

"Good. I should hate to think you a poor loser." His eyes gleamed wickedly. "Or that you wouldn't want to spend a day with your husband, as we agreed."

Charlotte flashed him a wide smile. "Of course not, Your Grace."

Philip inclined his head. "Come, then. Let us begin."

He pivoted on his heel. Charlotte looked with longing at the front door, then turned and followed him. She cleared her throat. "You never informed me when you were leaving."

"Leaving?"

"Yes, to London."

He held the door to the music room open for her. "There is no need to sound so dejected, my dear. I would not dream of abandoning you in the countryside."

At this announcement, she stumbled across the threshold. He caught her easily against his chest. "You wouldn't?"

Philip gave her a disarming grin. "No. I fear I would miss you far too much. And by the way the tears are gathering in your eyes, I can see you would miss me as well."

Charlotte blinked. Her eyes were completely dry. "Have you gone daft?"

He kissed her cheek—a short, sweet peck that was over before she could think to draw away. Then he released her and winked.

Charlotte's jaw dropped open.

It was the single most ridiculously trivial thing Philip had ever done. She hadn't realized he even knew *how* to wink.

His index finger tapped against her chin, and she promptly closed her mouth. "Your concern for my sanity is truly heartwarming. I had no idea you cared so much."

Charlotte rolled her eyes. "Yes, I've hidden it well, haven't I?"

He ignored her sarcasm and took her hand. "Come. I have something to show you."

Her feet dragged as he led her to the far end of the music room—for the most part, a room very similar to any of the drawing rooms, except in here an enormous grand piano sat in the middle on the large blue and gold Persian carpet.

Philip stopped, and Charlotte peered around his shoulder at a mysterious draped object.

"Close your eyes," he said.

She obeyed him without hesitation. Then, realizing she had done so, she immediately opened them.

The cloth dropped from Philip's fingers back into place. "I realize that you can't stand for a moment to allow me out of your sight, darling, but if you want to see your surprise, you must bear the agony for a short while."

"Humph." Though suspicious of Philip's intent, she closed her eyes again.

There was a rustling, a stirring of air, and then she felt Philip move behind her. His hands covered her eyes.

"Are you ready?" His breath lifted the hairs at the nape of her neck.

"Yes."

"You didn't peek, did you?"

"No." Well, only a little bit—a slight crack of the eyelids. Not enough to see anything beyond the blur of Philip's dark form.

"Very good. Now. Open your eyes." His hands fell away, and Charlotte gasped.

"I decided I would enjoy hearing you play for me every night. After you rub my back, of course."

Charlotte managed a halfhearted elbow to his ribs as she stared at the harp.

A beautiful golden harp.

"Go on." Philip nudged her. "Pluck a few strings. I will give you a moment before I expect you to bow before me in gratitude."

She dared not ask him the reason for the gift, for fear he would change his mind and take it away. She didn't remember when she had ever told him her wish to play a harp, but somehow he knew.

Charlotte walked forward, her hand outstretched. It was silly, really. She could have bought one for herself a long time ago, but somehow it had seemed wrong, as if she hadn't deserved it. As if she thought she had to be as pure as an angel to possess such an instrument, and her fingers were too soiled by her life of indulgence to be allowed to play upon its strings.

She drew her hand along the strings with slow, careful reverence. They vibrated beneath her fingers dully, a quiet, disharmonious mockery of the heavenly chorus it should have been.

Only the knowledge that Philip watched her kept

her from snatching her hand away. Tentatively, she tried again.

"I have arranged for an instructor to come from London once a week to give you lessons. I hope that pleases you?"

Charlotte nodded, not daring to look at him. She suddenly felt more vulnerable in his presence than ever before. Not even when he'd seen her fully nude had she wanted to retreat, to hide away as she did now.

"Ahem."

She strummed her fingers from right to left, then backward from left to right. And again.

*"Ahem."*

Pinching a string between thumb and forefinger, she glanced up at Philip. She let it go, unable to keep a small smile from her lips at the sound of the long, quavering note.

"I believe now would be a good time to properly express your gratitude."

"Yes, of course." She inclined her head. "Thank you, Your Grace."

"I'm afraid that is not sufficient."

"No?"

He shook his head sadly. "Not at all."

"And I suppose you have something specific in mind?"

"Indeed." He prowled toward her, his gaze intent.

Charlotte stiffened. Of course. He'd taught her before that his every action was selfish. With Philip, nothing ever came without a price.

She edged around the harp as he neared, determined to maintain a measure of distance between them. "Is it one of the nude sketches? I'm afraid all of those have already been distributed. Although, if you are willing to wait for a few days, I'm certain I can convince Astley to travel to Ruthven for a new set. Perhaps I should pose outside this time instead of in the house. The gardens here are so very lovely, do you not think—"

"*No.* I did not mean one of your nude sketches," he growled.

"Oh." She considered him carefully. He was looking at her lips. Good Lord. Surely he didn't expect her to thank him by kissing him—after all, hadn't he said he wasn't interested in her in any physical sense?

Charlotte couldn't help it. She licked her lips, then bit her lower one.

Yes, his eyes definitely darkened. Why, the cad! To make her feel as if he no longer found her desirable, all the while sneaking glances and touches she would have made other men beg for.

Charlotte thrust her shoulders back and lifted her chin—a confident, alluring pose meant to draw a man's attention to her chest's abundant endowments and to the slender length of her neck.

This time she studied him even more closely, saw how his hands pressed against the outside of his thighs, as though he resisted the urge to clench them into fists, saw how his features tightened briefly before he forced his expression to relax.

Charlotte nearly laughed.

He was trying so hard to fight his attraction for her. How it must kill him inside to realize that no matter how much he despised her for acting the whore, his baser male instincts would always react to the appeal of her body.

The knowledge was delicious. Purely, simply, utterly delicious.

She had been correct in her original assumptions. Philip was just like every other man; even though he chose to deny it, it was obvious he was led around by the

muscle between his legs, not by a higher sense of moral-
ity or any measure of ducal honor.

Perhaps spending the entire day with him wouldn't
be as tedious as she'd believed it would be after all.

"I don't want any of your nude sketches," Philip repeated gruffly, eyeing Charlotte warily as she suddenly
reversed direction and began to walk toward him.

"If nude sketches are not what you wish, how can I
fulfill your desires then, Your Grace?" she asked, pausing no more than a foot away from him.

Bloody hell.

If her eyes hadn't sparked with defiance, or if her tone
had been a little less sarcastic, he would have thought
she was purposely attempting to seduce him again.

He held her gaze evenly. "I would like your forgiveness. For what happened in the past, for lying to you, for
abandoning you for my mistress . . ." Before she could
comment, he quickly added, "I am weary of your continued ill humor. I have come to the conclusion that a little
peace would go a long way between us."

Her smile mocked him. "Ah. Another manipulation,
Your Grace? I fear you will never understand you can't
control me. You certainly cannot bribe me into thinking you are anything less than a selfish, egocentric
bastard."

Philip disguised his flinch by meeting her false, sweet
smile with a forced grin of his own. She would not see
his wounds. He leaned toward her, until they were nearly
nose to nose. "Then pretend," he bit out.

Her eyes flew to the harp, then back to him. "Very
well. I forgive you for being a terrible lover and ruining
my wedding night. But I shall not forgive you for lying
to me, or for flaunting your mistress, or—"

"I beg your pardon?" It had taken Philip a moment
before he could assure himself that yes, she really had

said what he'd thought she said. His shoulders stiffened and he straightened slowly until he towered over her. "A terrible lover? You didn't seem to think so three years ago. I distinctly recall how you cried out—"

"For God's sake, Philip, I was a virgin. You hurt me."

He paused, then shook his head. "No, after that. The second time."

Charlotte snorted. "Oh, that's right. I forgot the first lasted for only two minutes."

Philip could feel his face turn red. He knew she was just trying to provoke him, and he knew he should take this as a good sign—after all, at least she was speaking to him instead of ignoring him as she could have done after he'd abducted her. But even with this knowledge, he still rose to the bait, pride demanding that he defend himself. "I tried to make it as short as possible for you, so you wouldn't—"

"Yes, Your Grace." A sly smirk crossed her lips, her eyelashes lowering as she glanced downward at his breeches. "I must agree with you there. It did seem rather short."

It was in that instant that Philip realized he'd gone about this the wrong way. She didn't need to be wooed or courted nearly as much as she warranted a good, healthy slap to the backside.

"You little hellion," he growled, advancing toward her.

Charlotte's eyes widened and her lips parted. She darted away when he was a mere hairbreadth from her.

She laughed as he stalked her around the room—circling the harp, a settee, the grand piano. And all the while she taunted him as she held up her hand, her index finger and thumb a mere two inches apart.

"I regret to say I had expected more of you, dear husband." She extended her thumb and finger as far apart as they would go. "Yes, quite a *lot* more."

"I *will* catch you."

Charlotte frowned as she skirted a group of chairs. "Oh, dear. You're trying to intimidate me again. I have to admit, that fierce scowl is far more threatening than your cock was the last time I saw it—"

"Charlotte!" He lunged.

She hopped to the side with a surprised squeal, and Philip clutched at the hem of her petticoats as he fell to the floor. He immediately rolled, yanking on her skirts in an effort to knock her off balance.

"I said I forgave you, Philip! We called a truce, remember?"

Her belated attempt at peacemaking would have been far more convincing if she hadn't ended each sentence with a kick of her foot.

Philip cursed and tried to protect his head.

"No . . . truce . . ." he gasped, dodging the thrash of her skirts and another well-aimed kick.

She gathered her gown in her hands and jerked free of his hold. Philip came to his knees. They stared at one another, both breathing heavily.

"What now?" she panted. "Are you ready to be civilized once more?"

"Perhaps. Would you like to apologize?"

Charlotte tilted her head to the side. "For what? Telling the truth?"

He studied her for a long moment. She appeared utterly delectable, her cherry red lips pursed in a teasing pout, strands of her hair escaping from the safety of her pins, her gown sliding off one shoulder.

She was a woman accustomed to abandoning the strict rules of society for her own pleasure, someone who embraced her wild inclinations no matter the risk to her reputation or the censure of her peers.

Philip envied her ability to brush off the weight of

everyone else's expectations, to know the freedom of indulging her own wishes and desires.

To be uncivilized.

"No," he answered, rising to his feet, "I am not near ready." He surged forward again.

Skirts fisted in her hands, Charlotte neatly eluded him as she ran out of the music room and down the corridor. Philip loped after her, his pace hindered by a pain in his right leg. He must have twisted it when he'd lunged for her.

She skipped backward, her cheeks flushed and her smile wide as she beckoned him on with a wave of her hand. "Come now, Philip. You are hardly trying at all. I'm sure Fallon could run faster than you, and he's nearly three times your age."

Philip fought a grin at the sound of Fallon's muffled gasp of outrage behind her, near the front entrance.

"I am only giving you a fair chance, my darling," he said. "For when I catch you—"

She turned around, her dark hair streaming down her back. "You shall never catch me," she called over her shoulder.

Fallon tried to block her as she reached the front door, but she feinted around him, her movements too quick for the old butler's stiff joints.

Philip was right behind her. His gaze focused on her retreating form as she jogged to the left, past the mani-cured lawn and down the far slope, toward the banks of the small stream which ran through the edge of his property.

She disappeared from view. Philip increased his pace, wincing with each jolt to his right leg. As he topped the stream's bank, he saw Charlotte cautiously picking her way across a fallen log.

She must have heard him approach, because she

glanced up with an impish grin, her arms held out to her sides for balance. "I thought you'd gotten lost."

The ground was slick beneath his feet as he hurried down. "I didn't want to win too easily, that's—"

A grunt of surprise escaped him as his feet went out from under him, and he landed on his back. He tried to sit up, but his right leg throbbed in renewed protest. Groaning, he fell backward once again.

"Philip?"

He blinked up at the sky. Was it possible that was concern he heard echoed in her voice? For *him*?

He opened his mouth to assure her he was fine, but immediately thought better of it. Instead, he closed his eyes and let his head loll to the side.

"Philip?"

He heard a soft thud as she jumped to the muddied ground beside him. Her skirts swayed against his leg while she prodded him with her toe.

"Do not think for a moment I believe your unconscious act. Have you forgotten I have four brothers? I've been taken in by much better ploys than this."

He sighed. At least he'd tried. "Have pity, woman. I'm in pain."

He turned toward her as she knelt beside him, her brow furrowed. "Did you hit your head? Here, watch my finger."

Perhaps he had. In truth, he couldn't remember where he ached any longer. Her head was bent toward him, her beautiful blue eyes—those eyes which seemed to change shades moment by moment—focused on his as she peered at him in concentration.

Her fingers snapped, jerking him out of his trance. "My finger, Philip. Follow my finger."

The movement of her mouth drew his attention to her lips. Those perfect, sin red, luscious lips.

"That's not my—"

His mouth fused to hers, his hand pressed behind the nape of her neck, holding her still for his plunder.

The taste of her was sweet, exotic, and heady, evoking memories of their wedding night long ago. Memories he'd forced himself to forget.

"No," Charlotte mumbled against his lips, but she didn't try to push away, and Philip remembered how he'd driven her to the brink of ecstasy again and again, how the sound of her cries of pleasure—and she had cried out, whether or not she chose to admit it—had made his revenge all the sweeter.

Philip angled his head, his tongue sweeping over the seam of her lips, and now, just as she had then, she welcomed the invasion—tentatively at first, then with greater passion.

He'd given himself one night of victory to slake his lust with her tender, untried body. Afterward, he'd convinced himself he no longer wanted her.

Philip used his other arm to draw her nearer, growled as the fullness of her breasts crushed against his chest.

He had let her go, believing his own pleasure resulted in the knowledge that he was the first and only man ever to bed her, that the thrill of possession when he claimed her would soon fade.

And so he had returned to his mistress, never considering how great a lie it had been.

Until now.

For she was no longer innocent, and yet his blood still turned to fire in his veins when their lips met. He knew she'd lain with other men, and yet his desire for her could not have burned brighter.

At that moment, he realized it hadn't mattered that she'd been a virgin, or that he'd used her for his revenge. He hadn't made love to her three times that night for any other reason than because it was her.

It had always been Charlotte, and her alone.

Her touch, her smile, her scent.

Her beauty, her grace, her—

"Isn't there a rule about fornicating in broad daylight? Surely you could have chosen some other location—a tree, or a boulder, perhaps, instead of on the edge of my property."

Charlotte's mouth wrenched from his, and Philip opened his eyes to find her staring down at him, her expression frozen in shock.

"I can still see you, you know. You're not invisible simply because you stopped kissing."

Charlotte's eyes widened and she jerked out of his grasp, leaving Philip with a clear view of the other person, who stood on the opposite bank of the stream, her hands propped on her hips.

He stifled a curse. "Good morning, Lady Grey."

Charlotte surveyed the tall woman at the top of the embankment. She was the very picture of straitlaced gentility, every button in place, not a wrinkle to be seen. Even the wind dared not disturb a wisp of her hair.

Smoothing her own muddied skirts, Charlotte pasted a pleasant smile on her face, as if she hadn't mere moments before been cavorting on the ground with her estranged husband.

No doubt she appeared as wild and wanton as everyone believed her to be.

She nodded her head, uncertain how to address the woman who had been destined from birth to become the Duchess of Rutherford. The woman who Charlotte had, by turns, admired, envied, resented, and eventually pitied.

Joanna. Their childhood friend, Philip's former fiancée, and Ethan's almost bride.

And now the widowed Lady Grey.

It would have been a cozy reunion if it hadn't been so . . . well, so damned awkward.

And, of course, if Ethan had been present as well, instead of off in India or China or some other godforsaken heathen nation.

"Your Grace," Joanna answered, curtsying toward Philip. She then turned to Charlotte. "And Your Grace."

The silence seemed to stretch endlessly as they each waited for the others to breach the stifling tension, to venture beyond the brief, stilted exchange of greetings.

In the end Charlotte picked up her ruined skirts and, sending the fallen log a rueful glance, splashed her way through the stream and up the opposite bank.

"Joanna," she said, "I hope you don't mind my dirty skirts."

She lifted a brow. "No, I—"

"Good." Charlotte embraced her. "It is wonderful to see you."

Joanna's body stiffened in surprise at her gesture, but then her arms rose to return Charlotte's hug. "You naughty girl," she whispered in Charlotte's ear. "Now he will have to feign decency or appear an utter ogre."

"He is always an ogre." Charlotte released Joanna and looked sideways at Philip, whose expressionless mask had slid into place with practiced ease. Even with mud-stained clothes and mussed hair, he exuded masculine grace and authority.

Charlotte frowned. She should push him into the water. It would be well worth his wrath just to have him lose his composure, to have him sputter and curse like a normal person.

It was easier to contemplate how to anger him further than to think about their kiss. To realize that, for the briefest moment, she'd enjoyed the pressure of his mouth against hers, the hot rush of pleasure as he attempted to conquer her will with his lips and tongue.

She must keep her wits about her. After all, he was the man who had taught her to kiss. He was the one who had taught her the skills of seduction, how one's emotions could be completely distant from the acts of the body.

"Oh, do stop glowering," she called down to him. "I would have run away with someone else as well, if I'd had any idea how horrible you are."

"Charlotte!" Joanna's hand touched her arm.

Philip's eyes burned into hers before sweeping toward Joanna, then back to Charlotte. It must have been her imagination, or a trick of the sunlight. Surely she hadn't glimpsed a gleam of humor in their depths.

His gaze swung once more to Joanna. He made a gallant bow, the usual tension in his movements noticeably absent. "Lady Grey. I never did properly thank you for abandoning me four days before our wedding. Please allow me to do so now, for if you hadn't disappeared, I might never have known the joy of being married to my sweet, darling wife, my lovely Charlotte."

Joanna inclined her head. "You are most welcome, Your Grace." To Charlotte, she murmured out of the corner of her mouth, "I'd heard rumors you two hated one another."

"Oh, we do. He just hides it better than I do."

And she would do well to remember that his every action, his every word, was just another part of the game they played. Philip sought to control her by any means possible, whether through force, intimidation, or the sweet seduction of a stolen kiss. Or by attempting to gain her favor, as evidenced by the gift of the harp.

All she had to do was stay one step ahead of him until he tired of this farce and returned to London.

The best tool she could use to accomplish both goals of keeping distance between them and angering him stood right before her. All six feet of charm and propriety and broken promises.

"Joanna." Charlotte smiled. "You simply must come to tea."

"Now? Isn't it a bit early?"

"Now is a perfect time. Say yes."

Joanna glanced dubiously at Philip, who had stepped closer in an attempt to overhear them. "I'm not sure——"

Charlotte arched a brow. "Would you rather speak of Ethan? I heard that he——"

Joanna scowled. "Fine. Yes. I would love to have tea with you."

Charlotte clapped her hands and looked at Philip. "Oh, darling," she called. "Is it not wonderful? Dearest Joanna has agreed to be our guest for tea."

"Indeed, that is wonderful news."

His jaw clenched. Even from fifteen feet away, Charlotte could see it. She nearly clapped her hands again.

Charlotte wanted to strangle Philip.

If she hadn't believed he would laugh in her face at her attempt to do so, she would have.

She gritted her teeth as she watched him bend over Joanna's hand and place a lingering kiss on her fingers. Although she couldn't decipher his words through the fog of anger clouding her mind, it was enough to hear the low rumble of his voice, that deep purr he used whenever he thought to be charming.

How dare he make *her* feel uncomfortable, when he was supposed to be the one set off balance by the presence of his former fiancée.

Joanna waved as Philip escorted her out of the drawing room. "Good-bye, Charlotte. Thank you for the invitation. I hope to see you soon."

Somehow Charlotte managed a placid smile instead of the rabid snarl she was more inclined to give.

As soon as they disappeared into the hall, she paced to the window overlooking the front drive. She saw Philip hand Joanna up into the carriage he'd insisted she use to travel home, saw how they grinned at each other like two idiots enthralled by their own half-witted pleasantries.

It was one thing to know your husband found his pleasure in the beds of other women, and quite another to see him engage in such open flirtation, despite your presence.

The carriage rattled away, and Philip turned back toward the house. Charlotte gave him a mocking nod as his gaze found her at the window. No doubt he had arranged for them to rendezvous sometime tonight. Would he even wait for Charlotte to retire for the evening? Would he go to Joanna's house, or would she come here? Would Charlotte have to listen to their pants and moans as she tried to fall asleep?

The bloody bastard.

Philip merely grinned and waved his fingers until he once again disappeared from sight.

Charlotte counted twenty-two seconds before she heard his even footsteps enter the drawing room.

She continued to stare out the window, determined to maintain her dignity. She would not speak to him, for fear the bitter words which might come out of her mouth would make her appear jealous. Which she most decidedly was not.

She was simply angry.

"Charlotte."

Very, very angry.

"Look at me."

She turned around, her arms crossed over her chest,

unable to unfold herself from the defensive posture. "Yes?"

"I have given a great deal of thought to what you said."

"You have?" She arched a brow, her mind racing as she tried to remember what she could have possibly said that Philip would have given any heed to.

"Indeed. I have decided to grant your request."

Her heart gave a nervous kick in her chest. Request? She had only ever asked one thing of him. He couldn't possibly mean—

"I will divorce you."

# Chapter 6

At his words, Charlotte did something most unusual. She blanched, going completely white in a matter of seconds. Then she flushed, the color returning to her cheeks in a violent rush.

Philip would have held out his arms to catch what appeared to be her imminent fall, if she had not spoken at that very moment.

Her voice was hushed, her tone so low he had to concentrate on the movement of her mouth just to be able to understand what she said. "You will not jest with me in this manner."

He lifted his gaze from her lips to her eyes, saw the fury of disbelief unveiled there. "I promise you, my dear, I am not jesting." He turned from her. How was it he always somehow forgot the strength of her hatred? "However, there will be a caveat to my agreement. I will not concede to your request without receiving anything in turn."

"I see."

"Also, as the petition for divorce shall state the cause as adultery, you will bear the brunt of the scandal."

"I would expect no less, Your Grace."

He pivoted on his heel. "Is this not cause to rejoice, Charlotte? You have begged me for three years to give you freedom, and now that I am willing to do so, you sound dejected. Could you possibly have changed your mind? Do you wish to remain married to me?"

A small smile played around the corners of her lips. "Indeed not, Your Grace. I simply do not believe you will keep your word. After all, it would not be the first time you have cheated and lied to have your way. How do I know you'll not do the same yet again?"

Philip advanced toward her. "I mean what I say. I will even write my man of business today, if you like. I'll tell him to begin petitioning the courts in three months' time, at my behest."

Her eyes darkened as he neared. He liked that, liked seeing her awareness as he approached. "And I shall deliver it myself to a courier of my choosing," she countered.

He inclined his head, letting his gaze drift over the swell of her breasts for the barest moment. "As you wish."

"It's agreed, then. You will divorce me. What is your request?"

His eyes locked to hers. He wanted to see her reaction. He wasn't certain what he was looking for, exactly, but knew he wouldn't find it if he didn't look closely. "You advised me to find another wife, to release you. I have found her, Charlotte." He took another step toward her. "You will help me court Lady Grey."

"Joanna."

"Yes. Lady Grey." She would never be Joanna to him again, not after her betrayal.

Charlotte chuckled, a rich, warm sound that heated the marrow of his bones.

"You find it amusing."

She pursed her lips, teasing his resolve to stay away. "Yes, don't you? How ironic it is, that after all these years you would seek her out again."

"She would be the ideal wife."

Charlotte tilted her head, considering. "She does appear most proper."

"I have known her since childhood, and except for your brother, she has never done anything to bring shame to herself or her family."

"We Sheffields do have a tendency of influencing people for the worst, don't we?"

The very worst. Even now, there was nothing Philip wanted to do more than tumble her to the floor, to hear her scream his name, to convince her he was the only man she wanted. The only one she could ever possibly want.

Philip stalked away, turned at the last moment before he collided with the cream silk wall, and paced back toward her. He continued the odd patterned movement, his path radiating from her to the edges of the room, but always drawn toward her again. Even though she stood still, doing nothing, he could not resist the force of her allure. It was as if she were the sun and he some hapless, pathetic object bound to be destroyed by the pull of her fierce beauty.

And all the while, he spoke. "Perhaps she is not perfect, but she is very close to it. She has poise, grace."

"She's quite pretty, also."

Philip scowled at Charlotte over his shoulder. Her tone held no condescension or arrogance, and he was fairly certain she didn't intend to sound patronizing. Yet all the same, it was as though the sun, in all its brilliance and glory, was complimenting a star, a millionth of its size, for the small speck of light it shed.

Her words may have been sincere, but there was no

way Philip would believe Lady Grey could even begin to compare to Charlotte's exquisite beauty.

Charlotte tapped her chin. "Who knows? She might even read the *Times* to you. She does seem much more biddable than I could ever be."

"Yes." Philip nodded. "That is exactly my point."

"Yet, assuming you are serious and I agree to this mad scheme, there is still one particular issue to consider and overcome."

Philip arched an eyebrow.

"How do you propose to win her over? Even if you petition for a divorce, she is an intelligent woman. She knows the type of man you are."

It was not a wise idea, but he couldn't seem to keep himself from stepping closer to her. "And what type of man am I, Charlotte?"

Her mouth curved. "You are arrogant, controlling, manipulative, deceitful, unfaith—"

He laid his finger gently across her lips. "Enough." Drawing his arm away, he locked his hands behind his back. "You would have me change."

"I'm not certain it is possible, to be honest."

Oh, but he would. For Charlotte, he would do anything. "How would you change me? If you were Lady Grey, if you were any other woman, what would I need to do to appeal to you?"

Charlotte shook her head, her dark hair swaying with the movement. "You do not want to change. You want to pretend, just like you did with me, when you made me believe you were—"

She cut herself off, averted her eyes.

"What, Charlotte?" he pressed. "I made you believe I was what?"

It was a long moment before she spoke. "When you made me believe you were someone I could love."

Philip felt his entire body tense at her words. "Do you remember when you came to tell me Ethan had run off with Lady Grey? You had returned for the wedding preparations, leaving London in the middle of your first Season."

She frowned. "I remember."

"You were shy with me then, scarcely able to look me in the eye for more than two seconds. You blushed at any compliment, no matter how inane."

"Is there a reason—"

"You've changed, Charlotte." He leaned toward her. "You're confident now. You've become a seductress, a woman who could tempt a priest to abandon his vows. It's not just your beauty—you've always had that. It's the way you believe in yourself, the way you make everyone around you believe there is no better place on earth than wherever you are. In the park, in a carriage, at the supper table, next to you."

Philip stopped suddenly. He'd said too much. Watching while her slender throat worked delicately as she swallowed, he cursed himself.

"Even you?" she asked.

He quickly removed all traces of emotion from his face. It was a habit he'd developed at a young age, when he discovered his grandfather beat him harder when he cried out or if he tried to laugh the pain away.

He ignored her question. "The point, my dear, is that it is possible for anyone to change, including an arrogant, deceitful . . . What was it? Oh, yes"—he gave her a self-deprecating smile—"manipulative bastard like myself."

She looked at him warily. "I'm not certain it's at all possible to make you any less arrogant."

"No, probably not," he agreed.

"And it doesn't seem very fair to Joanna to assist you."

"If you teach me, I will be the very best husband in all of England."

She sent him a sly glance. "Not all the world?"

"Very well. The entire universe."

Charlotte turned her head, gazed out the window.

Philip followed the movement, his fingers itching to touch the curve of her cheek, the delicate arch of her brows, the subtle pout of her lips. "And if you help me, the petition will begin in three months. Compared to the past three years, it's rather a short period of time. Soon, Charlotte, you could be free of me." His voice lowered as he added, "Is that not what you've always wanted?"

Her lashes fanned in a black froth against her skin as she looked down, then up again, out to some distant point on the landscape. "Yes," she murmured.

Philip drew in a deep breath. "Excellent," he said. "Then let us begin."

*At the first snap of branches underfoot, Charlotte bolted upright. Her fingers combed frantically through her hair for stray twigs and leaves, and when she noticed how her hands trembled slightly, an echo of the sudden pounding of her heart, she cursed beneath her breath.*

*Even before she saw him coming through the trees, she knew it was Philip. He had a certain way of walking: each step carefully measured, almost a warning to those ahead.*

*Climbing to her feet, she managed another swipe through her hair and one last flounce of her skirts before Philip edged into the clearing. It wasn't a large clearing, perhaps only ten feet in circumference, but in the middle of the dense forest between Sheffield House and Ruthven Manor, it was her favorite refuge. For Philip to come here meant that he'd intended to seek her out.*

*Again, Charlotte silently cursed the rapid pitter-pattering of her heart. Never before had she cared for his opinion, or been breathless in anticipation of his attention. But that was before the elopement, before he began looking at her in that unnerving, intense way of his . . . as if, for the first time, he saw her as a woman instead of as Ethan's younger hoyden sister.*

*Philip smiled when their eyes met. It wasn't one of the wicked smiles that she'd been given by other men, but a slow, intimate curve of his lips which made her cheeks heat and forced her gaze away, unaccountably shy. She disliked this new ability of his to provoke her blushes.*

*"Good afternoon, Charlotte," he said, sitting down beside her.*

*She looked at him, unable to ignore the pull in her stomach when his silver eyes stared straight into hers. "Good afternoon, Philip." He had always been Philip to her—never the marquess or, after his grandfather had died six years ago, the duke—but for some reason speaking his given name seemed too intimate now. "I suppose I should address you as 'Your Grace,'" she murmured, crumbling a leaf between her fingers.*

*"'Philip' will do," he said, then, as her gaze darted away again: "Am I disturbing you?"*

*"Oh, no. No. I just—" She shrugged, unwilling to explain how very much he did disturb her, yet how she desperately didn't want him to leave. It was the second time he'd sought her out since the failed elopement and his fight with Ethan.*

*The first time he'd told her he still considered her a friend despite what had occurred, and presented her with a bouquet of wildflowers—a gesture of peace and goodwill, he'd said. They'd talked and laughed, and Charlotte had been glad to be on familiar footing with him once again . . . until he was ready to depart. Then he had taken her hand, intertwined their fingers, and pressed his warm, firm mouth to the inside of her wrist. She would never forget the excruciating embarrassment of having all of her blood rush to simmer beneath her cheeks, nor the way his lips had curved against her skin as he watched her blush.*

*Charlotte pressed her back into the tree and forced herself to meet Philip's gaze. "No, it's fine."*

*"Good. Because I brought something for you."*

*As he reached into his coat, Charlotte held out her hand. "Thank you, but I don't think it would be proper—" She halted at the sound of his chuckle, an inviting intoxicant, warm and rich as brandy.*

*"Surely I misheard you," he said, his smile teasing her while his eyes did scandalous things to her insides. "Charlotte Sheffield, afraid of impropriety?"*

*She huffed and turned her hand palm upward. "Very well. Let me see."*

*"Oh, no. What if it's something truly wicked? A locket with a piece of my hair? A ruby necklace?"*

*She should have said something very clever right then, to dismiss his assumption that she would want such things from him, but she was blushing again, her pulse throbbing violently with the knowledge of his flirtation.*

*Philip leaned closer, until their faces were but inches apart. "Or a lace negligee?"*

*"Then, I think"—her eyelashes fluttered downward of their own volition, toward the masculine sculpture of his lips. Starting, she jerked her gaze upward again— "that would be m-most improper." She'd ridden horses bareback and worn trousers so she could climb trees, yet speaking with him in this manner seemed the most scandalous thing she'd ever done.*

*"I agree." He withdrew his hand, revealing a small package wrapped in brown paper. "That's why I brought you candy."*

*"Candy?" she asked suspiciously, eyeing the present with disbelief. As he placed the package in her palm and leaned back, she wished he didn't appear so calm, so*

*completely, entirely . . . undisturbed. She unwrapped her
gift, then stared. "Toffee?"*

*"You're welcome."*

*She glanced up at him and smiled sheepishly. "Thank
you."*

*"Butterscotch toffee, to be exact. Here, try some." Reach-
ing over, he extracted a piece from her hands and held it
up to her lips. "Open your mouth."*

*Her eyes locked with his piercing silver gaze. "You
can't mean to—"*

*"Feed you? Yes." His thumb brushed against her bot-
tom lip. His head dipped toward her, his breath warming
her skin. "Open your mouth, Charlotte."*

*With a slight gasp, she obeyed. The candy slid past her
lips and touched her tongue, the butterscotch flavor melt-
ing upon every taste bud. Still, she couldn't help being
more aware of Philip and the feverish heat of his fingertips as he traced the outline of her mouth. Although it
mortified her, she moaned when his palm moved to her
throat, his hand a gentle clasp about her neck as she
chewed and swallowed.*

*"Done?"*

*She nodded, unable to speak, and watched as he reached
for another piece. Before he could ask, she opened her
mouth again, anxious to feel his touch.*

*Reveling in the knowledge that it was Philip who
touched her so.*

*"Close your eyes."*

*She did, the moment almost erotic as she waited for
his fingers to nudge the candy against her lips. But instead of the toffee, it was his mouth which pressed against
hers. And it erased all the kisses the butcher's son had
ever given her behind the rectory. Gasping, Charlotte
wrenched her head away.*

*She stared at him, her breath heavy. "Why—"*

*"I know I should apologize, but I wanted to kiss you."*

*"You could have asked," she said, and hastily climbed to her feet. He followed, catching her wrist when she would have walked away.*

*"If I had, would you have said yes?"*

*Even as she instructed herself to tug her arm away, to not turn around, her body betrayed her. Her wrist remained in the pleasant grip of his hand and her feet slowly pivoted toward him. When she would have refused to speak, her mouth formed the word without her permission. "Yes," she whispered.*

*And then her back was against the tree again and his mouth was on hers. The press of his body held her up when her knees weakened, and when he asked her one more time, she opened her mouth to him, then trembled when his tongue touched hers.*

*"Butterscotch," he murmured against her lips. "Delicious."*

*He kissed her again, and again, his lips seducing her while his hands stayed still, cupping her face. Her own were not as polite, roaming up the hard planes of his chest, smoothing over the afternoon stubble of his jaw, twisting in the black crispness of his hair.*

*When he finally broke the kiss, she dragged in a breath, her eyelids too heavy to open.*

*"Would you like to know a secret?" he asked, his voice scraping delightfully over her senses, thrilling her anew.*

*Charlotte nodded.*

*He kissed one corner of her lips, then the other. "I am very, very glad I didn't marry Joanna."*

Charlotte sat across from Philip in the library, studying his bent head while the quill between his fingers scratched against the parchment.

She didn't trust him. Not one bit.

He might allow her to send the letter by her own courier, but would he then post another missive to his solicitor, canceling the first request to petition the courts?

He might try to charm her by spouting words about divorce and freedom, but he had deceived her once. She would do her best to ensure he didn't do so again.

"There." Philip put the quill aside and, after blotting the ink, handed her the letter. "For your perusal."

It didn't take her long to read the few paragraphs. Nothing was amiss—but then, she hadn't expected it to be. "Thank you," she said, and gave it back to him.

He sealed the missive and returned it to her. "Where will you find a courier to your liking?"

Charlotte tucked the letter to her chest and stood. "I have my ways."

Philip rose to his feet. "Tomorrow the harpist comes from London to give your first lesson. If you don't mind, we will commence with my husband lessons afterward. I have a few things to accomplish this afternoon before supper."

"Until supper, then."

"Yes."

She strolled toward the door, thankful for the brief reprieve from his presence. But as she set foot into the hallway, he called to her. "Charlotte?"

She halted, rolled her eyes at the marble bust across the corridor. "Your Grace?"

"Remember, you are not to leave Ruthven Manor without permission, or without being accompanied."

Charlotte blew out a long breath. How could he have spent so little time with her these past few years, and yet seem to know her so well? "May I please visit my family, Your Most Munificent Grace?" she asked through gritted teeth.

A pause. "I thought you were afraid to see them again. Would you like me to accompany you?"

Charlotte made a face at the marble bust. It was probably meant to represent one of Philip's ancestors, perhaps the first or second Duke of Rutherford. It had his likeness—all hard planes and sharp angles. "No, thank you. And there is no time like the present to face my fears."

Another pause. "Very well. Be sure to take Gilpin with you."

"Of course. Until later, Your Grace."

Finally, she was able to quit the library. As she walked past the bust, Charlotte could not resist giving it an open slap to the side of the head.

"Charlotte." Joanna rose from a lounge in her solarium. "I had not expected to see you again so soon."

"Are you planning a rendezvous with Philip?"

Joanna blanched. "What? Good God, no!"

Charlotte studied her, found nothing but genuine horror in her eyes, and nodded.

"Do you have a messenger I can send to London? I have a letter that must be delivered immediately, and I need someone I can trust. Someone Philip cannot intimidate."

Joanna halted the footman who had announced Charlotte with a lift of a finger. "Matthews, a moment." To Charlotte, she said, "You may entrust whatever you have to Matthews. He will see that your letter is delivered safely, without any interference from the duke."

Charlotte hesitated before drawing the paper from her reticule. "How long will it take him to arrive in London?"

Joanna looked at her footman, who lifted three fingers. "Three hours, it seems."

Charlotte looked down at the letter and released it to the gloved fingers of the footman. "Thank you," she murmured, and sank into a nearby chair.

Matthews left the room, and Joanna returned to her position on the lounge.

Charlotte glanced over her shoulder, then at Joanna. "It's strange, isn't it, that you've returned to Norrey Hill, instead of staying at Lord Grey's estate?"

"Norrey Hill is my home. The Grey mansion never was. And besides, my husband's heir didn't want me there." Joanna leaned forward. "But I have a feeling you didn't decide to visit just to find a messenger, or to discuss my current domicile."

"No." This was where things became a bit tricky. Charlotte still hadn't quite figured out what she should or should not reveal. "I would trust there is no grudge between us, Joanna."

Only a slight flicker in her eyes showed any hint of interest. It was true; if ever there had been a perfect woman for Philip, it was Joanna.

"Of course not. How can I hold you at fault for anything, when it was Ethan and Philip who took advantage of us both?"

Charlotte took a deep breath and then, without fully knowing she was going to do it, blurted, "Philip has agreed to a divorce."

Joanna blinked. That was the only sign she gave of being surprised. Yes, she was perfect for him.

"And he wants to marry you instead," Charlotte added.

She laughed. Finally, an emotion. "Is that why he was flirting so outrageously with me this morning?"

Charlotte gave a terse nod, a brief jerk of her head. The reminder of Philip fawning over Joanna's hand made her temples throb with renewed anger.

"If Ethan is the last man on earth I would consider

marrying, Philip is surely the second to last. Good heavens. Why would he even consider such a thing, after Ethan and I nearly eloped?"

"It seems he's decided you would make the perfect duchess." Perfect, perfect, perfect. Philip thought he was perfect, thought Joanna was near perfect. All of this, of course, pointed to the very annoying and obvious fact that he found Charlotte severely lacking.

She knew this. She'd always known he looked down on her. What made no sense, however, was why she should care at any point in time what his opinion of her was.

She was being irrational. Philip had promised her a divorce if she would help him win Joanna, and now she was *jealous*?

Impossible.

She just . . .

She simply . . .

Charlotte cast about in desperation for a reasonable explanation for her strange thoughts, entirely ignoring Joanna as she continued to babble on about why she could never possibly allow Philip to court her.

She only wanted to prove he was wrong about her. That was it. To make him see that Joanna, with all of her near-Puritan clothes and stiff behavior, was in no way better than Charlotte.

Just because Joanna was the daughter of an earl and a widowed marchioness, and Charlotte was the daughter of the local squire—well, it meant nothing.

Nothing at all.

Joanna likely had many flaws. Scads of them.

Charlotte scanned her from the top of her head to the hem of her skirts.

"Charlotte."

True, it appeared she did conceal them rather well, but she was certain they were there.

"Charlotte."

"Hmm?" She jerked her gaze back up to Joanna's face and frowned. Not even a freckle in sight.

"You must convince him to pursue someone else. Anyone else. I am not interested in marrying again, and especially not him."

"Don't worry. You won't have to marry him. You shall simply have to pretend over the next few months that you are growing to like him a little bit more. But most importantly, I need you to let me know if his intentions toward you seem genuine."

"In what manner?"

"Does he try to kiss you? Seduce you? Write you poems?" Charlotte frowned again. "Why are you laughing?"

"Poems? Seduction? I can no more imagine Philip rhyming two words together than I expect him to climb up to my window and declare his undying love."

"But it is possible. You saw how he flirted with you today."

Joanna gave her a considering look, then nodded slowly. "I did indeed."

"Then you must keep me informed if he continues doing so. And as I said before, you should pretend to like him. I do not trust he will keep his word to divorce me if he doesn't think he can win you over."

Joanna stared at her for a long time before finally sighing. "You must admit, this all seems rather ridiculous."

"I know. But he is giving me a chance to be free. I know you understand—you ran off with Ethan just so you wouldn't have to marry him."

"Ethan is the one who—"

Charlotte waved her hand. "Yes, yes, but do not tell me you weren't relieved."

A tiny smile lifted the corner of Joanna's lips. "Very well. I was. Immensely."

Charlotte reached forward and placed her hand over Joanna's. "Then help me. Please."

"It could be quite amusing to see Philip make a fool of himself."

"Highly entertaining. It shall be like watching a trained monkey perform. Only this time, we will be the trainers."

Joanna grinned. "I've always wanted a pet monkey."

The wind was picking up. It had blown her bonnet off so many times that Charlotte had finally given it up for lost. The gale whipped her hair every which way now, untangling tendrils from her careful coiffure, flinging them across her mouth, her cheeks, her eyes.

She had to cup her hands around her face to see the roof of Sheffield House, the home where she was no longer welcome.

Charlotte had left Joanna well over an hour ago. She'd raced her mount against the wind, leaving Gilpin the groom trailing behind as she made her way toward the narrow edge of Rutherford property where Sheffield House was just visible over the wide swath of forest and thicket below.

There had been a time when it had seemed Charlotte had three homes: Sheffield House, Ruthven Manor, and Norrey Hill.

The properties were so close to one another that it took little more than half an hour to ride from Sheffield House across Rutherford lands to reach Norrey Hill. A little over an hour and a half on foot. Two hours walking backward. Fifty-six minutes if one skipped the entire way.

It was strange, now, how none of the houses seemed familiar. Even though Joanna was still as kind as she'd ever been, Charlotte had been acutely aware of her position as guest instead of confidante. She couldn't see

Ruthven Manor as anything more than a prison, with Philip as the warden.

And Sheffield House—

Well, she'd stood here for a good twenty minutes, and all she could think was that this must be how the street children felt when they passed the wealthy houses in Mayfair. As if a home and a loving family were foreign luxuries only the rich could possess.

She missed her parents and her brothers. Nicholas, Roland, and Arthur . . . but Ethan most of all. He had been the oldest, the one furthest from her in age, yet he'd been her closest friend. Her protector. Her enthusiastic scapegoat, always willing to take the blame when their adventures turned into mishaps.

Until he had been disowned. And then he had deserted her.

Charlotte had told Philip she wanted to visit her family. Yet, as she looked down at Sheffield House, she knew she wouldn't be able to. Otherwise, she wouldn't have waited twenty minutes in an attempt to gather her courage.

She couldn't face her father's scorn, her mother's disappointment.

They would have heard the rumors, even this far from London. They would know everyone thought her to be the modern harlot of Babylon.

And while Philip was right—she *had* changed in the past three years—she knew her parents wouldn't consider the change to be for the better.

"Your Grace? Perhaps we should return now."

Gilpin's voice swirled around her, the wind catching the consonants and tangling them into a muffled rumble of sound.

Charlotte gave a jerk of her head—just enough of a nod to acknowledge she heard him—and vaulted into the saddle.

The clouds wrestled in the sky, great big black monsters, their bodies rippling like waves over the landscape.

If they were fortunate, they might be able to beat the storm back to Ruthven Manor.

As they trotted away from where Sheffield and Rutherford lands collided, Charlotte glanced over her shoulder at the house she left behind.

She'd been wrong to hope things had changed, that it would appear any more welcoming than it had when she'd last seen it.

No matter how many times she looked back, she knew Sheffield House would never be her home again.

# Chapter 7

"No, no, no, Your Grace. You must leave your fingers loose." Mr. Lesser plucked her fingers away from the harp strings and shook her hand. "Loose!"

Charlotte's teeth clacked together from the force of the movement, but she dared not draw her hand away from his grasp. The last time she had attempted to do so, he'd threatened to walk out the door and never return.

She'd lost count of the number of times Mr. Lesser had reprimanded her for pulling at the harp instead of gently strumming the strings. It had to be well over twenty by now. And each time he took her hand in his, his voice became a little more strident, his cheeks a little more red.

And somehow, even though she'd never seen him run his fingers over his head, his light brown hair had managed to rearrange itself into frazzled, wild tufts sticking out from ear to ear.

"Do you feel"—Mr. Lesser gave her hand another fierce shake—"the looseness? Are your fingers"—he bent until they were face-to-face, his spectacles skewed at a dangerous angle on the tip of his nose—"relaxed?"

Charlotte bit her tongue and nodded. She wouldn't tell him she couldn't feel her hand or, for that matter, much of her arm anymore. If she opened her mouth, she feared she would burst out laughing at the image of the perfect madman he presented.

She did not want to offend Mr. Lesser's sensitive, artistic spirit any further. She wanted to play the harp, and, God help the man, he had been hired to teach her.

With one final shake, Mr. Lesser moved her hand to hover over the harp strings. His breath rushed out in a harsh sigh, as if he were fortifying himself to face another nerve-wrenching battle.

Charlotte thought she heard him murmur a supplication to the heavens before he released her hand and said, "Again."

She curved her fingers ever so slightly, making sure to only lightly rest them against the strings instead of pushing at them as she'd been inclined to do earlier.

"Dear Lord, please," Mr. Lesser whispered above her shoulder.

Then, as she'd seen him do a dozen or more times already that morning, Charlotte moved her hand from one end of the harp to the other, allowing the strings to ripple in a vibrant melody beneath her fingertips.

"Yes," Mr. Lesser breathed. "Did you feel the difference? Again."

Charlotte's heart thumped hard against her rib cage as she reached forward. She hadn't felt the difference, not really. To her, her fingers were just as stiff as before. But if Mr. Lesser approved, who was she to think otherwise?

Drawing a quiet breath, she strummed her fingers along the strings once again, trying to mimic her previous performance.

And once again, Mr. Lesser whispered his approval. "Yes, yes. Continue."

One, two, three, four times in succession, Charlotte played it perfectly, her confidence and pleasure building with each quiet murmur from Mr. Lesser. Soon, she began to believe she could feel the difference in the way she moved. Perhaps it was because her wrist was a little more slack, her motions a little more fluid. Or maybe it was because her shoulder had relaxed after all the shaking, and was no longer hunched up around her ear.

"One more time, and then we shall move on from this simple exercise to plucking individual notes."

Charlotte nodded. At last. It had taken forever, but she had finally succeeded. They would continue the lesson, and Mr. Lesser would return from London next week as scheduled. He would not leave her to be alone with her stiff, tense fingers and a lonely, unplucked harp.

She stretched her arm and set her fingers over the first string. Then, with slow reverence, she drew her arm toward her. Closing her eyes, she listened to the chorus of notes, trying to pick out the Cs from the Ds and the rest of the harp-sized alphabet.

Then, a third of the way through, she faltered. Her fingers plunked over the strings, and her eyes flew open as her index finger actually sailed through the space between the strings to peek at her from the other side.

"What?" Mr. Lesser's voice came from somewhere behind her. "What happened?"

Charlotte whirled around on her small seat and searched the music room. Her gaze lingered on the open doorway, her heart pumping in rapid, staccato beats.

She'd thought—

Charlotte shook her head.

She'd been certain Philip had entered the room. How else could she explain the sudden prickle of her skin, heating her every nerve as if someone had lit a fire in the hearth?

Shrugging, she turned around. Perhaps he'd simply walked past.

Mr. Lesser immediately picked up her hand and held it close to his face, examining it. "Your fingers are no longer loose," he said accusingly.

"I'm sorry."

Disappointment made the narrow angles of his face even harsher, and he dropped her hand to straighten his spectacles. "I do not think you are yet ready to move on, Your Grace. You must perfect this exercise before you can begin the next. One more time, or a hundred if it must be. Again, again!"

Charlotte nodded and willed herself to relax. But that odd feeling, the one that alerted her of Philip's nearness, would not disappear.

Drawing a deep breath, she threw a glance over her shoulder, hoping to catch him as he spied on her, but no one was there.

"Your Grace?" Mr. Lesser asked.

Charlotte slipped a small smile to Mr. Lesser and lifted her arm.

"Your fingers," he warned.

Before he could reach for her, she shook her own hand. For the thousandth time.

"Very good," he said. "Once more. Begin."

No other duke would lurk in shadows. Philip was certain of this.

Yet he couldn't help himself, hiding in the corridor outside the music room, listening to Charlotte attempt to play the harp. A shudder racked his body as she drew out another wretched, painful sound from the instrument.

She was horrible.

Completely, absolutely, utterly horrible. And somehow, it made him love her all the more.

Every few seconds, her fingers would come to a startling halt, the last plucked string vibrating forlornly with its dull echo.

Still, he couldn't bring himself to walk away. It would be another half an hour until her harp lesson ended and his husband lessons were scheduled to begin, but Philip could think of nothing he'd rather do than stand outside this doorway.

It was fortunate he had remembered their discussion of her wanting a harp long ago. Sadly, it was one of the few distinct memories he had of her when she was younger. He clearly recalled the way her face lit up, her mouth curving with wistfulness as she spoke of seeing a woman play a harp and thinking she was one of God's angels come to earth. He'd forgotten that day until recently, when he'd begun plotting ways to woo her again. The harp was one of his more brilliant ideas.

Very well. It had been his only brilliant idea. In comparison, the nausea-inducing poem of epic proportions he'd written in three days had been an utter catastrophe. Thankfully it hadn't taken nearly as long to burn. Now if only he could think of another thousand gifts to erase the innumerable ways he had hurt her . . .

Charlotte suddenly appeared around the edge of the door frame. "Aha! I knew you were spying on me."

She was so beautiful. God must have been having a very, very good day when he created her. Philip just stared for a long moment, until he could catch his breath. "I was doing no such thing."

Charlotte crossed her arms over her chest and tapped her foot.

"I was—"

"Spying on me," she repeated firmly.

"—merely ensuring you were behaving yourself," he finished.

Charlotte narrowed her eyes. "I doubt Joanna would

appreciate a husband who constantly monitors her behavior."

Philip bit back a grin. So this was how she wished to play the game. He cleared his throat and gestured grandly to the music room entrance behind her. "No doubt you are correct, my dear. Do proceed, and I shall return in half an hour to begin our other lessons." He paused, lifting an eyebrow. "Or do you suppose Lady Grey would take pleasure in having her husband watch her continue her music lessons?"

Charlotte glanced over her shoulder, supposedly at the waiting figure of Mr. Lesser. When she turned back, a frown tilted the corners of her mouth downward. "I don't think Joanna has music lessons."

Philip took her elbow and gently tugged her inside. "Well, if I were her husband, I would give her anything she wanted. And I think she might like to learn to play the harp as well, do you not?"

"Well, I suppose she might—"

"And she would want to have her husband's support."

They came to a standstill a few feet from Mr. Lesser, who tactfully looked away as he pretended to study the various bits of bric-a-brac around the room. Charlotte pulled her arm out of his grasp. "Nonsense. I do not need your support—"

Philip wagged a disapproving finger in front of her face. "Ah, ah. You are thinking of yourself. I know you do not need me. But I am thinking of Lady Grey. If she is to consider marrying me, if I am to be the perfect husband, I must begin now. I must act as I should in the future." He flicked a hand toward Mr. Lesser. "Go. Pretend you are Lady Grey and I am . . ." He paused, then grinned. "Well, I am a much better version of myself."

Charlotte gave him a withering glare. "No more than three months."

Philip inclined his head. "Only three months."

She wrinkled her nose. "Bloody hell. It sounds like such a long time. Why not two?"

"Remember, you are Lady Grey. And Lady Grey—"

"Let me guess. She doesn't swear?"

He looked over her shoulder, tried to muster some sort of dreamy expression. Hopefully he didn't appear as much of an idiot as he felt. "No," he said, "Lady Grey is an absolute angel. I have never heard her utter one word—"

Charlotte snorted. "Horseshit."

Mr. Lesser coughed in the background.

Philip returned his gaze to Charlotte, stared at her down his nose.

"Who always won the cursing contests when we were younger?" she asked.

Philip hesitated before answering. "You did."

Her lips curved in a knowing smile. "And who came in second?"

"Joann—Lady Grey?"

"Exactly." Charlotte nodded, then paused and cocked her head to the side. She took a step toward him. She might as well have thrown herself at him bodily, for the instant jolt of arousal that rocked his senses as she neared. "It is most curious."

"What is?"

She took another step forward, and Philip took a deep breath as he inhaled her jasmine scent.

*Do not touch her. Do not touch her. Do not touch her.*

Charlotte leaned toward him and peered into his face, balancing herself by placing her hand on his shoulder.

She really should not have done that.

He'd give her ten seconds to step away before he hauled her over his shoulder.

Even though he had cast aside his first plan to imprison her in his room, he would not be averse to reverting to that old idea. Using his lips and his tongue and his hands to convince her to stay appealed to him far more than some desperate, impulsive proposal that she teach him to become a better husband for his next wife.

"I never noticed it before. But you're cross-eyed."

Philip jerked his hand away—mere inches from making contact with the deliciously rounded swell of her hip. "I beg your pardon."

She held up her finger, waved it in front of his face as she had done yesterday when she thought he'd hurt his head.

Philip gripped the annoying appendage and, only through the most supreme amount of self-restraint, resisted the urge to draw it into his mouth and suck on her soft, tender flesh. Instead, he lowered it to her side, relishing the brief contact. "I am not cross-eyed."

"You are when you look down your nose at me that way."

Philip growled and pushed her toward Mr. Lesser. "Continue your lesson."

Charlotte grinned and crossed her own eyes before turning away. She murmured something to Mr. Lesser which had him looking at Philip curiously, his mouth crooked as he tried not to smile.

At Philip's scowl, he immediately returned his attention to Charlotte. "Ten more minutes, Your Grace. Surely you can master the exercise in ten more minutes."

Philip had told himself he would be nice. Indeed, he had woken up this morning feeling refreshed and renewed, ready to begin with a new outlook. Even his injured leg had healed quite nicely overnight. He had decided he would charm Charlotte, show her how he had changed, how he could behave like the man she wanted him to be.

But he didn't feel nice any longer. And he didn't want to restrain himself.

He stalked around the perimeter of the room, his hands behind his back, his gaze pinned to Charlotte as she studiously ignored his presence.

Amazingly, her performance on the harp became worse.

Despite Mr. Lesser's desperate last words of encouragement, her fingers flailed over the instrument, getting tangled together until Philip feared she would either somehow mutilate herself or break every last string.

"Enough!" Mr. Lesser threw himself in front of the harp before she could reach forward to try again.

Charlotte's gaze flew to Philip, and he saw the flame of anger and defiance in her eyes before she looked again at Mr. Lesser. "Perhaps if His Grace would be so kind as to take a seat or remove himself from the music room, so I may concentrate . . ."

Mr. Lesser glanced back and forth between them as he pulled on his gloves.

Philip paused in his circuit of the room to stand behind Charlotte, purposely allowing his breath to sway wisps of her hair as he spoke. "Is my presence disturbing you, my dear?"

The only answer he received was the stiffening of her spine.

"Very well, then. I shall take a seat, as you suggested."

Philip grazed his hand along the vulnerable skin at the nape of her neck as he moved past.

He chose a nearby chair, positioning it so he faced her, the harp obscuring his view of the left side of her body.

Mr. Lesser, however, seemed disinclined to continue the lesson, even with this show of good behavior from Philip. "I will return next week. You must practice, Your Grace. Practice until your fingers grow numb and your arms grow heavy. I expect much improvement." Then, because Mr. Lesser was, above all, a wise and prudent man, he gave a flourishing bow and added, "It has been a pleasure to work with you today. I have never had such a lovely pupil." He turned to Philip and bowed again. "Your Grace."

Philip inclined his head and watched the harp instructor leave, all the while pretending not to notice Charlotte's intent stare.

Finally, when a full minute had passed and he could feel the palpable touch of her glower begin to brand the side of his jaw with its heat, he turned to her and raised a brow. "Yes?"

She gestured toward him, a motion he supposed was meant to encompass his chair and the two feet of space around him which he dared to darken with his evil, ducal presence. Her wrist flicked, a question mark to her unspoken inquiry.

Philip wondered whether she even realized her lips were pouted. Probably so. She had become an expert at bringing men to their knees, and if anything could make a man beg, it was the sight of her mouth. Full and plump, teasing a man to lose his sanity for just one taste.

A weaker man would have been unable to resist such a temptation. He would have run, walked, perhaps even crawled to her, would have obeyed every last one of her wishes and desires, to be able to take her mouth with his own.

Philip was not a weak man. If he kissed her, it would be on his own terms.

He shrugged. "I wanted to be close to you. See what a dutiful husband I am?"

Charlotte lowered her arm and scowled. "I am not Joanna. You need not spout such foolishness to me."

Philip searched his sleeve for an imaginary piece of lint. "Of course. Apologies. I suppose I got carried away with the rehearsal."

He looked up, tried to muster his best innocent expression. From the way she regarded him, as if horns and pitchfork were a natural part of his ensemble for the day, he assumed his efforts were not successful.

Which was a damned shame, for he wanted so much to be good. But the more she looked at him like he was the devil incarnate, the darker and more dangerous his thoughts became.

His body began to ache beneath the torch of her gaze, and even the threat of eternal damnation could not curb his overactive imagination from devising a multitude of new sins he wanted to commit.

With her. On this chair. On that chair. On the damned floor. Above him. Beneath him. All around him.

She made it bloody difficult to be a gentleman, when she dared him with those brilliant blue eyes and that pouting mouth to be anything but.

"Philip." The mouth moved.

"Charlotte." *My love.*

Her fingers tapped against the column of the harp. "I do believe it is time to begin your first lesson."

Sometimes Charlotte really wished Philip had green eyes. Or blue eyes. Or, even better, plain old brown eyes.

There was nothing intimidating or unnerving when a person with brown eyes stared at you.

But silver eyes—

Charlotte tapped her fingers again against the harp, a purposeful motion meant to disguise how her hand was wont to tremble beneath that intense silver gaze.

"My first lesson." Philip leaned forward, and Charlotte had to stop herself from pressing against the back of her own chair, or ducking her head behind the harp where he couldn't see her anymore.

"Please go on. I earnestly await your instructions on how to be a better husband."

Charlotte rose from her seat—calmly, so he wouldn't be able to tell how he affected her. She stopped at a low side table and picked up the gloves she had discarded when Mr. Lesser arrived.

It was silly, really, but for some reason she didn't feel quite as vulnerable with Philip when she wore gloves.

Turning back toward him, she held up a finger. "The first thing you must learn is how to behave properly when you have guests. You must not—"

"We. When *we* have guests."

Charlotte sent him a pointed look. "You and Joanna. Not we."

"If I am to practice and do it well, you must pretend you are Lady Grey. It is as we discussed before."

"Very well." Charlotte gritted her teeth and raised her finger higher in the air. "When *we* have guests, you must act with the appropriate, proper behavior."

Philip nodded solemnly. "I can be very proper."

She ignored him. "You must not stalk around the room—"

"Stalk?" His brow wrinkled.

"—as if you were a lion and everyone else is your prey."

"Do you really think I stalk? I must say, that is quite a stroke to my ego. I assume I appear quite dangerous when I do it?"

Charlotte rolled her eyes and continued. "You must not mock your guests—"

"*Our* guests."

"—And you must certainly not mock your wife."

"You think I mock you? I assure you, my dear, I—"

There was nothing for it. Charlotte marched toward him and clapped her hand over his mouth. It was almost comical, the way his eyebrows inched up his forehead. Or it would have been, had those silver eyes not been so close, and had she not been able to feel the heat of his mouth searing her palm through the thin layer of her glove.

"And you must never—I repeat, *never*—interrupt the way you are doing now. It is most rude, and shows that you believe yourself superior to those around you."

He mumbled something against her hand, and Charlotte drew her arm away.

"Yes?" she prompted impatiently.

"But I *am* superior to almost everyone around me." His eyes flashed with amusement. "After all, I am a duke."

Groaning, Charlotte dropped her face into her hands. "I begin to feel I am doing Joanna a very great harm by helping you."

"You are not helping me in the least. You are giving me rules about what not to do, but you are not telling me how to correct my behavior, or what I should do instead."

Charlotte lifted her head and glared at him. "If you are unsatisfied with my instruction—and I still think this entire idea is absolutely ridiculous—then perhaps you should tell me what you desire to gain from these lessons."

Philip stood and moved toward her, brushed his knuckles across her cheek. It was a gesture so unlike him, so gentle and unexpected, that Charlotte's breath caught in her throat at his touch.

"I know how to be a duke," he said softly. "I know how to sneer, how to freeze a man cold in his step. I know how to be harsh and cruel, how to manipulate others to serve my will. All of these things were taught to me, and I learned them well."

His fingers smoothed the hair at her temples.

"Being a duke comes easy to me. Knowing how to be a husband does not. It is too late for us, but I would like for you to teach me. And for the rest of the time we are married, I will try to be a better husband to you, and you will help me be a better husband to my next wife—whoever she may be."

Charlotte lifted her hand, eased his fingers away from her face. Soft words and gentle touches were too much, coming from Philip. "You seem sincere."

His eyes searched hers, cautiously, earnestly, as if he needed to see that she believed him. "I am sincere."

Only time would tell if it was the truth. She knew well how easily lies slipped from that quicksilver tongue. But all that mattered to her right now was that he kept his promise to divorce her.

Time would tell on that account, as well.

She was a fool to trust him, but did she have any other choice? She could either go through the pretense of teaching him how to be a husband, with the possible outcome that he would carry through on his promise. Or she could refuse, and he would leave her at Ruthven Manor, imprisoned in the countryside, without any hope of freedom in the foreseeable future.

He had played her well; she was a pawn disguised as a duchess.

Philip edged forward. "Pretend Mr. Lesser is still here. In fact, twenty other guests are here, come for a harp recital. You have become the best harpist in the world, and everyone is eager to see you, to hear you play."

Charlotte couldn't help it—a tiny smile tugged at her lips at the fanciful image he drew for her.

"You and I are husband and wife, but we are different people. We are happy. We love each other." He gave her a glance of warning, his own lips curved. "Don't laugh."

Charlotte held up her hands. "Never. Do go on."

"Your performance, of course, is amazing, and I am proud to have you as my wife. I boast to all of our guests—"

Shaking her head, Charlotte said, "No boasting."

Philip stared at her. "Nothing at all? But what good is it to have a wife such as you if I cannot—"

"Nothing at all."

"Well." Philip tucked his hands behind his back, then swung them forward again, gesturing to some imaginary guest by the fireplace. "Lord Cohen has been leering at you all evening. I continue to glare at him, but he doesn't take the hint. I'm beginning to think I will have to have him escorted off the premises by Fallon and a footman or two. And if he doesn't comply, perhaps I will be able to persuade him by other, more forceful means."

Charlotte cast the empty space a considering glance. Was it by pure coincidence that he used the name of one of the men rumored to have been her lover?

She turned her head to look at Philip. Even though his stance was relaxed, his eyes glittered with possessiveness, ever watchful, ever secretive.

Charlotte fought to control the shudder that inched along her spine. Either Philip was a damned good actor, making himself believe he was jealous of another—even imaginary—man, or something had changed between them.

Something intimate, and new, and altogether frightening.

"No." Charlotte forced the word past her lips. "It would be more appropriate to ignore him altogether. Stay by me, fetch me another glass of champagne, banter wittily with the guests who meander our way. Touch my shoulder, my hand, my waist—not often, and not conspicuously, but enough to show that we belong together." She swallowed, wishing she had one of those glasses of champagne right now. "That we love each other, as you said."

Philip raised a brow. "This is how a proper husband behaves when we have guests?"

"Yes."

"Hmm." He looked pointedly over her shoulder. "And what do I do if a, shall we say, very well-endowed lady tries to catch my attention and lure me from your side?"

Charlotte craned her neck to search the spot where he indicated. Somehow it was very easy to imagine the busty and worldly Lady Harrington, Philip's mistress, beckoning to him behind her back.

She returned her gaze to him. "First of all, a good husband wouldn't have even noticed that another woman was 'very well-endowed.'"

"You mean a blind husband."

Charlotte bared her teeth in a smile. "A good husband," she repeated.

"Then you expect me to look at you and only you for the remainder of my life?"

She narrowed her eyes at him. Something in his tone of voice made her suspicious. "Yes . . ."

"You expect me to be faithful." He drew out the last word, bending toward her as he did so, and Charlotte stiffened. But at the last moment before his lips could brush her cheek, or her ear, or her hair, he pulled back, paced away from her.

"Of course," Charlotte murmured to his back, overly aware that her heart had stopped beating and had only resumed its fierce pounding when a goodly amount of distance was put between them.

"And do you think if I were a good, proper, faithful husband, that my wife would be good and faithful as well?"

If she had any talent as an artist, she would sketch Philip right now, just as he was, all vertical lines. And she would use a thick, black piece of charcoal to indicate the stiffness and tension evident in his posture. "I assume you are referring to yourself and Joanna, and not to you and me?"

He moved his head by only a fraction, just enough so she could see the hard, sculpted plane of his jaw. "Quite so."

"Then yes, if you were faithful and, as you said earlier, you loved one another, then I imagine she would be faithful to you also."

Philip turned around then, his expression inscrutable. He spoke as he strolled toward her. "You have told me how to behave when we are in public, when we have guests. But what about when we are alone, Charlotte?"

He was getting close, far too close.

"How should I behave then? Or should I behave at all?"

Her instincts told her to leave, to sashay away, to use the movements of her body to distract him from whatever devious purpose he intended.

"Would a good husband touch you like this?" Philip raised his arm, cupped her cheek tenderly in the palm of his hand.

"Or perhaps like this?" He laid his other hand at the small of her back. Charlotte wasn't certain whether he used it to pull her toward him or to keep her still as he stepped closer to her, but suddenly she had no space to breathe, to move. He was there, everywhere, surrounding her.

"Philip—"

"Tell me, Charlotte. If I were a good husband, would I kiss you like this?"

# Chapter 8

Charlotte should have been prepared.

She knew his kisses. As much as she wished she could have forgotten them over the past three years, they had stayed fresh in her mind, the memory of them taunting her when some other man tried to kiss her.

Certainly no other man's kiss could be as devastating as Philip's. As soon as his lips met hers, the careful detachment she had trained herself to feel was nowhere to be found.

She'd told herself he'd caught her off guard by the banks of the stream, and that was why she hadn't immediately pulled away.

She couldn't use that excuse now.

She'd known, with all the certainty of seeing clouds pile up over the horizon, that a storm was coming. She'd known he was going to kiss her.

And yet, still she was surprised.

Surprised that he didn't plunder and conquer, as she'd expected.

There was a wealth of restraint in his touch as he plied her mouth with soft, seductive kisses, nipping gently at her bottom lip, teasing her with light little pecks to the corners of her lips.

She could feel it in the firmness of his hands, one at her cheek and the other at her back, as he held her motionless for his tender assault.

He wanted her.

And the only reason she didn't pull away was because she wanted to push him. Past his rigid, ducal boundaries of expected behavior and into the realm where desire ruled. She wanted to see the man who had taught her to separate emotion from passion brought to his knees with the force of his need.

Begging her for another kiss, another touch.

This was why she allowed him to cover her face with soft caresses from his lips.

This was why she held still, the heat from his body seeping into her skin, warming her blood and slowing her pulse to a heavy, languid flow.

"Is it like this, Charlotte?" Philip swept his lips across her forehead, the bridges of her cheeks. "Is this how a husband properly kisses his wife? Tell me, Charlotte."

"No," she whispered, closing her eyes as his mouth drifted over her eyelids, pressing soft, whisperlike kisses there.

"No?" His voice was husky, a deeper timbre than usual. It made her want to sink into him, to have that velvet-bass voice wrap around her, rough and sensual.

She was glad for the brace of his arms holding her in place, keeping her from leaning into him. Her mind knew better, but her body was traitorous, yearning for him. This man who knew how to strum her body, how to make her cry out with pleasure with his deft, knowing fingers.

It had been three years, but still the memory was there. It had always been there.

He drew back, held her gaze as he used his thumb

to nudge her lips apart. Her blood quickened, and she watched him as she moved her tongue forward, slid it against the tip of his thumb.

His eyes gleamed as he lowered them to her lips. "Shall I kiss you properly, then? Teach me, Charlotte." He bent his head, and his breath soughed against her lips. "Show me how to be a good husband."

Charlotte waited until the very last second, after he removed his thumb and closed his eyes. When he kissed her, he kissed instead the index finger she had raised to her mouth. His lips were a scant inch from touching hers.

His eyes flew open, so close she could see black flecks, like obsidian, floating in the silver pools of his irises.

"Am I to understand you do not want to teach me?" he asked, his lips moving against her finger.

"A proper husband and wife will show their affection for one another within the confines of their bedchambers."

Philip straightened, but not before he drew her palm to his mouth for another kiss. "Is that what you desire of a husband? Propriety? Good manners?"

Charlotte gave a delicate shrug. "I am not thinking of myself, of course, but only of dear Joanna, and what she would want in a husband."

He flinched when she said Joanna's name. The movement was small, almost imperceptible, but it was there.

"Yes. Of course. Lady Grey."

Charlotte laughed. "Did you forget her, Philip? I'm afraid this doesn't bode well for your impending marriage. That is, if she even agrees to your proposal."

"She will agree."

"You think so?" Charlotte stepped to the side, ran her fingertips along the back of a chair in a pretense of checking for dust. "Your confidence is admirable, I suppose, although probably misplaced."

"I appreciate your concern, but you need not worry on my behalf."

She glanced at him sideways. "Perhaps I am more concerned for Joanna. If you cannot even remember the purpose for your lessons—"

"It is that damned gown you're wearing," Philip growled. "Even a saint would not be able to keep his wits about him when a woman wears a dress such as that. Somehow it appeared far more modest before you put it on."

Charlotte looked down. It was one of the gowns Anne had said Philip chose for her, one she'd never seen before this morning. In fact, it was much more conservative than any of the dresses in her London wardrobe. But arguing with him about the style of her dress would not be nearly as entertaining as provoking him.

Pursing her lips, she blew gently at the imaginary specks of dust lining her fingertips. "My apologies, Philip. I didn't mean to tease you. I'd forgotten it's been . . . oh, four or five days since you've had a chance to visit your mistress."

When he said nothing, she peeked at him beneath her lashes. He stood still, silent. Not as a statue, but as a predator watching his prey. Waiting for her to take a misstep, to say anything he could use to his advantage.

Charlotte edged around the chair. It was a nice, reasonably-sized buffer.

"I wonder how Joanna will feel about your keeping a mistress."

"I doubt she would be surprised. Many men keep mistresses because they cannot find pleasure with their wives."

Charlotte jerked her chin up at the suggestion that she hadn't been able to please him. How well she remembered the first week after their wedding, the solitude and the crying, when she loved him and hated him all at the same time. Knowing he had bedded her only to consummate the marriage, then had gone off to Lady Harrington.

She pushed the chair aside as she advanced toward him. "How dare—"

"I don't keep a mistress any longer."

Charlotte froze a foot away from him. The scathing retort she'd prepared slid bitterly down her throat.

"I haven't kept one for six months."

He was chock-full of surprises recently, wasn't he?

She began to clap her hands. "Bravo, Your Grace. Bravo." When he did not move, did not speak, only continued watching her, Charlotte stopped. "I do hope that was an appropriate response. You were looking for my applause, were you not? Perhaps congratulations are in order, instead?"

Finally, his mouth quirked at one corner. He inclined his head. "Thank you, my dear. I can always trust you to—"

He stopped. Shut his mouth. Then he pivoted on his heel and strode from the room, leaving his sentence unfinished and Charlotte gaping after him.

"No. Not that one. Another." Philip pushed the necklace back over to the jeweler.

The door jangled behind him, signaling that another village vulture had dared to enter the small shop and gawk at him.

Perhaps it had been a mistake to come to Henley-in-Arden. Yet if he'd stayed one moment longer with Charlotte, he would have risked her scorn and foolishly told her everything.

All of his plans, laid to waste, only because of his damnable pride.

He wouldn't have let her leave the room until she believed him. Not only about his mistress, but also the reason why he had not lain with another woman within the past six months.

Why he'd kidnapped her and brought her home, to Warwickshire.

Why he'd bought her the harp.

It was terrible to consider, but he might have even sent a servant into his study to retrieve the new piece of poetry his wretched soul insisted he try to write.

Of course, she would have laughed at him. Or worse, pitied him. Neither of those possibilities bothered him nearly as much, however, as the knowledge that he would then be back to the beginning, frighteningly in love with her yet with no idea how to gain her forgiveness and make her love him in return.

"Perhaps Your Grace would like to see a bracelet or our collection of rings instead? Or perhaps a brooch? I have one which—"

"The brooch will be fine," Philip said, cutting the jeweler off. The man was short and squat, and his entire face quivered when he spoke, from his bushy gray eyebrows to his fleshy chin. Even worse, he seemed to be of the opinion that the louder he spoke, the better. "And pray, do not speak again unless I require you to do so."

"Yes, Your ..." The jeweler's voice trailed away under Philip's fierce gaze, until it was nothing more than a whisper. "... Grace."

Philip cut a look toward the horse-faced old matron and her equally horse-faced daughter, who had crept nearer and nearer in the past five minutes, until he imagined he could smell the scent of hay and clover upon their breath.

It took no more than a narrowing of his eyes for each to squeal in dismay and immediately depart the shop, nearly treading upon the other's heels in haste.

Philip released an inaudible sigh and turned back to the jeweler.

"I say, Mr. Spofforth. Does His Grace not remind you of his grandfather? God rest his beloved soul."

At the sound of Lady Grey's cultured tones, Philip tensed again.

Across from him, the jeweler paused to peer up at Philip. "Why, the spitting image, my dear." He turned to beam at Lady Grey. "Just the spitting image."

Philip lowered his chin and spoke out of the corner of his mouth, so only she could hear him. "That was unnecessarily low, my lady."

The jeweler bent and popped back up again, extending his hand. "Ah, here it is, Your Grace. The finest brooch we have."

Philip cast an eye toward the wretched, gaudy piece. Gems of every color were stacked one upon another to form the shape of a peacock. It was a horrific monstrosity, larger even than his fist, and he feared any woman who dared to clasp it to her bosom would immediately fall face forward with its weight.

"Oh, how lovely," Lady Grey cooed beside him. "A proper gift from a duke, do you not agree, Your Grace?"

Philip refused to look at her.

"Indeed, it is remarkable you would say so, my lady," the jeweler continued, his face quivering with enthusiasm. "His Grace's grandfather once commissioned a similar piece for his wife, although that one was even more exquisite than this."

He glanced up, and at Philip's scowl, he hurried on. "Of course, if you don't find it satisfactory, we can create another, something even more extravagant than your grandfather's gift, if you like, Your Grace."

"I'll take it," Philip said.

The jeweler began a small smile, but quickly stifled the expression at Philip's continued glower.

"A strutting peacock . . ." Lady Grey murmured softly beside him.

"Do you have any earbobs?" Philip asked. "Something simple. Elegant." He remembered how Charlotte's eyes had flashed angrily at him that morning. "Sapphires, perhaps."

The jeweler nodded thoughtfully. "If you will excuse me for a moment." He bowed and backed away, stumbling over his feet as he bumped into a stack of boxes behind him.

Philip stared straight ahead. "You are wrong," he said quietly. "I am nothing like my grandfather."

Lady Grey said nothing, only stood beside him as they waited for the jeweler to return.

After a short while, he shuffled forward, solemn and contrite. "My apologies, Your Grace. These are the only sapphire earbobs I have at the moment. I fear they are too small." He opened a box to reveal two sapphire ovals, the size of teardrops. "I can arrange to go to London—"

"That won't be necessary. I shall take them as well."

"Oh, very good. Very good, Your Grace."

It was only a few minutes more before Philip and Lady Grey exited the jewelry shop, his packages tight beneath his arm.

Lady Grey was the first to speak. "I have never been much of a fan of peacocks or sapphires myself, you know. If you decide to purchase jewelry for me in the future, I would advise you to choose pearls. Or have you decided not to court me after all?"

Philip continued to walk, his step never slowing. His thoughts, however, immediately went to Charlotte and her obvious propensity to talk too much.

"Do you intend to do it then? Will you divorce her?"

A man in livery stood across the street, slumped against the side of a barouche. His shoulders were hunched, and his hands hung listlessly against his sides.

He tried to make himself inconspicuous, but Philip wasn't fooled.

He was the same man who'd dogged him to the edge of Henley-in-Arden, then turned back.

Philip stilled, turned toward Lady Grey. "Is that your servant?" He indicated the man with a slight inclination of his head.

Lady Grey's eyes flicked toward him, then back to Philip. "Yes."

"You had him follow me."

"I desired to speak with you—"

"Do not do so again. I am not a fox to be hunted."

As he turned away, Lady Grey grasped at his sleeve. "Damn it, Philip! Will you—"

At her use of profanity, Philip spun to face her. "What did you say?" She opened her mouth to answer, but he spoke first. "You cursed."

"Yes? It's not as if I've never done it before. When we were younger, I—"

"You placed second in the cursing contests," Philip finished. "Right after Charlotte."

Lady Grey gave a tentative smile. "I would have won first, but I was not as fortunate as she was to have four older brothers to educate me."

He chuckled.

The sound surprised him. But it felt good. Slow and deep, it lightened the tension in his chest, lifted his mood. Charlotte had done this. She had helped him to laugh again. "It's strange, but I cannot remember ever hearing you curse before."

Lady Grey's smile faded, and her eyes turned watchful, wary. "I cannot say I am surprised, Your Grace. You rarely paid much attention to anyone other than yourself. You were always more concerned with what others thought of you, especially the old duke." Her voice turned soft, yet was no less cutting for its gentleness. "Why did you buy the brooch, Your Grace?"

Philip ignored her question, all of his good humor having disappeared with her criticism. How quick she was to judge him, when she had been the one to jilt him so shortly before their wedding. "I find I have been erroneous in my judgment of you, my lady. Forgive me."

He lifted the package from beneath his arm and withdrew the small box containing the peacock brooch. He thrust it toward her, loath to touch her and force her to take it in her hand.

"You are far more insightful and intelligent than I gave you credit for. Take the brooch. And take your damned opinions with it."

She made no move, only stared at him with reproach and scorn and, damn it all, pity in her eyes.

Shrugging, Philip released the box, and saw with grim satisfaction that her hand stretched to catch it before it could fall to the ground.

"Good day, Lady Grey."

Charlotte searched the library, the drawing room, Philip's study. She even went so far as to creep around outside the door of his bedchamber, listening for any sound of movement inside.

It was amazing. Philip had left her, alone, at Ruthven Manor.

Her first impulse was to saddle Bryony and ride hell-for-leather back to London.

But she knew he would catch her, and even if she tried to hide, he would find her. Dukes had all sorts of connections. No, as long as she remained in England, she would never be able to run away from him.

She had once considered sailing off to America or even to the Orient to escape Philip and try to find Ethan,

but she had promised her best friend, Lady Emma Whitlock, that she would wait until Lady Emma finished her
current novel. Then they would go together. And Charlotte would never break a promise to Emma, not when
she had been the only woman in London to befriend her
despite the rumors of her licentious behavior.

Without escape as an option, Charlotte decided to
act upon her second impulse, which was to ride to Norrey Hill and discover whether Joanna's footman had returned from delivering the missive to Philip's solicitor.

"Hullo, Scrope," she said as Joanna's butler opened
the door.

"Miss Sheff—" Rheumy old eyes rounded in embarrassment, and he coughed as he corrected himself.
"Your Grace. What a pleasure it is to see you. It's been
a long time."

Charlotte frowned and took a step forward as he
swayed. "You're ill," she accused. "Why are you not in
bed? Surely Joanna would allow one of the footmen to
answer the door."

He shooed her hand away from his arm and tried
to straighten. "Lady Grey and Matthews have gone
to Henley-in-Arden, and Matthews is the only one I
trust—"

"Matthews. He's returned from London, then?"

"Yes, Your Grace. Not over two hours ago."

Charlotte leaned in and snuck a kiss on the old butler's cheek. She hid a smile as a blush rose over his
paper-thin, wrinkled skin. "Thank you, Scrope. Now go
get some rest."

Scrope sniffed, loudly, probably more out of indignation than illness. "Yes, Your Grace."

It took Charlotte no more than five minutes upon ar-
riving in Henley-in-Arden to locate the footman Matthews. He was the only man who stood in the street as

if frozen, allowing the small stream of villagers to mill around and past him.

She stayed Bryony a few yards distant from him.

As she waited for Joanna to appear from one of the shops, she noticed how he shifted his stance. It was slight, only a subtle transfer of weight from one foot to the other, but it was the first movement she'd observed of him in the past few minutes.

She followed the direction of his gaze to find Joanna and Philip in the center of the street.

Charlotte's hands fisted on Bryony's reins.

They had arranged for a rendezvous, after all.

No wonder Philip had left so suddenly. He had been worried he would be late for his appointment to meet with and woo his next wife. And how well Joanna played the part Charlotte had asked of her, her gaze locked intimately on Philip.

The whoosh of Charlotte's breath seemed impossibly loud in her ears as Philip withdrew a small package from beneath his arm and held it out toward Joanna.

Charlotte turned away.

She counted the hills as she raced toward Ruthven Manor, Bryony's legs steady and sure over the hard-packed earth and the brown swells of autumn grass, across well-traveled roads and through flower-laden meadows.

She counted her breaths, tried to make them match the heavy, striking sound of Bryony's hooves.

In. Out. In. Out.

It was ridiculous, really, to feel this way.

Jealous—as if Joanna weren't simply acquiescing to her request.

And betrayed—as if Charlotte hadn't known Philip was interested in the widowed marchioness.

No matter how she tried to pretend—to herself, to everyone, but especially to Philip—the knowledge that her marriage was an utter disaster still hurt. And the pain of seeing him with another woman, even if it wasn't his mistress, was just as sharp as ever.

Perhaps it was because seeing them together reminded her of how naive and foolish she'd been three years ago, to believe theirs was nothing less than a fairytale romance.

Or maybe it was because some misplaced sense of wifely outrage demanded she make him remember that, though he might have agreed to divorce her, English law nevertheless held them bound to one another, even if it was for only another few months.

God help her, she certainly didn't want to believe it was something in Philip that still awed her. Something that continued to attract her to him and, despite her thorough knowledge of the kind of cold and calculating bastard he could be, made her want to believe there was hope for redeeming him.

Whatever the reason behind the dull, dreadful ache hitched high in her chest, Charlotte didn't like it.

Only as the Rutherford stables came into view did she realize she had long since lost count of the number of hills they had traversed, and her breathing had deteriorated from a controlled pacing to unsteady, rambling gasps of air rife with curses.

One of the grooms offered to take Bryony and rub her down, but Charlotte opted to do the task herself, needing the methodical routine to calm down.

When she finished, as she was walking toward the house, she spied Philip riding toward her. He slowed when he saw her.

"Jackass," she muttered beneath her breath, and swept toward Ruthven Manor, determined to ignore him.

She might not have been a model of genteel maturity, but it sure as hell made her feel better. A little righteous indignation went a long way.

"Your Grace," he called behind her.

Charlotte snorted and kicked a pebble out of her way, pretending it was Philip's head. Or his pea-sized brain.

*Your Grace. Humph.*

Always the proper duke, making certain he addressed her formally in front of the servants.

But she wouldn't be the Duchess of Rutherford for very much longer.

Charlotte took a deep breath and exhaled, closing her eyes briefly.

Thank God for that.

The thundering of hooves across the ground compelled her to open them again, and she glanced over her shoulder. An unknown man rode past Philip as he dismounted from his stallion and drew up near the front entrance of the manor.

Before the man could knock, Fallon opened the door and glared through the slight crack. "Yes?" he queried suspiciously.

"I've a message for the Duke of Rutherford," the man panted. "From Mr. Humbert A. Jones, Solicitor."

Charlotte looked back at Philip, only to find his gaze already fixed upon her.

# Chapter 9

"I am the Duke of Rutherford," Philip said, stepping past Charlotte to tower over the courier.

She hurried to his side. She wouldn't dare allow him to read the missive without her there, wouldn't give him the slightest opportunity to hide from her whatever the solicitor said.

If he had double-crossed her and sent a second letter canceling his first request to petition for a divorce, she would know about it.

"Your Grace." The messenger lowered his head and dug into the pouch at his waist.

Philip took the letter from his fingers and nodded to Fallon, who, upon his master's arrival, had swung the door wide open.

"Give him two shillings for his trouble," Philip ordered, then walked past Fallon into the foyer.

Charlotte skipped to keep up with him. "I demand that you allow me to read the letter."

Philip never slowed his step as he approached his study, nor did he turn his head to address her, but continued walking, his back stiff and straight. "Come, Charlotte. I cannot dally all day, waiting for you."

She would have dressed him down with a scathing retort, or an equally imaginative curse, but she found she needed most of her breath in order to jog her way to his side.

Of course, by that point, they had reached his study.

Philip opened the door and gestured inside, his arm outstretched, the letter pinched between his fingers. "Dearest."

Huffing, Charlotte strolled past him, pausing briefly to snatch the missive from his hand as she did so.

The door slammed shut. He growled behind her, but she danced away from him. She broke the seal and unfolded the parchment. A hum of satisfaction filled her as she quickly scanned the note.

His shadow fell across her. "Give me the letter."

Charlotte glanced upward. She held his gaze as she released the paper, allowing it to float downward. "I fear you'll have to pick it up from the floor," she said, smiling sweetly.

Philip's eyes flicked to the carpet, then back to her face. The curve of his lips was nothing if not predatory, not at all what she had expected, and she turned toward the row of windows overlooking the lawn.

Charlotte leaned against the space between the windows and pretended to admire the landscape, but in actuality she studied him from beneath her lashes.

He had already bent to retrieve the missive, his expression half concealed, half exposed by the late-afternoon sun as he read. And all she could think while she watched him was that the play of shadows and light upon his face was like a mask upon a mask. She could see nothing of his thoughts from the line of his brow or the careful stillness of his mouth.

After a few moments of silence, when his eyes had

stopped moving but still he kept his head bent, she spoke. "It seems you kept your word."

He looked up then. "You sound surprised."

She gave a delicate shrug of her shoulders. "In truth, I am. You are a serious man, which some believe implies that you are also honest, but sincerity has not often been a part of your character."

"Philosophy, my dear? How . . . educated you have become." Philip folded the parchment again and slipped it into his pocket. He widened the distance between them by moving to sit in the chair behind his desk.

Charlotte flattened her palms against the wall as she recognized his move for what it was: as a king had his throne, so a duke had his desk. He was reminding both of them of his status as her superior.

They stared at each other across the room, and she couldn't help but remember how much he had frightened her that morning, how easily he could awaken desires she'd rather have presumed dead.

And it was precisely because his kisses lingered in her memory that she determined to be at her most alert and cautious. She would not give him the opportunity to use her desires against her once again.

Philip reached in his pocket, and Charlotte thought he was going to take out the letter again, but instead he drew forth a small package. He laid it on the desk in front of him and placed his hands on either side.

"I must confess, my darling, I am wounded that you continue to think so ill of me. I have become a changed man, remember?"

Charlotte narrowed her eyes. "You are *trying* to change."

"Yes. Of course."

"I saw you in Henley-in-Arden, with Joanna."

He lifted a brow.

"You gave her a gift."

Philip laughed, a charming, easy laugh, one that put her on edge. "You're jealous," he said.

She wanted to laugh right back at him—a laugh of wonder that he might suggest such a thing. But instead her pulse raced and she had to force herself to not look away.

"No, not jealous," she replied. "Just surprised."

He cocked his head to the side, inviting her to come closer. Charlotte didn't budge. "Why are you surprised? You knew I intended to woo her." He paused. "Perhaps you wanted a gift as well?"

"My freedom is all I need. Besides, you already gave me the harp."

"Ah. Well. I suppose I am simply a very generous man, because I did indeed purchase a gift for you in addition to the one for Lady Grey."

Her heart hammered at his words, and though she told herself he was only trying to purchase her continued cooperation, it refused to return to a normal pace. Why must she become so excited when Philip sought to give her something? She'd received countless gifts from other men over the years, and none of them had brought this same breathlessness or anticipation.

"Come here, Charlotte."

She stayed at the windows.

"Please."

It might have been the deepening of his voice in that single syllable, or perhaps the fact that she couldn't recall the last time he had said "Please." First her hands left the wall and then her feet moved soundlessly over the carpet, until she stood before him.

He picked up the package and held it out to her. Wordlessly, she took it, her fingers sliding against his. Charlotte removed the paper wrapping and looked down at the small box in her hands, then up at Philip.

"I won't like you any better for this, you know."

"No, I did not expect you would," he answered quietly.

Her curiosity piqued, she lifted the lid of the box.

"They are a bit more reserved than your usual pieces," he said.

"Yes." She could not look at him. Whereas the harp had been the fulfillment of a childhood dream, the small earbobs were somehow much more intimate.

As if he had searched for the oval sapphires specifically, pictured her wearing them.

"Why did you buy these?" she asked, her voice soft.

He said nothing, until she finally had to lift her head and meet his eyes. "Philip?"

She didn't know what she was looking for—a hidden message in his gaze, a glimpse of vulnerability, maybe—but all she found was the calculating gleam of his silver stare.

"I hope you will wear the earbobs for our supper tomorrow evening."

Charlotte closed the box, berating herself. She should know by now that he always had an ulterior motive. "You have kept to your end of our agreement. I will also keep to mine."

"The supper will be a test of sorts, to see what I have learned from your lessons thus far."

"The ideal-husband lessons, you mean."

"Yes. Up to now we have been alone. Tomorrow evening we will have guests, and you must help me to be at my most"—he paused, tapped his finger on his jaw, then grinned—"dashing."

"And the earbobs—"

He stood abruptly and advanced toward her, around the desk, until he was no more than a few inches away. "Simply a gift for a beautiful woman."

Charlotte lifted a hand to her brow. "Why, Philip, I do believe I feel a bit faint. Such flattery, such kindness."

"Shall I catch you?" His gaze had risen to follow the upward movement of her arm, and his expression stilled, his eyes shuttered as he focused behind her.

Charlotte lowered her arm and peered over her shoulder. All she could see was a portrait hung upon the wall over his desk, of a man whose silver eyes matched the streaks in his black hair. His face was hard and lined, and the same sense of unease crept over her skin that she'd felt whenever she saw him as a child.

The old duke. Philip's grandfather.

She glanced back at Philip. "He always was rather scary-looking, wasn't he?"

His attention never wavered from the painting. "I'd forgotten it was there," he said, his voice low and distant, almost as if he didn't realize she was still in the study.

Charlotte gave a half laugh. "And not only there, but in the drawing room, the music room, the dining room. Not to mention my bedchamber. I cannot tell you how discomforting it is, trying to go to sleep while he glares down at me."

Only then did Philip shift his focus to her, a small quirk showing at the corner of his mouth. "I can imagine. You may not remember, but there's another portrait in my bedchamber as well. After he died, I could not sleep for weeks. I was convinced his ghost would come out of the painting and haunt me."

He turned, a cautious movement, but Charlotte noticed it was enough so he could no longer see the portrait behind him.

She wasn't certain why, but she felt suddenly protective of him, of the young man he'd once been. She edged closer, until their arms touched. She looked with him toward the opposite end of the room, at the low fire burning in the hearth, a buffer against the chill of the darkening sky.

"He thought very highly of himself, didn't he?" she asked.

"Yes." Then, after a small pause, as if he felt obliged to give an explanation, he added, "He was a duke."

"You're a duke, also, but you're nothing like he was."

Even as she said it, it came to her as a surprise. She knew the sort of man Philip was: selfish and manipulative. The old duke had been the same way.

In the past, she would never have defended him, rather claiming that they were cut from the same cloth.

And yet now there were differences. Perhaps Philip had changed, despite her initial disbelief. There were glimpses of kindness and warmth, of real humor and generosity, that she could not even remember seeing in the time he had courted her. Oh, he had been gallant then, and considerate, but not nearly as . . . as human.

Philip made a mirthless sound, something that others might have mistaken as a chuckle. Charlotte, however, recognized it for what it was: a warning, to her, to the entire world, not to come too close. Not to show sympathy for a man who neither needed nor desired any.

She brought her hands together in front of her, joined by the box which contained the elegant sapphires.

"Thank you for the earbobs," she said.

She felt him shrug against her side. "As I said, it was simply a gift for a beautiful woman."

Charlotte nodded, though she didn't think he saw it. Then, without another word, she crossed in front of him and left the room.

Philip wasn't prepared for the abrupt sense of loss he felt when Charlotte left the study.

If he'd been a maudlin sort of man, or a poet—which God knew he wasn't—he would have thought she'd taken his soul with her.

He stared after her, at the empty doorway, and considered calling for her to return. To not leave him alone.

She would come back, and tell him again in that soft voice that he was not like his grandfather. He would take her in his arms, crush his mouth to hers, and pretend she was right.

He would never admit he knew she was wrong.

Despite what he'd told Lady Grey in the jeweler's shop, Philip held no illusions about himself, of who he was or was not.

He was a duke, just like his grandfather. And he was a damned good one, for the old bastard had taught him well. And just like the eighth Duke of Rutherford, Philip would do whatever was necessary to have his way.

A heavy knock sounded on the wooden door frame, and he straightened. "Enter."

Fallon appeared, bowing as soon he stepped into the room.

"Close the door." Once assured of their privacy, he beckoned the butler to come closer. "You gave the two shillings to the messenger, as I instructed?"

"Yes, Your Grace." Fallon withdrew a piece of parchment from within his coat. "Here is the second letter."

"Very good." Philip took the missive and motioned him away.

He waited until Fallon disappeared and shut the door behind him before he sat at his desk again.

The letter was as he expected: Mr. Jones confirmed he had received Philip's second letter, voiding his request for a divorce from Charlotte. He also wrote of his relief upon the arrival of the second letter, as he had feared the duke was setting himself up for a catastrophic scandal.

Philip scowled, the edges of the parchment crumpling in his grip. To hell with the scandals. He only wanted Charlotte.

After quickly scanning the remainder of the note, he crossed to the hearth and fed it into the fire.

Time would tell whether his precaution in canceling the directive for the petition had been necessary. If he was successful in wooing Charlotte as he planned, she would have no need to know he never intended to divorce her.

Charlotte had no doubt Philip was trying to suffocate her.

After years of wearing the most scandalous gowns she could, she found that the high-necked, long-sleeved, stiff taffeta dress left her no room to move, let alone breathe.

Not only that—there had already been a time or two in the past few minutes when she was certain she'd heard him snicker.

But every time she looked his way, he casually glanced at the clock nearby.

"I'm sure they'll be here soon," he offered, with the smallest trace of a smile. "Have I mentioned tonight how very . . . wholesome you appear?"

Charlotte tipped her chin up, partly for relief from the tight fabric scratching against her throat and partly as a show of indifference. "You have yet to mention who our guests will be this evening. I hope you did not invite Joanna. That would be quite awkward."

"No, Lady Grey was not invited. I suppose I should warn you—"

A clatter of horses' hooves and jingling harnesses arose outside, and they both got to their feet.

Philip crossed the room to stand beside her. "I should have told you before, but I didn't want you to be upset."

Charlotte ran a finger along the inside of her collar. "Why ever should I be upset? If I'm angry, it's because you made me wear this horrid dress. Well, from this night forward, what I wear and what I do not wear has nothing to do with our agreement. I shall throw out every one of—"

"Forgive me." Philip gripped her hand and squeezed. "I only wanted to help."

His plea had her swinging her gaze up to search his. "What do you—"

"Your family, Charlotte," he whispered harshly, and dropped her hand as a shadow darkened the drawing room's entryway.

Fallon bowed with a creaking flourish. "Squire Sheffield, Mrs. Sheffield, and Messrs. Roland, Nicholas, and Arthur Sheffield."

As he stepped to the side, Charlotte's heart plummeted to the pit of her stomach with such speed she nearly cast up her accounts.

"Philip," she whispered, her fingers frantically searching for something to hold on to.

He grasped her hand and laid it gently over his arm. "I'm right here," he answered quietly. "Everything will be fine."

She wanted so much to believe him—equally as much as she wanted to hit him for arranging the entire affair. But she feared that even with a proper dress and an elegant set of earbobs, her parents were certain to see past the ladylike accoutrements to the tainted woman she'd become.

Her mother was the first to enter the room, followed closely by her father. The skin beneath her mother's eyes was dark, her cheeks sunken—though the downward turn of her mouth and the bulk of her girth told it was not from hunger but from sadness. There was no sadness in her father's eyes—only the same burning anger, his eyebrows perpetually slanted.

Charlotte swallowed and gave them a weak smile. "Hullo, Mum. Hullo, Papa."

"Charlotte, dear," her mother said, then looked away.

Her father cleared his throat and glowered first at Philip, then at her. "Charlotte."

Philip's other hand came up to cover hers and, instead of jerking away, she was never more grateful for his strong, solid presence.

Roland, Nicholas, and Arthur trickled in behind their parents, each with expressions that indicated they'd rather be in hell.

At some point a nervous tickle crept up her throat, and as she stared at the miserable faces of the family she loved and had missed for so long, she could not keep herself from laughing.

This, of course, only made her father glare at her all the more, his mouth narrowed suspiciously. "Is this what you learned in London, Charlotte? To laugh at your elders?"

"N-no, Papa," she answered, and had to cover her mouth over a small hiccup.

It was amazing. She might as well have been eight years old again, readying herself for another whipping and lecture on why good little girls did not sing in church. Especially not while the sermon was being delivered, and *especially* not a song such as "Bessie's Flying Skirts."

It made her want to laugh again, but even more, it made her want to cry.

"Shall we go in to supper, then?" Philip asked, rescuing her at the very moment she would have launched herself into her father's arms and hugged him.

It was very good of him, as she wasn't sure what her reception would be should she act upon such an impulse.

They filed silently into the dining room, Charlotte pulled close to Philip's side.

"Remember. I'm right here," he whispered before

they parted to sit at opposite ends of the table. She shouldn't have taken comfort in his words, as he'd been the one to invite them, but she did.

As footmen brought forth the first course, she wondered what kind of world it had become, when she and Philip were no longer adversaries, but had somehow formed a fragile allegiance.

It did not escape her notice that he seated her parents at his end of the table, with Nicholas in the middle and Roland and Arthur on either side of her.

Although she was glad for the human buffers her brothers presented to keep her parents from blustering too loudly at her, Charlotte could not keep her eyes from lingering on the empty chair across from Nicholas.

The seat where Ethan should have been.

Spoons tapped a tense, steady rhythm against bowls, the only sound she could hear against the backdrop of her mother's sighs and her father's grumbling.

Her brothers—intelligent men that they were— wisely kept their heads down, staring with fascination into their soup.

Charlotte met Philip's gaze down the length of the table. At the inquiring lift of his brow, she shrugged helplessly. He gave her a short nod and turned toward her father, murmuring an indecipherable question.

Her father banged his spoon upon the table. Charlotte jumped.

"Damnation! We're here, aren't we? What else do you expect?"

Philip's answer carried evenly to her ears. "Perhaps a little civil conversation would be best. Do you not agree, Mrs. Sheffield?"

Interrupted in midsigh, her mother blinked at the charming smile sent her way. Charlotte could well understand her reaction. Even viewed in profile, the curve of Philip's lips sent her own heart racing.

"Yes, Your Grace. That would be best," her mother echoed.

"Excellent," Philip said and, catching Charlotte's eye, sent her a wink. Like the first time he'd winked at her, the movement caught her by surprise.

Over the next hour and seven more courses, they spoke of the ordinary and mundane topics of everyday life: of the good rains this summer and the flooding last year; of old Mr. Carlisle, who had finally died in May; and also of the youth deserting the village in favor of finding employment and excitement in London or nearby Birmingham.

It was a stilted, drawn out affair, full of awkward pauses and hasty glances thrown down both ends of the table.

No mention was made of the past, nor of Ethan, nor of any rumors her family may or may not have heard about the way she'd behaved over the past three years, for which Charlotte was grateful.

At the end, everyone watched and waited as Arthur carefully and painstakingly savored the last of his pineapple cream, apparently oblivious to the impatient throat clearings sent his way. Charlotte was tempted to reach over and remove it herself, so anxious was she for the meal to be over.

Finally, as Arthur's spoon slipped from his mouth for the last time, Philip turned to Charlotte's father and said, "Mrs. Sheffield mentioned your gout has been acting up terribly, with the rain coming. What do you say? Shall we leave the port and the cigars for another evening, Squire?"

He swung his head toward Philip, then to his wife, then back again. "Gout? I do not—"

Philip narrowed his eyes.

"I . . ." Her father allowed the remainder of his sentence to trail away. His face reddened, even to the tips of his ears. "Yes, Your Grace, my foot has been bothering me greatly tonight. Perhaps, as you suggested, another evening would be better."

A polite smile spread across Philip's face and he rose, signaling for the others to rise with him. "Then we shall bid you farewell."

They moved to the drawing room and waited for Fallon to fetch Mrs. Sheffield's shawl. Charlotte and Philip stood near the hearth while her family clustered together in front of the doors.

When Fallon appeared, Charlotte swallowed past the nervous lump in her throat and stepped forward.

"Mum. Papa. Please—" She had meant to plead for their forgiveness, but at her father's cold blue stare, and as her mother averted her gaze to busy herself with her shawl, she faltered.

Instead, she moved to her brothers. "Roland—"

He gripped her in a bear hug. "Lottie," he whispered in her ear. "Give them time."

She nodded and pulled back, and Nicholas and Arthur were there, waiting to embrace her.

Nicholas tousled her hair as he released her.

"We missed you," Arthur said when he took his turn to hug her.

As he dropped his arms to his sides, Charlotte looked over, hopeful, searching for her parents.

They were no longer in the doorway.

Nor, when she peeked out of the drawing room and into the corridor, could she see them walking toward the front entrance.

She turned back to her brothers and tried to smile, but failed miserably. "Papa moves unusually fast despite his gout," she joked.

They laughed politely, not quite meeting her eyes, and then said their good-byes. Then they, too, left the drawing room.

She leaned on the door frame, unable to tear her gaze away from their departing backs. Yet she didn't call for them to return, or to wait for her, so she could go with them to Sheffield House. It seemed she belonged nowhere.

Charlotte closed her eyes when Philip's hand brushed the back of her neck, along the edge of the high collar.

"You were marvelous tonight," he said, his voice low and soothing, tugging softly on her bruised heart, just as his fingers tugged at the stray wisps of hair falling from her coiffure.

For once, she didn't try to shrug him off. Neither did she choose to be assertive or bold, but stood still and silent beneath his gentle touch. Absorbing his strength, the warmth radiating from his fingertips to her skin, the masculine scent of soap and leather which filtered through her nostrils and intoxicated her blood.

He sighed, and the rush of breath skimmed along her ear, almost like a caress. "I understand you are angry," he said. "Gilpin had told me you never went to see them that day, and I thought—" His fingers stilled at her neck, and he withdrew his hand. "I wish to apologize, Charlotte. To tell you the truth, I thought it would go much better than that. I didn't realize how hardheaded, how utterly stubborn—"

"Don't," she cried, her tone harsher than she intended. Turning, she lifted to her toes and swiftly kissed his cheek.

She swayed there a moment more, longer than she should have, inhaling the scent of his skin and tempting herself with his nearness. Finally, she forced her feet to step away. "You have no need to apologize. Tonight, Philip, you were a wonderful husband."

Then, before he could ruin the moment—for she knew he would if she stayed—and before the tears burning at the backs of her eyes betrayed her, she whirled around and fled the room.

# Chapter 10

Six months, two weeks, and three days ago.

That's when Philip had begun to fear for his sanity, when he realized he wanted his wife.

At first, he had been stunned. After all, they barely spoke to one another; perhaps on a good day, as he was passing from the breakfast room and she was coming in, they might murmur formal greetings before they went their separate ways.

He certainly hadn't given any credence to his attraction in the beginning. If he delayed his morning ride by a few minutes so he could be at the breakfast table, still eating, when she entered, it wasn't because he looked forward to a few more silent minutes spent in her company. He was only hungrier than usual.

And when he began coming home earlier in the day, around the time when she usually received visitors in the drawing room, his only reasoning was that he wanted to see the types of people she brought into his house. He had heard rumors of dockworkers, actors, and foreign merchants, not to mention the run-of-the-mill viscount and earl.

At times he told himself he was lonely; after all, when a man neared thirty years of age, it was understandable if he began to think of family, and of permanence, and a child or two underfoot to ensure the continuation of the Rutherford legacy.

But no excuse he could make was reason enough to explain why he'd become suddenly enchanted by her.

*The fact that Philip had deliberately investigated the details of Charlotte's social calendar was ludicrous enough. But now he was attempting to manipulate her into spending time alone with him.*

*He might have been concerned, if it wasn't overshadowed by the appalling way his pulse raced when the footman opened the carriage door and Charlotte climbed inside.*

*"Good evening, my dear. To the Livingston soiree?"*

*She gasped, a scream that was cut short when her gaze jerked to his corner of the vehicle. "Your Grace." Deprecation in two little syllables. It was very well done.*

*The door closed behind her, and Philip motioned to the other seat, disliking how his body reacted to the jasmine perfume she wore. He had breathed the same scent from her skin on their wedding night, warm and soft as her flesh beneath his palms.*

*Lust. It was an irritation, especially in conjunction with Charlotte.*

*"I thought we might take the carriage together to the Livingstons', instead of one of us going in the coach." That was the justification he had invented for himself, and he found it amusing that it sounded as weak spoken aloud as it had in his mind. He simply, strangely, wanted to be alone with her. He couldn't explain the compulsion, had no reason for it and couldn't remember whence it had come, but there it was all the same.*

*He waited, wondering if she would exit the carriage*

*before it could go on, but she didn't move. "As you wish,"
she said and except for the slight curl of her lips, disguised her hatred well. She turned her head to the side
and looked out the window, even though the night was
too dark beyond the light of the coach lamp to see much
of anything.*

*Although being ignored the entire fifteen minutes to
the Livingston mansion hadn't been his intention, Philip
didn't know what to say to her. The only vocabulary that
seemed to exist between them now was words like "divorce," "scandal," "adultery," and "Ethan."*

*He sat stiffly as the carriage wheels rumbled through
the street, unable to look away from her. She was beautiful. He'd rather she be ugly. It would have been easier to
dismiss her; he probably wouldn't feel the recent possessiveness he had at the thought of her lovers. Or perhaps
he would; after all, she was still his wife.*

*Perhaps it was her rebellion which now drew him to
her. To take lovers, then laugh in the face of polite society.
It was an odd sort of courage, but courage nonetheless.
A weaker woman might have cowed before him, slunk
away into isolation after what he'd done, but not Charlotte. She was determined to force him to agree to a divorce petition. She knew what she wanted, and was strong
enough to continue even when he pretended to disregard
her scandals.*

*He couldn't respect her for it, but at the same time he
couldn't deny he felt a certain amount of admiration at
the way she defied him.*

*Lust and admiration. He didn't like having to admit
to either.*

*She turned her head. "What do you want?"*

*He wanted to hate her as much as she hated him, or,
even better, to return to his previous habit of ignoring
her. Anything would have been better than this sudden*

*awareness of her, this near obsession to know her every thought, her every emotion.*

*Philip consciously loosened his shoulders. He shrugged. "Nothing."*

*"Why are you staring at me?"*

*He arched a brow. "Where else should I look?"*

*She sighed in exasperation, and the sound was so similar to the one she used to make when vexed at Ethan that he almost smiled. But he subdued the inclination before it could emerge on his lips. He'd made himself think of her as a stranger, a woman he hadn't known before Ethan and Joanna's failed elopement. Had he begun to allow himself to see her differently now? Was that why he wanted her?*

*His anger at Ethan or Joanna hadn't faded. But Charlotte—she had never deserved . . .*

*Philip banished the errant thought. What was done was done. Even if he wished it, he couldn't change the past.*

*She turned her head away again, and Philip continued to stare at her. She wore a blue dress, the color bright as midday even in the gloom of the night. A diamond necklace encircled her neck, lying at the base of her throat. The expanse of ivory skin beneath the glittering jewels and the immodest bodice of her gown led the eye to stray.*

*Philip silently cursed his lack of discipline even while he indulged himself in looking. As he did, her body shifted subtly, her breasts suddenly lifted higher than before, and he knew she was aware of where his gaze lingered. Although her head remained turned toward the window, he was sure she meant to taunt him.*

*No, it was only his imagination, his lust-crazed mind, feverish with desire.*

*God, how he wanted her.*

*The carriage slowed. They'd reached the Livingston residence. As they waited for the vehicle to pull up to the front of the mansion behind the long line of other guests,*

*Charlotte spoke again. "It's been a long while since we've attended the same function." Her tone held a weary note of boredom, which somehow made Philip grow even more frustrated. "I trust you won't expect a dance?"*

*"No. As I said, I only wanted the use of the carriage. We needn't spend any more time in each other's company." They were all the right words, but he didn't mean a single one. He wanted every dance for himself, abhorred the thought of her with any other man.*

*"Good," she said, then flashed him a sultry smile. "I'm certain Lord Cullen is waiting for me."*

*The carriage stopped. Philip fought to maintain his usual air of remoteness, unaccustomed to this jealousy. Before she could leave, he said, "Thank you for informing me. However, I'd like to remind you—even if you cuckold me with every man in all of England, I won't divorce you." Her affairs were one thing, an insult to him, but a divorce would be a defamation of the Rutherford duchy. And . . . there was the matter of his lust. He wouldn't be able to seduce her as easily if she were free.*

*Her smile wilted. "I don't understand you."*

*"You don't need to."*

*But Philip understood, and that was all that mattered. He might not know why he wanted her now, after all this time, but he would have her. He would seduce her, so well and thoroughly that she wouldn't want any lover but him. And then he would be content.*

*The night of seduction came two weeks later. Philip had planned it down to the last detail: the wine prepared, dim light provided by only a few candles set throughout the room, pillows at the ready should he be successful.*

*He gulped down a glass of wine, then grimaced. He would be successful. He would be charming, and nice, though he would be careful to protect himself, to not give too much away in case she rejected him.*

*Even with the continual doubts playing in his head, Philip sent Fallon to retrieve Charlotte. He had looked at her calendar; she had nowhere to go tonight.*

*After several minutes, until he thought she would refuse to answer his summons, Charlotte entered the study. He could see her wariness as she approached. Others might not have known; they might have assumed by the sway of her hips and the open invitation in her eyes that she desired him as much as he did her. They didn't know her sensual parade was nothing more than a mockery of the marriage they could have had.*

*But Philip knew. He'd taken her to bed before, when she professed her love for him. And while he watched her walk toward him and then lean forward, displaying the sumptuous wealth of her curves, all he could think about was that he wished she would laugh with him again.*

*"You asked for me, Your Grace?" Her voice was too low, all wrong. He didn't want the temptress, damn it. He wanted her.*

*"Yes, I—" He couldn't do it. He couldn't bear the knowledge that behind the seductive facade, she hated him.*

*After all of his plans to seduce her, he'd rather have spent the entire night on opposite sides of the room, talking with her—of her life over the past three years, minus the adultery, of course; of her goals and dreams for the future; asking her if she, too, desired children. And he wanted to coax her to laughter—not the deep, throaty chuckle she gave whenever a man's eyes were on her, but the natural sound of joy and pleasure he remembered: when she laughed so hard her eyes filled with tears, and her hands pressed to her sides, trying to contain it all.*

*For the first time in a long while, he allowed himself to see her again as Charlotte, the girl who had once been his neighbor, his friend. And he wanted her smiles, her confidence, her trust, her respect—everything he didn't deserve.*

*He lusted after her, yes. But much more than that, God help him, he . . . loved her.*

Philip sent her away that night and began his pursuit the next day, full of fear, but also of hope and determination. He knew it would be difficult, after all he'd done, but he would not give up.

Over the past six months, two weeks, and three days, his hope had slowly dwindled, until determination was all that remained. If he hadn't loved her, he would have given up. But though he tried, he couldn't stop this craving for her. As mad as it was, he would rather have had a thousand nights sitting together, simply playing a game or talking, than one night in her bed.

It was determination—and an equal measure of desperation—which drove him to kidnap and seclude her at Ruthven Manor, far away from London and her admirers and the city's decadent enticements.

For so long, he had waited. He had loved her, without any hope that her heart would soften toward him and she would love him in return.

Only now, as he watched her flee from him, his skin still warm from the gentle touch of her unexpected kiss, did a spark of new hope flare to life.

# Chapter 11

"You do not need a lesson on kissing," Charlotte said four days later. "You do it quite well, and if you need any practice, it is Joanna you should be seeking out, not me."

She waved to the maid arranging the tea service in front of them.

"Or if you must, practice with one of the maids. Such as this one."

The maid knocked over an empty cup, and her eyes flew to Charlotte, then Philip. "A-apologies, Y-Your Graces," she stammered, then without even righting the cup, scampered away.

Philip cocked a brow. "Should I be insulted?"

"You should be pleased," Charlotte answered, pouring the tea, "that you have managed to terrify the staff to such an extent." She handed him a cup. "Isn't that what you wanted?"

"It is rather useful at times. Such as now, when I wanted to be alone with you."

Charlotte peeked at him over the rim of her cup. He

looked . . . rather adequate today, in a navy blue waist-coat, gray coat, and gray pants.

He leaned forward to snatch a biscuit off the tray, and his pants stretched tight over his muscled thigh for one throat-drying moment.

Charlotte took a gulp of tea, absently noting the hot liquid flowing over her tongue and scalding the roof of her mouth.

Dash it all, if she must admit it, Philip appeared far more than just adequate. He was stomach-fluttering, breath-hitching magnificent.

Clutching her cup in one hand, she reached out with the other and ran her fingers through his hair, from the back of his head to the front.

He jerked beneath her touch, then stilled until she pulled away. "I presume there's a reason why you did that," he drawled.

A flush of heat warmed her cheeks. "I merely wanted to see your cowlick. It is charming, in a boyish sort of way."

"Ah."

There was nothing boyish about him. Contrary to her expectations, his ruffled appearance did nothing to diminish his appeal. If anything, his intense gaze and mussed hair made her think of a man who had just risen from bed. And by the way he looked at her, no doubt he would happily take her back there with him.

Cursing softly, Charlotte glanced away. She must not think of Philip and beds together.

She started when he spoke, his tone low and confidential. "By the way you leaned toward me, I must confess I had hoped for a kiss."

She stared at the wall.

"Charlotte?"

"Hmm?"

"Would you like to kiss me?"

"No." She was being too much of a fool already, as it was.

He sighed and shifted beside her, placing his cup on the tray. "Very well. Since you refuse to assist me in kissing lessons, we shall move on. Yet I cannot continue in good conscience without pointing out that you have been woefully remiss in teaching me how to be a proper husband."

He paused, and did not speak again until she looked over at him. Sighing again, he said, "I can feel myself becoming less attentive and considerate day by day. Why, when I woke up this morning, my first thought was to wake you up as well so you could rub my back. It was only through supreme self-discipline that I refrained from entering your bedchamber."

Charlotte gritted her teeth, refusing to allow the devilish gleam in his eyes to lure her imagination down forbidden paths. "How . . . gallant of you."

"Yes. I thought so."

"Indeed. You seem to be very gallant of late." She set her cup of tea on the tray beside his. "For instance, you single-handedly attempted to reunite my family. Without asking my opinion or telling me in advance, even."

Philip leaned forward, until their noses were mere inches apart. "If I were a good husband, this would be the time when I fell to my knees and begged for your forgiveness, would it not?"

"Do not forget the gift to soothe my hurt feelings. You gave me jewelry already, so I suppose flowers will do."

He rose to his feet.

Charlotte gaped. "You're truly not going to—"

He stretched out his hand and, without thinking, she placed her palm against his.

"No, I'm not going to kneel at your feet. I am not in the least repentant of my deeds." He pulled her up to stand before him. "The truth is, Charlotte, even though it went terribly, in the past three years I've never seen you as happy as you've been since they came to supper."

"Nonsense. I've been wonderfully happy." Even as she said it, her chest tightened at the thought of how miserable she'd been, how lonely her life was. But she gave him an enthusiastic smile, nonetheless. "Truly. Giddy, even."

Her smile faded at his serious expression, and she tugged her hand from his. She whirled away, then back again. "Besides, why wouldn't I be happy? I've dozens of lovers, hundreds of admirers. If my family didn't want me, why should I want them?"

"No." He captured her shoulders. "Listen to me."

"You." Her voice shook. He dared to talk to her about how unhappy she'd been the past three years, when he was the one who'd made her so. She was surprised he'd even deigned to notice her from the height of his lofty ducal throne. *"You?"* Her hands lifted to his chest to push him away. "Let me go—"

He ignored her. "It will take a while. God knows, forgiveness is difficult to find in your family. But I had to take the chance."

She continued to struggle, tried to block him out, but it was useless. It didn't matter; whatever he had to say, she didn't want to hear it.

"Damn it, Charlotte! Can you not see? Do you not understand? I ruined your life. I know this. But this—helping you with your family—this is the only thing I could think of to make it right. To try and make it up to you."

He released her suddenly, and paced away. When he turned around, he remained at a distance. His fingers raked through his hair, leaving it even more disarranged than before.

And still he looked wonderful.

Charlotte clenched her fists at her sides and forced herself to meet his gaze. "Philip—"

"Hate me if you will. Loathe me. I do not expect much more than that from you. But do not begrudge me this. Do not deny yourself happiness only to spite me."

She waited for him to continue, waited for him to do something. When he neither moved nor spoke, but only stood there watching her, she went to him.

She stared up at him, silent, and searched his eyes. She didn't know if it was because he truly was trying to become a better person, or if perhaps she had never really known him as well as she thought she had, but he was different.

And it was odd, to consider that after everything, after spending so much time together as children, and then three years as husband and wife, she could discover that he was a stranger to her.

Finally, she lifted her hand and cupped his jaw. His gaze consumed her, ever intent, ever steady, as her thumb brushed across his cheek.

"Philip," she murmured. "You have changed, haven't you?"

"Some," he said, stiffly. "In some ways, I'm much the same."

She reached up and smoothed her fingers over his hair, so that it lay naturally in place once again. "Thank you. You did what I could not. I didn't have the courage to see them, to approach them first. Thank you."

When she drew away and he said nothing, she prompted, "This is the time when you're supposed to say 'You're welcome.'"

"You're welcome." He paused; then a small, sly grin slid across his face. "Does this mean you'll kiss me now?"

\* \* \*

"It's very childish of you not to tell me where we're going," Charlotte said an hour later, peering through the carriage window.

"And I will not tell you. You kept your kisses to yourself, and I'll keep my secrets. Besides, it's meant to be a surprise."

Charlotte threw a glance at him. "I thought it was intended to be another lesson for you."

"It is."

"Then wh—"

"We're here," he announced, even before the carriage began to slow. He reached across to place a finger against her lips. "Close your eyes."

She hesitated. Philip grimaced. "You still don't trust me."

Before she could say anything, he removed his finger and leaned back, closing his own eyes. "Now are your eyes closed?" he asked.

"Yes," she answered, doing so.

"Then listen."

At first she could hear only the sound of her own breathing, the jingle of the harnesses as the horses stirred, the creak of the wooden seat when the coachman climbed down.

"Do you hear the children?"

As if coaxed into existence by the warm resonance of Philip's voice, the sound of children's laughter crept to her ears.

"Yes."

"And what else?"

She smiled; this was another facet of Philip she couldn't remember ever seeing before. He'd never been one to participate in whimsical guessing games. "I hear music."

A fiddle, joyful and quick, accompanied by a swell

of voices as the musician played the chorus of "The Wednesbury Cocking."

Then, in between the strains of the fiddle, she heard a loud noise from her right. "And cattle lowing," she said.

While she was trying to distinguish another sound, similar to someone crying, or perhaps someone yelling, a heavy, rich, spicy scent drifted to her nostrils.

She shifted closer to the door, and it grew stronger.

Across from her, Philip chuckled. She opened her eyes. "Meat pies and sausages," she said, turning to him. "You've brought me to the fair—"

The expression on his face halted any other words she might have spoken. There was a warmth in his gaze that she'd never seen before, a look she couldn't describe as anything other than yearning.

For her.

Charlotte's heart thudded hard and fast in her chest as she leaned forward. "Philip—"

He opened the door and climbed outside, and when he turned to assist her in stepping down, all traces of longing were gone.

She took his hand, dismissing the thought that his emotions might run deeper than mere lust. For if they did, she would have to examine her own heart as well, and that thought was singularly frightful. No, if he was kind to her and tried to kiss her, it was because he desired her in the most carnal sense. It wasn't because he loved her. In fact, she would go so far as to say that he might very well despise her as much as she despised him.

Only . . .

Only she wasn't sure if she did despise him anymore. She certainly didn't like him, and she didn't trust him, but he was no longer "Philip the bloody bastard" in her mind.

He was simply Philip. Philip, who gave her nice things and made her laugh and arranged to have her family over for supper.

Philip, whose voice made her want to lean into him. Whose smiles tested her self-control and made her yearn to kiss him.

Her feet stumbled on the carriage steps, and she lurched forward.

"Whoa. I've got you." Philip caught her easily, pivoting so that he was in front of her, his arms around her hips, her hands catching his shoulders. "I'm right here."

And all she could think was that his embrace felt entirely natural, and it would be so easy to wrap her arms around him and bring her lips to his.

Charlotte snatched her hands away from his shoulders as if they were burned.

Dear God. She liked her husband.

Philip lifted her off the steps and planted her on the ground before him. "Are you all right?" he asked. "You look a little sick."

His hands were heavy on the small of her back, keeping her in place, and Charlotte swayed forward—only a little, enough that her breasts rubbed across his chest.

"Charlotte? Are you going to faint?"

And then, swiftly on the heels of the knowledge that she liked her husband, came the realization that she also—

No, no, no. She had to be more intelligent than this.

Philip tightened his arms around her, and she nearly groaned when his hard, warm body pressed against hers.

Yes, she was sick. Yes, she was going to faint. And no, she wasn't nearly as intelligent as she'd thought.

Because as horrible as he'd been to her in the past and as ridiculous as it was for her to even think such a thing, she wanted to make love to him.

Not seduce him because she wanted to wield any sort of power over him, or to prove that he couldn't hurt her any longer, but simply because she wanted the decadent pleasure of putting her hands and her mouth all over his body.

Everywhere.

"Dobbs," Philip called to the coachman. "Get back on the carriage. We're going home."

"No!" She pushed against his chest until she could stand up straight, trying not to notice the firmness of the muscles beneath her palms. "I mean, no. No, we're staying here." She gave him a wide smile. "At the fair," she clarified, toning down her smile lest he think her mad.

Which she had no doubt she was. But thankfully, even though she liked him and wanted to make love to him, at least she still had enough wits lying about to know that returning to Ruthven Manor—or, dear God, being alone with him in the carriage—was not a good idea at this point.

"Are you certain?" Goodness. Was that concern in his voice?

She nodded. "Yes. I feel perfectly well. And you need your lesson."

"All right, then. We'll stay."

Charlotte couldn't help noticing his hold seemed just as tight on her as before. "Philip, release me," she hissed, glancing to her right and her left, hoping her role of preserving propriety was a convincing one.

For a moment, his eyes darkened as he looked down at her, as if he would refuse her request, but just when she decided to give up, throw her arms around him, and damn the consequences, he let her go and stepped away.

He motioned for her to begin walking. "Am I to understand a good husband doesn't embrace his wife in public places?"

"You are correct," she said, looking back at the groom, who followed them, pretending not to see the arm Philip offered her.

A grand mill of people roamed around them, over the grounds. Some were on horseback, some walked as they did, some carried children on their shoulders or their hips.

Six miles of open fields stretched away from Henley-in-Arden; the fairgrounds had to be large to accommodate not only the locals but also the hundreds of visitors from Alcester, Stratford-on-Avon, Wootton Wawen, Birmingham, and the other nearby towns and villages.

The sights and sounds and smells were welcome friends, old memories from her childhood. She'd always loved the spring fairs held on Lady Day and during Whitsunday week, but the annual fair in October was her favorite.

The crying and screaming she'd heard outside the carriage were the sounds of the men and women hawking their wares on either side. There seemed to be no logical order to the rows of booths and tents. Ribbons, hops, and hardware; sheep, gingerbread, and gowns; rope, cattle, and hats: all were interspersed here and there. Surprises to be met at every stall.

Charlotte inhaled the crisp, acrid tang of smoke upon the air, so different from the dense London smog which smothered her lungs. Underneath it lingered the ripe, mellow scent of autumn, of harvested earth and newly chopped wood.

"Look there," Philip said, pointing to the left.

A crowd of children and adults surrounded a magician's platform, their eager faces upturned. Some of them, like Charlotte, had no doubt seen many of his tricks before. But still they stayed, transfixed not by the mystery of his illusions, but by the wonder of the evening, the spell that seemed to be cast by the oncoming dusk and the atmosphere of gaiety.

"Charlotte." He grasped her hand and pulled. "Over here."

She followed after him, enchanted by the excitement in his voice. "You act as if you've never been to a fair before," she called loudly, in an effort to be heard above the shouts and songs and music.

He pulled up short and glanced down at her, a cautious light in his eyes. "Only once." He looked over his shoulder. "There. That is what I wanted to show you."

"Philip, wait." Intrigued by his vagueness, she tried to slow him by dragging her feet, but he only turned to her and grinned.

"Come on," he urged, and she forgot to question him further as she hurried to keep up with his long strides.

They came to stand in front of a small tent, well lit with oil lamps. In the center was an artist with his easel, and before him sat a grizzled farmer with his apple-cheeked wife upon his knee.

The easel was angled so that the visitors to the tent could see the artist and his canvas as he worked. With deft strokes he sketched the man and woman, transferring the couple's image but not the man's potbelly, nor the woman's wart over her left eyebrow.

A wisp of hair tickled Charlotte's neck as Philip bent down to murmur in her ear. "I cannot imagine how he could make you any more beautiful."

Flattery.

She'd heard it before. Some said she was England's version of Helen of Troy—that the brilliant sapphire of her eyes could have launched a thousand ships, that her hair was soft as a dove and dark as a raven's wing.

Of course, she had not been able to resist pointing out that her hair was, in fact, a dark brown, and that ravens

were black, at which point the gentleman who had made
the absurd aviary comparison only continued to stare at
her, a tiny line of confusion marring his brow.

But she hadn't received any flattery from Philip in a
very long time. And even then there had been a note of
irony, a mocking knowledge in his eyes that his compliment was but one among the dozen given to her every
day.

Her heart thudded heavily in her chest, and she
watched, mute, as the artist continued his sketch. She
was aware of Philip's gaze on her face, and she willed him
to look away, to believe she had not heard his comment.

Out of the corner of her eye she saw him open his
mouth and—

Oh, God, surely he wasn't going to say it again.

She wouldn't be able to pretend then, especially if he
said it louder, and then she would have to look at him,
and if she saw that wariness in his eyes—or worse, the
contempt he always seemed to have for her . . .

Well, she simply would not be able to bear it. For one
moment, one fleeting, selfish moment, she wanted to believe that his compliment had been sincere, that when
he looked at her, he didn't see her as the woman she
had made herself become, but rather a woman whom he
respected, whom he liked—

He leaned toward her, and her tangle of thoughts immediately halted as his lips brushed her ear. "I think I
would like a sketch of you, just like this."

Charlotte sucked in a quiet breath and forced herself
to turn toward him, her eyes lowered carefully so they
wouldn't meet his. She lifted to her toes and when she
spoke, her mouth intentionally brushed against his in a
soft, whispered caress. "Are you certain you don't want
one of Astley's nudes instead?"

In the silence that followed her words, Charlotte
knew she'd made a mistake.

She told herself it was instinctive, that she'd taught herself for so long to defend herself with seduction and innuendo. To protect any moment of vulnerability in a manner which would turn her into the aggressor, instead of someone to be taken advantage of.

And yet as Philip took a step backward—as if he couldn't stand to be near her—and as his expression shuttered, leaving not mockery or bitterness but an inscrutable, careful blankness, she desperately wished she could take back the words.

"Philip, I—"

He smiled, a lopsided, three-quarters smile which possessed much more charm than sincerity. He offered his arm once again. When she hesitated to take it, he snatched her hand from her side and fit it snugly into the crook of his elbow.

She'd always been aware of him, always prided herself in being able to estimate his proximity to the nearest foot—for how else would she know when to raise her shield about her?

Yet she'd also been able to maintain a certain distance from him, so even when he was close by, she was still the one to decide the extent to which she would be affected by his nearness.

Tonight, however, she seemed to have lost that ability. She couldn't block out his dark, earthy scent, subtle yet somehow stronger than the smells of sausage and smoke upon the night air. The heat from his body warmed her right side more thoroughly than any of the fires around them could have done. And the brush of his leg against her skirts as they walked—that simple movement was far more intimate and alarming than any wayward drunkard's hand she'd ever had to swat away.

And as they passed a cheerful, shouting throng of children, she was somehow able to hear his soft murmur.

"Damn you, Charlotte."

*        *        *

Yes, by God, he did want one of Astley's nude sketches. He wanted all of them, every last one, to collect and hoard them in some secret, private place where no man's eyes but his own could gaze upon her loveliness. At times he wondered if she'd posed for the portraitist simply for the scandal, or to enrage him, or both. Whichever motive it was, she had succeeded.

He would gladly spend every last farthing he had to purchase them, or steal them when the owner could not be convinced to sell. He would also break Astley's hands, so that he would never dare to sketch Charlotte from memory.

Better yet, he would gouge out the eyes of any man who had ever seen her naked ... but that would not stop them from imagining her, from fantasizing about her.

Yet none of that would matter, not if Charlotte refused to allow him close.

What a fool he was, to think for a moment he had actually caught a blush upon her cheeks, the spectacular color a result of his compliment instead of the excitement of the fair and the heat stolen from the firelight.

He damned her, for her stubbornness and her courage and the slight shine of fear he had spied in her eyes before she lowered them, before she opened her mouth to taunt him again.

And he damned himself even more thoroughly, and with many more violent, inventive curses, for this weakness of his.

It consumed him, this wanting of her. And he needed to consume her in turn—not just her body, though he would take it, and claim it, and, by God, he would be the last man to ever lie with her—but also her mind and her heart.

To be cherished by Charlotte—it was laughable of him to even conceive of such a thing, but it was something he desperately desired. No matter how he tried, he couldn't banish this longing.

For her.

And for her to want, to need . . . to love . . . him.

One day he would be the only thing she could think about, an obsession so deep and so fierce it would be—

*Bloody hell.*

Philip came to a sudden halt, wrapped his arms around Charlotte, who nearly tipped forward with surprise, and kissed her.

Not the sort of kiss he dreamed about at night, mind you, but still, a good, solid kiss right on the lips.

He counted to ten before he drew away. Or rather, before Charlotte jerked backward in his arms.

And then he released her, waiting, willing her to prove his suspicions were correct.

She brushed a hand over the top of her head, as if her hair had somehow gotten mussed up in his embrace. Which it had not. He should know. He had wanted to muss it up.

"Philip!" she said, then quickly lowered her voice as she glanced around.

He bowed. A gentlemanly thing to do. "Yes, my dear?"

She scowled, and she appeared infinitely lovely doing so. Philip could not tear his eyes away from her, for this time—yes, she *was* blushing, and she refused to meet his gaze. Almost as if she were embarrassed. Or shy. Or an innocent.

Charlotte folded her arms across her chest. Philip obliged her by following the movement with his eyes, a small sigh escaping as he noted the uplifted curves of her bosom.

"Philip!"

"Hmm." And in case she thought he might not have heard her, he also lifted a brow as he continued to stare at her chest.

This could quickly become his new favorite pastime. He hadn't allowed himself to stare at her chest before, but it was really quite . . . fascinating.

Especially when he watched her breathe. He could tell she was angry, just by the way her chest rose and fell at short intervals. It made him wonder if her chest would rise so quickly when she was aroused, or if her breathing would slow with the languid flow of her blood. He wished he could remember. Alas, he had not taken note of such things back then. He had simply—

"You kissed me," she hissed, rearranging her arms so most of her torso was hidden.

Sighing again, Philip reluctantly lifted his gaze to her face.

Oh, yes. He had been correct after all.

*You push my buttons, my dear, and I shall push yours in turn.*

He smiled innocently.

Which must not have appeared to be very innocent, for her brows slanted at a greater angle and her mouth formed a neat little purse, the corners refusing to become pinched.

Even when she tried, she could not look ugly.

And just because he knew it would annoy her, Philip brought his hand to his lips and kissed his palm, then pretended to blow it in her direction. "My apologies, of course, darling. I thought kissing you was something a proper gentleman would do at the moment."

Her lips parted, her eyes narrowed, and she flung her arms out to her sides.

Ah, yes. There was that lovely bosom again.

"At a fair, Philip? Arggh! Stop looking at me like that!" Once again, her arms wrapped around her chest protectively.

He couldn't help it. His lips curved into a smug little grin all on their own. "You did flirt with me," he pointed out. "Teasing me about naked portraits and such." He leaned toward her, and his grin grew wider as she leaned back. "Do you truly think I could find one of Astley's sketches?"

"What I think is that you should stop leering at me. And no, you cannot kiss me at a fair. We are in a public place."

Philip's smile faded, and he allowed all the desire, all the love he had for her to surface. And when her eyes widened and softened, confusion crossing her expression, he knew she saw it.

He nodded. "Very well." He reached forward and took her arm.

She started. "Very well?" she echoed, her arm tense beneath his grip.

"We will go to the carriage at once."

# Chapter 12

Philip didn't have a clue where the coachman had taken the carriage. Not that it mattered. All he cared about was inciting Charlotte to . . . to . . . well, something besides the pretense of seduction and indifference she cloaked herself in whenever he was near.

And he rather thought he was doing a fine job of it so far, if her flushed cheeks and little muttered protests were any indication.

And curses. Truly, she had quite a talent for swearing.

He had never known his head resembled a horse's testicles.

Rather a fascinating comparison, that.

Still, as he moved her along beside him, casually urging her to appear as if she were actually happy, he mused that if he were indeed fortunate enough to find the carriage—

Well, there were simply an innumerable number of things one could do with one's wife inside a carriage for an entire hour or so.

He was nearly overwhelmed by the possibilities.

Philip quickened his step, determined to find the carriage immediately.

"This is not"—Charlotte paused to huff a pair of breaths before continuing—"what I meant in the least."

Philip stopped and reared back in feigned affront. Not exactly straight back, but more of a lean to the right and then to the back. This, of course, was calculated to make Charlotte's lovely body collide with his.

She pushed herself aright and attempted to shove her hair in place, as it had grown rather fond of the left side of her head. "You really must stop doing that."

Philip raised a hand to his chest and fixed her with a wounded expression. "Please don't tell me proper husbands do not kiss their wives in the privacy of their own carriages."

Her hand froze on her hair, and her blue eyes lit with such a telltale gleam of "Aha!" that he nearly laughed outright.

"Yes!" She poked him in the chest. "That is exactly the case. A man who expects his wife to engage in such . . . such . . . lurid acts—"

"Lurid acts?" He arched a surprised brow. "Do tell. Which lurid acts are we speaking of?"

If anything, her cheeks turned an even brighter shade of red. "No, I—"

She shook her head violently, so that her hair now tumbled down on both sides, and Philip had to suck in a fortifying breath to keep from reaching out to run his fingers through the dark, lustrous strands.

She stiffened. Withdrawing her poking finger from his chest, she nearly glared a hole through him. "You know quite well what I mean. You expect me to get back in that carriage with you, with you looking at me like that, and I know what you're thinking. You want to kiss me, and—"

"But I will not. After all, you've already said it's not

proper to do so in front of a crowd, and if you say it's not right to kiss you inside a carriage—"

"It's not!" she cried. "Only in the privacy of one's home. Only, in fact, in one's . . ." Her voice trailed off so slightly, the "s" lingering for so long that even if he hadn't been paying strict attention to her words, he would have known what she'd intended to say by the hesitation in her tone and the darkening of her eyes.

"Charlotte." Her name was whisper-soft on his lips, but his mouth tilted into a rogue's grin. "Are you inviting me to your bedchamber?"

He'd expected the swift rise of her hand—he had, in fact, raised his arm to deflect her blow before he even finished the question—but he didn't expect for her hand to drop just as quickly, nor for her to turn away in a swirl of skirts and a vehement wish for him to go to a very unsavory place.

"But I do not want to go to hell," he called to her back.

To which she made a very rude gesture with the crook of her elbow and her fist.

Lovely, lovely woman.

Philip strode after her—he did not run, of course; he was still a duke. He neatly dodged a clump of children loping between the vendor carts before he made it to her side. Then, when she didn't slow but continued to march toward an unknown destination—chin high, eyes forward, hands clenched in her skirts as if she'd rather wrap them around his throat—he dared to step in front of her and block her path.

She jerked to a halt. Her narrowed eyes glittered her disdain and . . . again, there was that sliver of fear.

If he was any sort of decent man, he'd give her the space she so obviously desired.

But he wasn't decent, and he desired *her*. He was a

duke. He had no qualms about being selfish. Or indecent.

Her mouth remained closed, but her eyes demanded an answer to her unspoken question: *why do you not go away?*

He couldn't tell her.

Their gazes were locked and the silence between them seemed to drown out the gay, chaotic noises of the fair around them. It was a rare intimate moment, but he couldn't tell her the truth.

That he wouldn't go away because he could not, that he needed her, that the very air around her was sweeter because she breathed it.

And in that moment, even though neither of them moved, he could feel the distance he had closed over the past few days growing wider. The sounds of the fair slowly crept back into his consciousness, until he was just a man and she was just a woman in the crowded mass of people.

And he couldn't stand for her to think of him as just another man.

Desperately, as though caught in some mad fever, Philip turned. He glanced around, searching for something, anything—although he didn't know what.

And then he saw it. A group of dancers, caught in the fading dusk. Firelight flung their shadows across the gathered circle of observers. Sweat and pleasure flickered over the dancers' faces—some round, some gaunt, others young and old.

This wasn't a London ball, with its waltzes and quadrilles. The attendees weren't guests selected by special invitation; here there were no rules about whom one danced with, or even what sort of dancing was allowed.

All that mattered was that your feet moved in time to the sprightly notes flying off the fiddle, and that you didn't stop.

Philip stared in fascination. Except for the men who had been recipients of Charlotte's favor, he had never before been so envious of anyone.

And yet there was the irony; for despite all of his wealth and status and supposed happiness in this world, he could not remember ever before feeling as *alive* as those dancers appeared.

No, not quite. He had felt alive before. Every single time he was with *her*.

Philip turned toward Charlotte. She was also looking at the dancers, the light from the fire shadowing her face and highlighting the delicate curve of her neck, the ivory slope of her shoulder.

Then, as if drawn by his gaze, she turned to him. And even though the blaze was nearly behind her now, he could see little sparks of blue fire reflected in her irises—an invitation which he doubted she even knew she issued.

He extended his hand, palm upward.

"May I have this dance, Your Grace?"

Charlotte was two and twenty years old. Old enough to know the dangers of the world, and experienced enough to feel herself leaning toward doing something entirely foolish.

And though she usually delighted in doing foolish things, she was also a creature of self-preservation.

She knew, as thoroughly as she knew the many quirks of her husband's smile, that to dance with Philip would be a mistake. Not only because she already felt more vulnerable in his presence than he had a right to make her feel, but also because she had never, *never* thought once in her life that she would hear Philip Burgess, the ninth Duke of Rutherford, ask to dance with her at a country fair.

It was unfathomable. Completely plebeian. Coarse. Common. Vulgar.

Exactly like her, and nothing like him.

And yet the foolish part of her—oh, there were so *many* foolish parts when it came to Philip—refused to allow him to retract the offer.

If Philip chose to lower himself to the level of the masses, to kick up the same dust as maids and farmers and wheelwrights, then she would be there to ensure he didn't change his mind.

That was the reason why she laid her hand firmly over his, performed a small curtsy, and answered, "Why, of course, Your Grace."

*Not* out of any particular desire to dance with him. And certainly not because she wished to allay the awkwardness between them which had arisen moments before.

Perhaps—and here she was willing to admit this bit of spitefulness was part of her self-preservation—he would dance poorly and make an utter fool of himself.

Smiling a bit to herself and ignoring the warmth creeping from his hand to hers, then up her forearm to her elbow and beyond, she allowed him to lead her toward the dancing.

Some people in the crowd around the dancers were like her, straining toward the music, their toes tapping anxiously as they hummed along. And though they were fewer, there were also some like Philip: steady, silent, unmoving as they watched the performance with rapt attention.

The music ended with a hearty cheer from both the dancers and the observers, and those nearest the open circle quickly jumped in to claim their places. Since she and Philip stood near the middle of the crowd, they were required to wait again.

The main fiddler—a short, squat man with a bald head and a bushy beard that took up nearly half his face—bowed to the onlookers and then to the newest round of dancers. He lowered his head over the bow and began to draw out a few long, melancholy notes—the beginning of a ballad, or a dirge, but definitely not a reel.

He halted, raised his head expectantly, and in a chorus of voices, the dancers and the crowd around them heckled him, hollering for a "nice tune, Billy."

Charlotte cupped her hands around her mouth and joined in, whooping a time or two.

Then, with a wink and a grin which turned his eyes into little half-moons, Billy lowered his head again. This time, however, once his hand drew the bow dramatically across the strings in a prolonged prelude, the music immediately dissolved into a fierce, frantic pulsing of melody.

And almost as quickly, the dancers began to move their feet, anxious to keep the pace of the fiddle.

It was a breathless moment, the kind that froze one in place with wonder: the music and the swirl of colorful skirts and the flashing of firelight and shadows, dark and light merging together, then separating in an almost hypnotic cadence.

She didn't know what caused her to look at Philip. A slight shift of his body, or a brushing of his sleeve perhaps. But she lifted her gaze to his profile and traced each feature slowly, one by one, from the wing of his brow to the hard jut of his chin.

He was utterly still, his face a stark plane devoid of emotion as he stared at the dancers. A keen disappointment swept through Charlotte as she watched him. It was ridiculous for him to affect her so, but part of her joy in the night was now diminished because he didn't share in it.

Sighing at her own foolishness, Charlotte touched his

arm, resigned to beckon him away. Certainly by now he had changed his mind about dancing with her.

Yet when he turned toward her, every thought of leaving fled her mind. It was his eyes. When she had looked at his profile, she had not been able to see the expression in his eyes.

*They are gray,* a little voice inside her scoffed. The same voice that had saved her through the torment in those early days, the one that kept her safe, distanced. The reasonable, pragmatic voice. *Gray, gray, gray.*

But another voice swiftly dismissed the dry summarization,

Silver eyes. Hot silver eyes, molten with passion. Not of desire, not of lust, but passion for *life.* It was as if everything she felt while watching the dancers was magnified ten times over   the excitement, the joy, the pleasure.

And she couldn't look away. Her gaze locked with his, and though neither spoke a word, a measure of understanding seemed to pass between them.

It was almost physical, the touch of his eyes. As if she could feel him prying, prodding, searching her.

Charlotte took a deep breath, tried to remind herself that this was *Philip,* and surely he couldn't understand anything about her. Perhaps he thought the dancing was pretty, but that did not mean he knew *her.* And then . . . and *then—*

Dear God, he smiled. A languid, radiant curve of a smile, and Charlotte couldn't help but return it. And as they stood there facing one another, *smiling,* Charlotte wished for her reasonable, pragmatic voice to return. To berate her for allowing him to pierce her vulnerability, for letting herself respond to him. Not in a seductive manner, but in every other way, in every way that counted.

God *damn* him and his silver eyes.

She was the first to look away, her emotions far too

unsteady and tangled. She would not give him the pleasure of seeing her discomposure.

The music was ending, the dancers performing their
final steps.

"Charlotte." His voice was a quiet beckoning. A command spoken softly, but a command nonetheless.

At the sudden cheer of the crowd, she turned blindly
toward him and grabbed his hand. "Come," she urged,
pulling him forward to the front of the spectators. "It's
our turn to dance."

For a few minutes at least, there would be no time to
talk, no time for him to stare into her eyes and search
for her secrets.

When they entered the circle cleared for dancing, Charlotte released his hand and walked to the line where the
other women stood.

The fiddler raised his arms in the air, the signal that
the music was about to begin.

Charlotte dipped her knees in a deep curtsy and bent
her head. When the women straightened, the men responded by bowing.

Philip arched a brow, a slight smirk on his lips, and
Charlotte gave him a saucy grin.

Only he did not see her grin. Or if he did, he thoroughly ignored it. Instead, his focus shifted over her
shoulder, somewhere to the right of where she stood.
The first strains of the reel began. But again, the fiddler
teased the crowd, turning it into a melancholy piece.

Charlotte leaned to the right, tried to catch Philip's
eye, but his brow had lowered and his lips had thinned,
and he seemed to look right through her. She frowned.
Surely he wasn't going to change his mind, not at the
very last moment.

Yet as the people around them raised their voices
to encourage the fiddler to play properly, that's exactly
what he did.

Among the hoarse shouts and piercing whistles, Philip slipped out of line. Without a backward glance in her direction, he pivoted on his heel and disappeared.

Charlotte walked toward the woods between Ruthven Manor and Sheffield House.

She had waited for the rain. The darkening clouds had teased her at the fair, and on their return to Ruthven Manor, a few fat droplets spattered against the carriage window. The sound hadn't been near enough to drown out the overbearing silence, yet it was the only reason she had for staring outside instead of meeting her husband's brooding silver gaze.

Now the rain cascaded over her. Long, cool rivulets of water streamed down her face, plastering her hair to her head, her clothes to her skin. Her feet made little squishing noises as she neared the edge of the woods, the place where civilized manicured lawns were swallowed whole by the untamed wilderness.

She loved the rain.

She refused to think of it as some sort of solace, though. She needed no solace, no refuge, for she had no grief, nothing to run from. The rain simply . . . was. It never demanded anything from her, never toyed with her emotions. She never had to pretend with the rain, never had to lie or manipulate.

A swell of water rushed over her brow and into her eye, and Charlotte stumbled. Her vision blurred, she threw out her hand and found the crisp, rough edge of bark.

"Damn it to bloody hell." The curse was empty in its bitterness, for she felt no pain at all, but it certainly made her feel better. And so she cursed again. "Damn. Damn. Bloody. Bloody—" And then, for some inexplicable reason, she began to laugh.

And then to cry.

She tried to convince herself it was just the rain, the

lovely, wonderful rain, but she couldn't deny that her lips were crumpled up and the rain certainly wasn't causing her brows to pull so hard together.

Charlotte fisted her hand and swung at the tree trunk. "God da— Ow! Bloody *hell*!"

It was a foolish thing to do, to try to inflict pain on such a hard, solid object, when her husband's equally hard head was the source of her—

Charlotte sank to the ground, her back against the tree.

Her what? Anger?

She halted another sniffle. Sadness?

Her eyes closed, and images of Philip's face flashed in her memory. Expressions of joy, curiosity, eagerness, all wiped away by that mask of nothingness. Blank, bland ennui.

Philip would never dare to venture out into the rain. He would never understand why anyone would prefer to be chilled to the bone and have their skin shrivel from the damp when they could instead be warm and dry in front of a fire.

Why had she thought he'd changed?

Perhaps he'd been nice a few times, but that couldn't erase the years of apathy and arrogance. Tonight had proven that.

How could she have believed he thought differently of her?

It was more than obvious that she still meant nothing to him. It was laughable, even, that she could consider such a thing at all. Philip caring? About anyone?

She was only a means to an end. That was all she'd ever been, all she ever would be.

And he was . . . Philip. Not even worthy of her anger or any sadness or, if she admitted it—and she did so, but begrudgingly—her disappointment.

Yes, it was laughable. Quite. Only she did not feel like laughing anymore. Or crying.

She simply sat in the rain, her hands and feet slowly becoming lost in puddles of mud and water. She shivered, but she welcomed the cold, concentrating on the numbness of her fingers and toes, the heaviness growing in her limbs. She would welcome anything that helped her cease thinking of him.

An hour could have passed, or minutes, or even mere seconds as she sat, listening to the steady patter of rain as it rustled the few remaining leaves overhead. Watching the intermittent shadows of raindrops as they splashed against her eyelids, then slid away until only a faint grayness remained.

"I don't understand why you are out here in the rain, when it is perfectly warm and dry inside the house."

Her breathing stopped at the sound of his voice, and she almost smiled. His words were a near echo of her earlier thoughts.

Slowly—for she didn't want him to think his presence affected her—she opened her eyes.

His legs filled her vision, his trousers plastered snugly against the muscled contours of his thighs. A low heat began to flow through her blood. It was as if the rain she had waited for had actually come for him, to fall upon him in loving streams, pouring down his body in a deliberate caress. The rain had always been meant to taunt and torment her, to remind her of the desire for him she tried so desperately to escape.

"Must you stand so close?" she muttered, pushing backward against the tree.

Although she refused to look up, she had no difficulty sensing his frown as he spoke. "I was only attempting to— Never mind."

As soon as he stepped away, raindrops fell anew on

her face. Rain she hadn't even realized had disappeared as he stood over her, creating a shelter for her.

The realization made her want to curse and cry again, all at once and with no reason for either. She stood. Perhaps she was becoming sick. There was no other reason for her to be so emotional of late.

Charlotte glanced up, met his silver gaze, and pronounced, "I believe I am ill." Turning toward the manicured lawns and civilization, she began to walk. It was a slow, hazardous affair, as her weighted skirts preferred to drag her back down to the ground, and her feet insisted on finding every hole and puddle available.

Philip, of course, did not take the hint; he strolled patiently beside her.

As she tripped over her skirts for perhaps the eighth or ninth time, his hand reached out to her shoulder and steadied her.

"I could carry you—"

His mouth closed abruptly at the force of her glare. The glare was one thing she would give him credit for; he was the best teacher in all things cruel and hostile.

She should have known he wouldn't let her be, but still she was surprised when, instead of releasing her shoulder, he pulled her toward him and said, "Dance with me."

Charlotte stared at him. Wayward strands of hair clung to his forehead, slicked over his brow. Tiny diamonds of raindrops glistened on the tips of his eyelashes and lingered on the edge of his bottom lip, drawing attention to its lush curve, so different from his stark, thin upper lip.

She hated the rain. She truly did.

"No," she said, and glanced meaningfully at the place where his hand held her firmly in place.

Somehow, perhaps because the rain was so cold, the warmth of his hand seemed a hundred times hotter than it normally would have. It seared her senses, and although her mind rang a shrill warning bell, she still yearned to lean in closer.

He didn't release her, but instead wrapped his arm around her waist and dragged his other hand down to capture hers.

Charlotte growled. It was something she'd heard him do a number of times, but somehow she didn't think hers came out quite as effectively. Even to her own ears, it sounded like she had a wad of phlegm stuck at the back of her throat which she was trying to clear.

"Charlotte."

She returned to glaring. It was much easier to get her point across, anyway.

His gaze didn't waver—damn him. "If I am correct, good husbands do not leave their wives at the beginning of a dance. Is that not true?"

She shrugged. "I certainly don't care if you are a good husband. I won't be your wife for much longer, and you were never much of a husband to begin with."

His arm stiffened around her waist, almost imperceptibly. She desperately wished she wasn't so attuned to him; his reaction nearly made her regret her words. Even if they were true.

Then, he did what she least expected: he leaned toward her, his eyes holdings hers captive, and pressed his lips to the corner of her mouth.

For a second—perhaps less than a second, really—her body betrayed her and she felt herself tremble.

She knew he must have felt it, as well, for he stilled for a long moment before he finally drew away.

"Dance with me, Charlotte. Even if it doesn't matter to you, I would like to show my sincere apology for leaving."

Perhaps she should agree. Then when the dance was over, he would have no reason to hold her so close.

"Very well. Lead on," she grumbled, trying to fix her eyes upon some less appealing part of him without appearing a coward.

"Of course, Your Grace," he murmured in a droll voice, then began to hum.

Her eyes immediately locked upon his mouth. Damnation. "Must you make noise?" she asked irritably. "It is very . . . distracting."

He halted in midstep, and she suspected he had intended for her to crash into him, for his arm tightened even further around her. "Very well," he conceded, almost as if her contrariness pleased him greatly, and began to dance again.

"You needn't hold me so close, either," she said shortly. She struggled against the near embrace of his arms.

He gave a low chuckle, and she could feel the vibration of it pulsate through her own body. "Would you rather I kissed you than danced?"

Instinctively clamping her lips together, she shook her head and relaxed as best she could, allowing him to hold her as close as he wished and lead her in slow, awkward movements around puddles and across the slick, wet grass.

Philip smiled, his gaze ever watchful and knowing. But he was silent as well, and didn't hum again. The entire earth seemed to be silent. There was no sound but the rush of water from the heavens as they danced.

He turned, and she followed. He led, and she matched his steps. It was a medley of crushed toes and stumbles, and they nearly fell to the ground several times, but still they continued.

Slowly Charlotte calmed, and she closed her eyes. Despite the treachery of the uneven ground, Philip's arms were strong about her.

His breath fanned across her ear as he laid his cheek

against her temple, and suddenly they weren't dancing anymore as much as they were simply swaying.

Her heart skipped inside her chest, and her eyes flew open.

Dancing in the rain with Philip was one thing, but this . . . this, whatever it was, was far too intimate.

"Well, then, you've done your duty. Is your conscience eased?"

She'd made her voice purposely bitter and angry, and was well rewarded when he dropped his arms and pulled away from her.

Philip bowed stiffly, his lower lip no longer as giving as it had been before. "You forget, my dear, I have no conscience."

Why did her chest insist on aching so?

She gave a brief nod and turned away, pausing only to murmur over her shoulder, "I haven't forgotten. I haven't forgotten anything."

# Chapter 13

Philip was being haunted.

Not by a ghost, but by memories.

And that was even worse, in a way. If a ghost had taken to following him down the hallways, or visiting him in his bedchamber, he would have sneered and scared it away.

But the memories ...

They came unbidden, shallow shadows of the past, unpredictable, straight from inside his head. And they would not be ignored.

They weren't all bad memories, these recollections of his grandfather, the estimable eighth Duke of Rutherford. They simply had the unfortunate habit of reminding Philip of his responsibilities as a duke, and also that Charlotte would never be a proper duchess.

His grandfather had never liked the Sheffields. "A rotting lot of self-pretentious commoners," he'd called them.

Sometimes, God help him, Philip couldn't tell if he agreed with the old duke because he'd heard it so many times, or simply because it was true.

"Charlotte," he whispered, knowing he was mad to be

here while she slept, as if being near her could chase the memories away.

It must have been close to dawn. The hours had melted into one another as he contemplated his next step. Desperation cluttered his thoughts. He had tried to be nice. He had attempted to disarm her with the pretext of the lessons. But neither had worked.

He refused to consider telling her he loved her. Doing so would give her too much of an advantage over him, and though he had tried to change, he could leave only so much of his pride behind. If any glimmer of the love she'd had for him in the past remained, he hoped he would be able to fuel it once again by making her jealous.

It wasn't the ideal plan, and admittedly, she might very well encourage him in his endeavors at courtship to ensure that he would grant her a divorce, but he had to try.

Now, though, he would steal these moments to watch her, to be with her. Though he doubted that the shadow of guilt he bore would ever fully disappear, in this moment at least there would be no bitterness and accusations. For a little while, he could pretend she had forgiven him.

The grayness of the lightening sky made her face appear even more beautiful, even more radiant than usual. Yet even in sleep, she was no innocent angel. Though her eyes were closed, still she presented a seductress, causing his body to yearn with the temptation of her parted lips, the subtle rise and fall of her breasts with each breath.

"Charlotte," he whispered again, this time so close he could see the path of his breath as it moved over her hair.

Just once, only once, he wanted her to look at him again with the earnestness, the sincerity he'd seen in her eyes before, without any of the calculation or manipulation he had taught her so well. If she could love him, then he could tell her how much he loved her in return, without fearing her scorn or rejection.

His hand strayed toward the curve of her neck, his fingers nearly grazing the soft, supple ivory skin revealed above her nightgown. But she stirred, and he stilled, his heart pounding as he waited to see whether she would wake.

She didn't, but only turned her head to the side, away from him.

With an unsteady exhalation, Philip drew his hand to his side, his fists clenching and unclenching with want. It wasn't worth it. He could dream of her inviting him eagerly into her bed, but it was more likely that it would be Charlotte the temptress instead of the woman beneath, the woman he loved.

It could have been tonight. He'd seen the way she'd looked at him earlier, at the fair. They'd teased, laughed, flirted, and he knew he was making progress when at times she'd seemed almost afraid of the way she responded to him.

As Charlotte was never afraid, he could only view it as a good sign.

But then, of course, he'd ruined it.

Standing there before her, waiting for the music to begin, he'd been aware of the curious stares of the crowd around him. So many people watching him, waiting for him to make a fool of himself. One man behind Charlotte in particular had laughed, and though Philip knew it was unreasonable to think it had been at him, still he felt ashamed. Gone was his anticipation of the dance, to show Charlotte he could be a different man than what she expected. Instead he looked at the laughing man, and all he could see was his grandfather's disapproval, reminding him that he was not one of them.

The old duke was dead, yet still Philip remembered.

Another night at the fair, long ago, when Ethan had come and stolen him from Ruthven Manor. When, after hours of eating sausages and tarts and shamelessly flirting with housemaids much too old for them, they'd returned to find the duke preparing a search party.

His grandfather hadn't spoken to him for the remainder of the night, nor even for the week next. He hadn't needed to, as the resulting whipping had well accomplished the task of ensuring that Philip knew his role in the world.

And it wasn't one in which he was free to go wherever he chose, to mingle with the servants and commoners, with people like the Sheffields.

Yes, he could have had Charlotte tonight, but he had chosen duty instead, miserable fool that he was.

It was his role, his right, his privilege, his burden.

Somehow, he would find a way to serve his ducal obligations and have Charlotte, too.

A harsh sigh escaped his lips as he turned away, the sound becoming a stifled laugh when he caught sight of another of his grandfather's portraits high on the opposite wall.

A multitude of scarves and stockings hung over the frame, draped over his face in haphazard disarray. Only one steely eye peered through the silky veil.

"Oh, Charlotte, my love," Philip whispered once more, and strolled out of her bedchamber with the beginnings of a smile on his lips.

"Joanna." Charlotte halted at the entrance to the sitting room. She had just come to . . . to . . . Oh, dash it, it didn't matter now. "Fallon didn't tell me you were here."

Joanna gave her a strained smile, her eyes flicking to the opposite side of the room. Charlotte found it all too easy to follow her gaze to the sight of Philip, standing tall and straight as ever.

"Charlotte," he said, gesturing toward a chair. "Please, sit down. Joanna has come to visit."

Charlotte started. He hadn't called her Lady Grey, but Joanna. She looked at Joanna again, and then once more at Philip. "No, thank you. I prefer to stand."

"Very well."

The silence stretched in the room, and she knew he was toying with her, waiting for her to take the bait. But she was done playing his games.

Smiling widely, she said, "Good day, then," and turned to leave.

"Charlotte," he called from behind her, not raising his voice at all, but merely using his ducal tone as if that alone would freeze her in her place. "I have told Joanna of our agreement."

It was a strange thing. Such an announcement should not have made her heart skip a beat, or the blood to drain so quickly from her face, but it did, and she had to put a hand to the door frame to steady herself.

Counting to ten, she willed her body to calmness, to give nothing away, before she turned around once again. She couldn't meet Joanna's eyes, nor her own in one of the myriad mirrors along the wall. She fixed her gaze on Philip's right ear. "Our agreement, Your Grace?" A question, as if they had any other sort of agreement between them.

He shifted subtly, just a slight movement, so that their eyes met. "Yes, our agreement. Regarding our divorce."

If there had been a time when Charlotte had ever doubted Philip's word, it was over. There was no going back now.

Even though she had spoken to Joanna about it, there was something so decisive, so final, in hearing him say the word aloud, in front of someone else.

Charlotte cocked her head to the side, a purposeful show of nonchalance. "And did you also inform her of your decision to make her the next Duchess of Rutherford?"

Philip smiled slowly, a smile which began with a twitch of his lips and spread until it crinkled the corners of his eyes. It was not one of his carefully controlled ten-degree smiles, but a full one. A real one.

He turned to look at Joanna, the warmth of that smile obviously meant for her alone. "Indeed, I have," he said softly, "and she has agreed I do not need any further husband lessons from you."

"I see." But truly, she didn't. How was it that not so long ago the two of them seemed to despise each other, and yet now they were smiling at each other like love-sick fools and sending secret messages with their eyes?

She looked at Joanna, waiting for some signal that she was merely playing along as they had agreed. But Joanna refused to meet her gaze, and Charlotte realized if Philip could have begun to thaw her heart, it must have been even easier for him to thaw Joanna's.

She shouldn't have cared, but somehow she felt as if he'd betrayed her all over again. Only this time, she'd thought he would fail with Joanna, had been so certain Joanna would be different. But apparently she wasn't, and the pain of their togetherness was almost more than she could bear.

Despite everything, he was still her husband.

Somehow her back had come to rest against the edge of the door frame, and Charlotte was glad for the support. "And when is the wedding?" she asked brightly. Joyfully. So much so that the high octave of her own voice made her cringe.

Philip stood behind Joanna's chair, his hand resting on her shoulder, her hand resting over his. It was such a lovely, domestic scene.

"Of course we shall have to wait until the divorce is finalized. I'll ensure there's no unnecessary delay, but it could very well take several months, perhaps even a year."

"And in the meantime, I will . . ."

Philip cocked a brow. "You will be free to do as you wish once the petition has begun. At that point, we won't be able to avoid the larger scandal. Until then, however, I trust for you to remain here, at Ruthven Manor, to the end of the three months as we had first agreed. As much as I can, I wish to delay the gossip, at least until dear Joanna has finished her period of mourning."

Dear Joanna.

Not much longer and he would doubtless begin composing sonnets to her beauty.

Still, Charlotte was suspicious of the sudden change. Just last night he had teased about kissing her in the rain, and yet today he acted as if they were as much strangers as they had been for the previous three years of their marriage.

Her fingers bit into the woodwork of the paneling beside the entrance, and she inhaled deeply. Then, matching his gaze with one equally arrogant, she asked, "And will you continue to try to kiss me until the end of the three months as well?" She darted a look at Joanna, who seemed frozen in her chair.

Philip's brow lowered. "That won't be necessary. Dear Joanna, I'm certain, will be happy to receive my kisses. Isn't that right, my love?"

Charlotte followed the movement of his hand as he trailed his fingers from Joanna's shoulder to the curve of her neck, to the sweep of her cheek, his thumb grazing her lips.

And as she spun toward the hall, the image of Philip leaning down toward those upturned lips remained imprinted, like a brand, upon her vision.

"Yes, yes, very good," Mr. Lesser said, nodding his head with approval. "You have been practicing, Your Grace. Very good."

The melody was a simple one. Charlotte could have played it with her eyes closed, her feet bound, and seven of her fingers amputated.

Yet if it hadn't been for certain . . . distractions . . . she no doubt would have been thrilled with the harpist's praise.

She cast a mental scowl in the direction of the hallway, imagined it traveling through the winding corridor until it reached the sitting room, until it smacked Philip in his manipulative, overbearing head.

And because the sound of Joanna's laughter had become quite the nuisance over the past five days, she then imagined it hitting Joanna, too.

Joanna. *Dear* Joanna.

Charlotte frowned. She could probably play the harp with all eight fingers and one thumb amputated.

"Your Grace!" Mr. Lesser exclaimed. He stilled her hand and wrapped his arms around the harp protectively. "The harp is not a drum! You cannot hit it with such—such—*ferocity*."

Sighing, Charlotte sat back, not much caring if she maintained the proper duchesslike posture or not. After all, her duchess days were nearly over.

"My apologies, Mr. Lesser. Perhaps you might teach me something a bit more challenging. A bit more . . . lively?"

"Ahh." Mr. Lesser's eyes glinted behind his spectacles. "Her Grace wishes for a challenge. She is bored with my poor attempts to instruct her—"

Straightening, Charlotte extended a hand. "No, that is not what—"

"I see." With a sly grin and a push of his spectacles back to the bridge of his nose, Mr. Lesser released the harp. "Let's begin, then. Shall we?"

Two hours later, Charlotte learned what a sly grin from Mr. Lesser meant. Callused, bleeding fingertips. Dull, aching shoulders and a strained back.

Groaning, she happily watched him leave. She doubted she could have survived another ten minutes.

She heaved herself off the seat, tensing as a muscle spasm gripped the area between her neck and shoulder.

A low rumble and an accompanying giggle filtered into the hollow silence of the music room. What on earth could they be talking about? Not just today, but day after day, as they visited in the sitting room, in the conservatory, in the library.

Of course, she supposed she should be grateful she didn't hear the dreadful silence instead. Those were the times when her head filled with lurid images, and her stomach writhed as if a nest of snakes had taken residence there.

And although Joanna usually left Ruthven Manor in the late afternoon, and Philip alone dined with her at supper, Charlotte couldn't help but wonder if afterward, when she had retired to her bedchamber, he then visited Joanna at her home. Through the night.

After all, Joanna might be much more wholesome and proper than Charlotte could ever be, but if she was so free with her kisses, would she not be free with her body as well? And Philip was a man who had always kept a mistress—though not in the last six months, *if* she chose to believe him. She couldn't imagine him being willing or able to wait until the petition began, and certainly not until the divorce was finalized.

Cursing beneath her breath, Charlotte quit the music room and headed in the direction of the sitting room. As she neared, she quieted her breathing and focused all of her attention on attempting to hear the conversation within.

"Soon this will all be yours, my darling," she heard Philip say.

"Oh, Philip"—rustling—"do not say such things. She is still your wife. You must be more circumspect—"

More rustling. "She doesn't care what I do. You know how she detests me. For once, let me be happy. Let us be happy."

This was followed by silence and yet more rustling, and Charlotte's imagination was quite happy to supply the intimate scene in her mind's eye for her as she stared at the opposite wall—Joanna sitting on the end of the sofa, her elegant, gloved hand captured between Philip's, their lips pressed together.

Humph. *Let me be happy,* he'd said. As if *she* had been the one to make his life miserable this entire time. As if he'd been anything *but* happy. He was the duke, and he had his mistress as well as a hundred other women who made themselves available to him.

Well, at least he was correct in one thing: Charlotte did indeed detest him.

Retreating a few paces in the opposite direction, she threw back her aching shoulders and pasted a smile on her face. When she was within the limit of hearing distance from the sitting room, she abruptly turned back around and began to whistle.

A loud, cheery tune that some sailor in a pub had taught her not quite so long ago. She whistled as she strolled with sashaying hips toward the sitting room, past the entrance, and all the way up the stairs to her bedchamber.

\*    \*    \*

Philip stared at the doorway of the sitting room.

"It's as I told you," Joanna said, lifting her hands and silencing the rustle of her skirts. "This isn't the way to go about it. At least allow me to tell Charlotte you love her, if you refuse to. It would be a start."

Philip shook his head. He hadn't spent the past five minutes with his lips a scant inch from Joanna's for nothing. His neck had even been crooked at an exact angle so that if Charlotte had happened to look in, she would have thought their lips were touching.

He'd risked too much already by asking Joanna for her help. She could have gone to Charlotte and told her everything, but thankfully, swallowing his pride enough to approach her and apologize for his past behavior had seemed to sway her to his side.

But he was so damn tired of playing the mindless chitter-chatter game with Joanna every day, tired of being near her, talking with her, pretending to be interested in her, when all he wanted to do was be with Charlotte. And God knew, forgiving Joanna for nearly eloping with Ethan had been the most difficult of all.

"How long do you intend on continuing this little farce, Philip?"

His hands lay flat on his thighs, despite his instinct to clench them into fists and punch the nearest inanimate object.

"A little while longer. She does care, you'll see. Just a little while longer."

"Fine." Joanna stood, smoothing her skirts. "I will return tomorrow. Not much longer, though, I hope. You are beginning to wear on my nerves. If you would but tell her you loved her instead of—"

Philip slashed his hand through the air. "Yes, I know. You've mentioned it before. Good day, Lady Grey."

For a moment, as she paused from pinning on her hat to stare at him, he imagined he could feel her pity. But then she gave a quick nod and turned away. "Good day, Your Grace."

"I've been considering it for the past few days, and I simply can't make up my mind. I wish your opinion, Philip. Where do you think I should go?"

"Go?" he echoed dully, unable to tear himself away from the sight of Charlotte's throat as she paused to take a sip of wine.

"Yes." She set aside the glass and returned her attention to the slice of veal before her. "The Orient? Italy? Africa? Russia, perhaps. I've always heard the Russian ambassadors are great lovers. If those are the politicians and diplomats, imagine what the real Russian men could—"

"Enough!" Philip slammed his fist on the table, causing the entire supper service to clink and clatter in protest.

Charlotte merely quirked a brow at his display. "Very well. Italy it is." She took a delicate bite, her lips pursed slightly as she chewed. Her eyes sparkled as she swallowed. "Although I never knew you hated the Russians so."

Philip bared his teeth. "I see you have forgotten the protocol for proper supper conversation. Thank God, I'm sure Joanna doesn't spout such lewdness while eating."

Lowering his gaze, he reached for his own wineglass, imagining the stem as the thick necks of all Russian men.

"Have you bedded her?"

Philip whipped his head toward her, disbelieving his own ears. "I beg your pardon?"

"It's quite a simple question. Have you bedded Joanna yet?"

Slowly, with great patience, he returned the wineglass

to the table. Bloody hell, was he *blushing*? "Do you not recall what I said only a minute ago about decorum—"

She waved his words away and continued to talk around a mouthful of food. "I've been wondering if you would be able to wait. You know, since you told me you haven't had a mistress lately. But I know your appetite is great. After all, you certainly didn't wait long to find another woman after we married."

Philip abruptly stood up, his chair crashing to the floor behind him. "Shall I ask for your forgiveness again? If I remember correctly, you refused to give it before."

She stared at him momentarily, her eyes wide, before she shrugged. "It is needless to speak of the past, as we won't be in each other's future. I used it merely as an example."

He couldn't think straight. She shouldn't be so calm, so matter-of-fact, so . . . apathetic.

"Well, Philip? Do not keep me in suspense. Have you or have you not bedded dear, *dear* Joanna?"

Her words rang in his ears—Russian lovers, no future between them, Joanna, Joanna, Joanna—and he pierced her with his stare, hoping to see past her smiling facade and into her heart.

She returned his gaze steadily, until it seemed she was the one who saw through him instead.

Finally, with a muttered excuse, he bowed and left.

Charlotte's head sank into her hands as the sound of his footsteps faded. Shaken, she looked down at her half-eaten meal, remembering only the bitter taste of each bite upon her tongue.

For a moment she'd thought he heard the sarcasm breaking past her manner of indifference, the sarcasm which served only to mask the hurt and betrayal.

How could she let him do this to her again? After all this time, after everything . . .

She had a chance at freedom, and yet she couldn't be happy about it. Oh, no, she had to torture herself by spying on him and Joanna, by wondering what else they shared besides hand touches and kisses and annoying little pet names.

She wasn't surprised he had refused to answer her question. She wasn't shocked, either, when he had resorted to gracing her with the coldness of his silver eyes before he left.

What had been interesting, and quite uncharacteristic, was the fact that he had nearly blushed, *and* pounded on the table, *and* thrown his chair back in anger.

She was becoming more adept at annoying him than she had thought.

But, God, she still couldn't help but wonder—had he left the dining room simply to go to Joanna? Would he even pretend to retire for the night? Had he already gone?

Rising from the table, Charlotte gulped a mouthful of wine, draining the rest of the glass.

She stepped carefully over Philip's chair and avoided making eye contact with the ever-present footman at the edge of the dining room.

Yet once she passed him, she stopped and asked quietly, "Did you see in which direction His Grace went?"

"No, Your Grace. If you like, I shall—"

"No matter. Thank you."

She looked in the music room, the study, the drawing room, the library—after fourteen more rooms and still no sign of Philip, she encountered Fallon in the hall.

He could barely restrain his frown at the sight of her. "Your Grace," he intoned.

"Fallon. Have you seen my hus— His Grace?" she corrected hastily. He was her husband, true, but it seemed odd to address him as such when he clearly no longer saw her as his wife.

The butler's eyebrows twitched as he spoke. "I believe he went for a ride, Your Grace."

"Oh." On a horse, or on a woman? "Very well. I believe I shall . . ." Do what? Run to a window in the hope of seeing him? Retire to her bedchamber, sit by the fire, and wait to hear the sound of his footsteps returning?

"Your Grace?"

She smiled at him. "I shall be in the sitting room."

"Yes, Your Grace," he answered and bowed, as if it were normal for her to apprise him of her intended location.

The sitting room. Not the drawing room, a place reserved for entertaining guests and making idle conversation. No, the sitting room was for intimacies—intimate conversations between close friends and family; days and nights spent with loved ones, simply doing nothing but enjoying one another's company.

As Charlotte entered the room, her gaze immediately fell upon the chairs, the sofa—the places where Philip and Joanna had renewed their own intimate relationship, where they had engaged in touches and kisses and words.

She made her way to the escritoire, defying the impulse to take one quick glance out the window. She would probably see nothing, and even if Philip were visible, it would change nothing.

He had spoken of freedom earlier, with the tone of a man who understood its importance. Of one who had been locked away, caged for too long. And he had spoken of finding happiness in his freedom away from her.

In this respect, at least, they were kindred spirits.

Charlotte opened the desk drawer, drew out a sheaf of papers. The fire was lit, but it was a dim, flickering light, casting more shadows than it dispelled.

She grasped a candle nearby, preferring its softness

to the bright glare of an oil lamp, and set it next to the papers.

A sharpened quill and a bottle of ink were next.

Before she had even written the first invitation, more than ten names entered her mind.

Philip enjoyed entertaining Joanna here at Ruthven Manor; Charlotte would enjoy entertaining her guests as well.

Philip wished for freedom and the happiness their marriage had long denied him; Charlotte was eager to partake of such liberty, too.

And while he and Joanna conversed and flirted in the sitting room, Charlotte would use the drawing room to host her own little intimate party.

# Chapter 14

*T*hree days later, at promptly two o'clock in the afternoon, Charlotte's guests began to arrive.

"Your Grace," Fallon said from the door of the drawing room, "may I present Mr. Wright, Mr. Bowlby, and Viscount Massey?"

"Thanks, old chap," Edward Wright said, clapping Fallon on the shoulder. "But dear Charlotte knows who we are. Don't you, Char?" Edging around the butler, he threw her a wink.

"Edward!" she cried, stepping forward to allow him to give her a kiss on the cheek, then waited as Andrew Bowlby and Lord Massey had their turns at taking her hand and sketching a bow.

"Gentlemen," she began, then halted as Massey nodded toward the door. Turning toward Fallon, she said, "Thank you, Fallon. You may be dismissed. I am expecting a few more guests. Please send them in. There will be no need for introductions."

"Yes, Your Grace," he said, and inclined his head as he walked backward into the hallway. There was no change to his usual dour tone of voice, but he made his disapproval more than clear.

"He's a cracked old bird," Andrew said from behind her. "Still, not much of a jailer if this is your prison."

Charlotte sent him a flirtatious grin as she turned and sat in the sofa in the middle of the room. "Then I imagine it shan't be difficult for you to help me escape."

Massey, the only one of the three men who had remained standing, lifted a corner of a curtain with a long, gloved index finger. "Holland and Stafford have arrived." His ice blue gaze switched to Charlotte's. "Have you summoned all your beaus from London, dearest?"

A shiver of unease ran down Charlotte's spine as his lids lowered to her mouth. Out of all the men she had invited, Stephen Avery, the fifth Viscount Massey, was the only one who had made it clear he considered it only a matter of time before she became his mistress. All the others were content with the harmless flirtation, happy for the simple pleasure of keeping company with a beautiful woman.

"Only my favorites, Stephen," she murmured, sweeping her lashes downward. Though he made her uncomfortable, his presence was important to the effectiveness of her little performance.

"You're a naughty, naughty girl, Char." Edward cut the tip of his cigar, rolled it between his fingers. "It's why we've missed you so."

"I must admit I feared no one would come. I thought you were all scared of the duke."

"Scared?" Andrew scoffed beside her, leaning forward with the obvious intent of staring down the front of her gown. "He's never done anything all these years. What would he do? Glare at us?"

Charlotte shifted until she faced him directly, cutting

off his view. "Of course, what you say is true. He has never cared about my ... indiscretions in the past."

"I was at Fontaine's that night." Massey's voice echoed from the corner. "He cares."

"Stephen." Charlotte ignored the pounding of her heart at his words and winked at Andrew. "I am touched you think so."

"Hullo, gentlemen! Dearest Duchess."

Thomas Holland and Richard Caversham, Viscount Stafford, strolled into the room.

Charlotte came to her feet and extended her hands. "Thomas, Richard, how pleased I am to see such friendly faces!"

On it went, greeting her guests as they came over the next half an hour, flirting and smiling and laughing at all manner of sexual innuendos.

Pretending not to notice when eyes strayed, adjusting her position subtly when hands attempted to follow eyes.

She was skilled in this type of performance, juggling each suitor's attention, taking care to make each man feel as if she preferred him over all the others.

Only she had changed since the night Philip had stolen her away from Fontaine's. She found herself fighting a yawn as Andrew and Thomas sparred, flinching at the overt glances Massey threw her way.

She knew she could handle the men, but found she no longer wanted to. It all seemed pointless now, when it was only a matter of time before she and Philip would go their separate ways. She had gotten the divorce she'd wished for.

And if she weren't bitter and just a little immature, she would never have hosted this little party, hoping for Philip to come and see that she deserved some freedom and happiness, too. She needed to prove to him—and perhaps to herself as well—that she didn't need him or care about his affair with Joanna. That she wasn't the same foolish girl she'd once been.

The clock on the mantel taunted her, ticking off the minutes ever so slowly. Philip should have come by now. Should have been alerted by Fallon to the inappropriate gathering in the drawing room. Told him that, once again, his improper wife was acting the whore.

They had left the door ajar. At the very least, he should have heard the voices and come wandering in.

Unless he and Joanna were too busy distracting each other in the sitting room . . .

Philip's thighs ached, his cheeks burned by the brisk October wind.

He and Argos were no strangers to daily rides, but taking the stallion out for a gallop two or three times a day was excessive even for him.

After spending several hours with Joanna at Ruthven Manor, he had escorted her home, but not before discussing his departure loudly with Fallon in the front hall. Not that it had done any good; he'd not seen Charlotte at all today. For all he knew, she might still very well be abed, entirely unaware of his continued companionship with their old friend.

For the past two hours he'd ridden Argos over his estate, despite the possibility that Charlotte might not even know he was absent.

The days were slipping away. With every minute he spent with Joanna, he was aware that he lost even more time with Charlotte. He second-guessed himself, an entirely new experience. He'd never been familiar with doubt before, and he didn't relish the feeling now. The desperation with which his plan had begun now consumed him.

If he'd meant to make her jealous, he had failed utterly. So far, his actions had served only to confirm her belief in him as an absolute bastard, a man unworthy of her.

And yet, he continued this farce. For what purpose?

He laughed, the sound harsh in his ears before the wind carried it away.

Because he had no idea what else he could do. Because all of his plans had been exhausted. Only twelve days remained until the end of the month, and there were only two more months until the time he was supposed to let her go free. Yet all he'd succeeded in accomplishing was falling even more in love with her, and giving her a greater reason to hate him.

With his heart lying heavy in his chest, Philip pulled on the reins and wheeled Argos back toward Ruthven Manor.

Perhaps he should let her go now. It was clear her view of him hadn't changed; why torture himself any longer than he must?

Except his intent to divorce her, as everything else, had been a lie. She would never be free of him, and dear God, he would never allow her to be.

As they neared the house, Argos gave an agitated snort, his ears bent forward. Soon Philip could see what the stallion had already sensed: three—no, four vehicles of varying sizes littered his grounds. Two broughams, a carriage, a curricle, a scattering of grooms in various colors of livery.

Philip dismounted at once and threw his reins to one of his passing stable boys. Already, he could feel heat beginning to surge at the base of his spine. He didn't need to ask, but some demon inside forced out the question. "What is going on here?"

The stable boy, with an expression of bewilderment on his face, answered in stammering halts. "The d-duchess, Your G-Grace. A party. Sh-She—"

It was enough.

Philip brushed by the stable boy and strode toward the front door. Somewhere, a window was open, and the smell of cigar smoke filtered through the air. A loud masculine laugh followed.

Fallon was not there to open the door. He was always there, nearly as permanent a fixture as the door handle itself.

"Fallon!" Philip roared as he entered, the sound of the heavy oak crashing against the wall a fitting punctuation.

The butler immediately appeared from around the corner, his cheeks blanched a startling shade of white. He had good reason to be afraid.

"Where is she?" Philip demanded.

"In the drawing room, Your Grace," Fallon answered, his breath wheezing while he followed on Philip's heels.

"How many?"

"I tried to reach you, Your Grace. I sent a footman—"

Philip rounded quickly. "How many?" he asked again, quietly.

The butler recoiled as if struck. "T-twelve at last count, Y-Your Grace."

Philip spun around and proceeded onward to the drawing room. He could see the edge of the entrance, hear the rumble of voices.

"Men? Women?"

"All men, Your Grace. And, of course, the duchess."

Philip halted outside the doorway and gave Fallon a grim smile. "Of course."

He stepped inside.

It took a moment for anyone to notice him, simply because all of the visitors were focused on Charlotte, who sat in the middle of the room.

In the middle of the bloody sofa, in between two of her admirers. It appeared she'd altered one of the gowns he'd bought her, a crimson dress which revealed more skin than it concealed.

She was the first to become aware of his presence. She smiled and waved, inviting him closer—damn her— as if he was one of *them*.

"Your Grace," she called, effectively quieting the room.

He didn't return her greeting. "Gentlemen, I believe it is time you left."

One of them made the mistake of rising to her defense. "See here, Your Grace. We know about the divorce. Charlotte told us—"

"I will count to ten. Anyone who has not removed himself from this house by that time should give notice to his second to meet me in the morning. I will kill you, by God, and I will defy any court which dares to punish me."

Charlotte stood to her feet, her eyes flashing. "If you force my guests to leave, I shall go with them."

"One."

No one moved.

"Two."

A man in the corner rose and bowed. Philip recognized him as Viscount Massey.

"Three."

"Adieu, my dear," he said to Charlotte. "Until next time."

"Four."

Two other men followed Massey out of the room.

"Five."

An argument began among four men to his left. Their voices quieted as his gaze fell upon them. One by one, they shuffled past him.

"Six."

Charlotte turned to the men on either side of her. "Edward. Andrew. You won't leave me with this ogre, will you?"

"Seven."

Three more men escaped. Only Charlotte, Edward, and Andrew remained.

"Eight."

Edward was the one with the cigar in his hand. The smoke curled in a wisp through the air as he spoke in hushed tones to Charlotte.

Philip had several interesting visions regarding what he would do with that cigar if the man should choose to stay.

"Nine."

Edward left. A pity.

"Ten."

The last man, the one named Andrew, the one who had spoken about the divorce, darted a glance between Charlotte and Philip. With a little squeak, much like a frightened mouse, he too scurried away.

Charlotte glared at Philip and tried to follow. He caught her around the waist.

He clucked his tongue. "Their lack of devotion must pain you."

"Your high-handed arrogance pains me more."

Philip's hand tightened over her hip. "You can't expect me to allow those men under my roof. They are like dogs after a bitch in heat, panting to be your lovers."

Her chin rose a fair two inches. "Why not? You parade your lover in front of my nose."

"Jealous, Charlotte?"

Her eyes narrowed, then softened. Her lips parted. "Jealous? Yes, perhaps I am."

Philip stared at her, certain he was imagining her words.

She turned into him, placed her hands flat upon his chest. "Did you want me to be jealous, Philip?"

A dangerous question. "I—"

"Shall I tell you how I wished, if but for a moment,

that I could be her instead? That I could be as proper, as elegant, as perfect for you as she appears to be?"

His voice became a hoarse whisper as his breath refused to leave his body. "Why would you wish such a thing?"

"Shall I tell you how I longed to be the one upon whom you showered your attention, your affection?"

His hands had somehow come to grasp her arms, pulling her closer inch by inch. "Why would you long for my affection?"

*Tell me. Tell me you love me.*

Her lips grazed the corner of his mouth, his cheek, as she spoke. "Shall I tell you how much it pained me to see her in your arms, to know she was the one you planned to spend the rest of your life with?"

"Why, Charlotte? Tell me why," he demanded harshly, striving to keep her at a distance as her body leaned into him. Even though he desired nothing more than to crush her to him, enfold her in his arms, and hold her until neither of them could remember, until both of them had forgotten the tragedy and the pain of the past three years.

He couldn't suppress a tremor as her lips brushed his ear.

"I shall not," she whispered. She rubbed the softness of her lips gently over the shell of his ear. "Philip, you bastard. How I detest you."

Pushing away from him, she shook loose of his grip. "How dare you! You *wanted* me to be jealous."

He watched her wide eyes and her gesturing hands as if from far away. Strange, how his mind chose to believe these words were the lies, and that her previous confessions were the truth.

Her voice rose as his silence continued. "Is there nothing you do that is not an effort to control me? Were you upset when you saw those men here, my lovers, as you call them? I hope you were, Philip. I truly hope you understand how it feels to be manipulated at every turn, to have your every action and emotion turned against you."

She had moved away from him, pacing across the room as the torrent of words rushed out, and now she whirled around. "Damn you, Philip! Say something!"

He couldn't. He had no defense.

Charlotte's chin lifted, and she averted her gaze. "Fine. Leave me be. Go to Joanna. Go to your lover. Just . . . leave me alone."

Perhaps it was his anger at her continued assumption. Or perhaps, despite how hopeless it seemed, he couldn't leave her alone, no matter how much she begged.

Regardless, he wouldn't allow her to believe for one moment longer he had been unfaithful to her again.

"Joanna isn't my lover. I never intended to marry her."

Her head lifted, a wary frown of disbelief marring her brow. "Then why did you agree to a divorce? Why did you bribe me into giving you those ridiculous lessons? Why would you pretend?"

"I—" His mouth was open. He could tell her the truth now and perhaps gain her respect. A doubtful possibility.

He could tell her the rest, that he had never intended to let her go. And he could lose any chance—slim though it might be—that still remained of winning her love.

"I wanted you." A partial truth, and yet still he regretted the words instantly. Hated the sudden vulnerability they brought with them.

Hated the curl of her lips, the silent accusation he saw in her eyes which said he was like all of the other men who only coveted her body.

Her voice shook as she spoke. "So the harp, the fair,

the kindness—oh, God, I should have known when you were *kind* to me—they were all ploys to get me in your bed?" She threw up her hands, yet the bleakness of her eyes spoke more than her dramatic gesture. "For heaven's sake, you're my husband, Philip. You own me, do you not? All you must do is unbutton your trousers and tell me to get on my knees, and I am expected to obey—"

"No!"

"You think I am a whore. Should I not act like one?"

His hands, his legs, his entire body trembled with rage as she swept her skirts aside and knelt on the carpet before him.

"Get up." He bent toward her, swiping away her hands as she fumbled at the front of his trousers. "Get up, damn you!" Gripping her elbows, he tugged with all of his strength. The force caused her to stumble against him, burying her cheek against his chest.

"Oh, I do apologize, Your Grace," she mumbled. "I forgot it is not *proper* to fornicate in one's own drawing room—"

Philip shoved her away. Too forcefully, perhaps, because a short cry escaped as she fought to keep her balance.

He stepped forward to steady her, but stilled when she lifted her head. The bright sheen of tears could not disguise the despair shining in her sapphire eyes.

"I'm sorry," he said. "I didn't mean to—"

Her laughter, wild and anguished, tore at his soul. "Of course you didn't. Just as you didn't mean to trick me into marrying you, or to take my innocence and then leave me so alone. You didn't *mean* to make my life a living hell—"

"And I never meant to fall in love with you. But I did. God help me, I love you, Charlotte."

\*     \*     \*

Charlotte stared at him. She lifted her hands, palms outward—an attempt to steady the sudden-tilting world as much as to stop his words. "Don't."

Philip moved toward her. "That's why I gave you the harp. That's why I took you to the fair. I tried to court you, to woo you, though, admittedly, I've done terribly at it. And Joanna—yes, I wanted to make you jealous. I wanted to make you want me—" He sighed, running his fingers through his hair. "I love you, and I wanted . . . I hoped—"

She shook her head as she retreated, her legs heavy, unsteady. "Don't. Don't lie to me. Not about that. I believed you once, Philip. I'll not do so again."

"I dismissed my mistress because of you. You're the only woman I want."

"Ha!" Charlotte pointed a finger, noticed it was shaking, and buried her hands in her skirts. "How noble of you. Or perhaps you merely tired of her and have yet to find another—"

Moving her hands was a mistake. He advanced upon her, closing the distance quickly as she somehow managed to stumble into every piece of furniture in the room.

"Did you not notice how I suddenly began to escort you to the theater, the opera? How you would accidentally find me at the same parties you attended, or how I would be waiting for you in the breakfast room every morning, when for the past three years we had never dined together once?"

"I—"

He smiled grimly. "No, you didn't notice. No matter how I tried to show you I had changed, you continued playing the part of the scorned wife, flitting from one man to another."

"Am I to regret my actions, Philip, to feel pity for you? I *was* the scorned wife, and those men—"

"You were *my* wife," he reminded her, his voice low and dangerous. "Those men had no right to touch you."

Her heart thrummed violently in warning, but Charlotte couldn't keep the sultry smirk from her lips. "But they did touch me, Philip. Here." She placed her hands on her breasts, lifting them up.

Philip's growl rent the silence of the room as he covered her hands with his own.

"Here." Though he tried to keep her still, she dragged her hands—and his—slowly down her torso, around to her buttocks. The movement brought him a step nearer, caused his chest to brush against her breasts.

Charlotte released a small gasp at the unexpected arousal caused by his nearness. His breath fanned the hair at her temple and his scent—so masculine, so dark—teased her nostrils with its decadence.

His hands turned and twisted so that they grasped her wrists, pulled her arms forward, between them. Charlotte held her breath as, with a sort of reverent tenderness, he kissed the fingers of one hand and then another.

Then he released her completely and stepped away, leaving Charlotte to wonder why she should feel so bereft at the space between them. As if she had wanted him to continue holding her, touching her.

She wondered what he would say if she told him the truth about all those other men.

God help her, was she softening toward him merely because he'd told her he loved her? What sort of fool was she?

It unnerved her how Philip watched her, his silver gaze heavy, brooding. His mask of stoicism had fallen into place once again; it was as if she'd imagined the anger and sadness in his expression before.

"If you'd like a maid to help you pack your bags, I will not stop you from leaving."

"Why should I leave?"

"Why would you stay?" he countered.

It was a dare, plain and simple. He pretended he didn't care whether she went or not. Charlotte would have easily called his bluff—why, indeed, would she want to stay?—except for the brief longing which flared in his eyes before he shifted his attention to the window.

Curious, uncertain of both him and herself, she remained silent.

"You have an hour or two before dusk. You could be on your way back to London before nightfall." He paused before turning back to her, a falseness to the curve of his lips. "I'm sure Denby and all your other admirers would be more than happy to see you."

Charlotte nodded slowly, as if she were considering his words. As if the promise of groping hands and leering eyes were any sort of temptation. Yet, instead of agreeing with his suggestion, she asked, "It is twelve days until the end of the month, is it not?"

"Yes."

"I agreed to stay for three months. If I stay to the end of this one, what shall we do in the next twelve days?"

His jaw tensed under her scrutiny. "Anything you wish. If you do decide to remain at Ruthven Manor, I only ask that you allow me to attempt to prove to you I am telling the truth. Let me court you. Let me show you how I've changed. Let me love you, Charlotte."

"And after the twelve days?"

"Whether or not you insist on the petition, I will continue to love you." His eyes burned fiercely as he held her gaze, and Charlotte felt a slow flush begin to make its way from her chest to her neck, and then spread upward across her cheeks.

The clock on the mantel ticked off several seconds as they stared at one another, the air seeming to hum between them.

If she were to base her decision on fear alone, she

would have already fled upstairs and rung for her maid. She was afraid of him, more afraid than she'd ever been of anything in her life. Fearful of the attraction which still remained between them, no matter how much she tried to deny it. Fearful of how quickly her emotions could be swayed by his vulnerability.

But it was too late to be governed by fear.

"Will you stay?" Philip asked finally.

"Yes," she whispered, giving him a brief smile which she hoped didn't betray her cowardice. "I'll stay."

# Chapter 15

Charlotte awoke the next morning with the devil on her shoulder. Philip had made a mistake by telling her she could do as she wished for the remainder of the month.

Instead of ringing for Anne to come help her dress, she pulled a wrap over her nightgown and tied the sash into a jaunty little bow.

Tapping her finger against her chin, she considered the drawer of stockings. Then she looked up at the portrait of the old duke and sighed. To her dismay, she had tossed the most decadent ones across the frame, and wasn't tall enough to pluck them down. Staring again at the plain woolen stockings in the drawer, she decided bare feet would be best.

She skipped down the stairs two at a time, her loose hair bouncing with the motion.

"Good morning," she called in a singsong voice as she entered the breakfast room. It was unnecessary to fake the grin that stretched her lips as she waited for Philip's reaction.

Although an egg and a half-eaten slice of toast remained upon his plate, he focused on a copy of the *Times* spread before him. Had he waited for her to waken and descend for her own breakfast, as he had claimed yesterday? It was odd—and quite thrilling—to think of him anticipating the pleasure of her company.

He lowered the paper. "Good morning, Char—" A choked sound issued from his throat as he scanned her attire, skipping from her tapping toes all the way to the long locks she had left hanging past her shoulders.

Nodding happily, she dragged out a chair from the table before the stunned footman nearby could assist her. Leaning forward, she planted her elbows on the table and cupped her chin in her palms. "You may be wondering why I am wearing only my nightgown and wrapper."

Philip's gaze jerked from somewhere below her neckline to her lips. "Indeed." He turned to the corner of the breakfast room and signaled Fallon. "Leave us," he ordered.

Once the servants had retreated, he returned his attention to Charlotte with a jerk of his head, a lock of black hair falling forward over his brow. "Did you lose your maid perhaps? Or are you simply trying to tempt me beyond control?"

She ran her fingers along the edge of the table. "Are you tempted?"

She frowned at the seductive heat gleaming in his silver eyes. "Never mind," she added hastily, and wished she had thought to at least pour a glass of juice to occupy her hands.

"Yesterday you said I could do anything I wish." She shoved away from the table, twirled around, and sank in a curtsy. "I've decided today I wish to wear my nightclothes for the entire day."

He folded the paper and set it aside. "I suppose you mean to test me. To see if I will forbid you or scold you for doing something unbecoming a lady of your standing."

"It is rather scandalous, is it not?"

He rose to his feet. "I shall join you if you like."

Folding her arms across her chest, Charlotte smirked. "You wouldn't. Your dukeliness would not allow you."

Philip deftly untied his cravat. "Do you not remember, Charlotte?" After he stripped off his coat, he laid it neatly over the back of his chair.

"Remember?"

The waistcoat came off next. He paused, sending her a wicked glance. "I prefer to sleep in the nude."

Her memory conspired with him to taunt her, flashing images across her vision of gleaming muscular flesh, shadowed only by the flicker of candlelight and the bold, eager strokes of her own hands.

"I wonder why you blush," he murmured.

Reminding herself that any modesty she'd once possessed had long since disappeared, Charlotte met his gaze evenly and willed away the heat beneath her skin. She gestured to his discarded clothing. "Although quite brave of you, I've decided your sacrifice isn't necessary. You shall be a duke forever. I will be a duchess for only a short while longer. We can't compromise your ducal propriety, can we?"

It was a good speech, especially for one delivered almost breathlessly. But even she knew it was far from convincing.

Still, Philip nodded and tucked in the hem of the shirt he'd been in the middle of removing. "As you wish, my love."

*My love.*

A simple endearment, yet painful to hear. How many times had he whispered those words in her ear before their wedding? How many times had she believed them to be true?

"I wish for you to call me Charlotte. Not 'my love,' nor 'Your Grace,' nor even 'Duchess.' Only Charlotte."

"Ah. Very well. If, however, you decide to address me as anything other than Philip, I must tell you I am particularly partial to 'O Supreme One' and 'His Great Magnificence.'"

Charlotte tilted her head. "Why stop there? Why not 'Your Majesty' then?"

He swept her a regal bow. "If you insist."

A swell of laughter caught at her throat. This was the man she'd fallen in love with: clever, wicked, too charming for her to resist. He made it so easy for her to believe, if even for a moment, that this was the sort of man he could be all the time.

He made her *want* to believe.

For some strange reason she had agreed to stay. Certainly there existed some mad, masochistic side of herself that she hadn't realized. After all, it was silly to remain, if only to see it through to the end. He had agreed to the divorce no matter what she chose.

She might stay for the next twelve days, but she must remember why they could never be happy together, and forget about the reasons why her heart claimed it was possible.

She would not allow herself to forget the agony and pain of his betrayal. She could not.

Philip picked up his cravat. Dangling it between his thumb and forefinger, he regarded it with a forlorn gaze. "I suppose I should put the rest of my clothes back on. But if you should change your mind in the future—"

"Why do you love me?"

The easy smile faded from his lips; his eyes captured hers, holding her immobile, refusing to let her pretend she hadn't just spoken the question aloud. One of his hands gripped the chair beside him, his knuckles white.

For a moment she thought he wouldn't answer.

"I love you because ... you are everything that is vivid and bright in this world. You teach me what it is to be alive. You see me as a man, not a duke, and ... I want to be one that is worthy of you. Every moment, I think of you. I imagine what you are doing if we're apart. I yearn for the next time I will hear your voice, smell your perfume, watch your eyes dance with laughter or flash with defiance. And when I am with you—" He cut himself off, his breath harsh and labored.

"Yes?" she prompted, afraid if he didn't continue he would realize her own breathing was just as erratic. Afraid he would see more than she wanted him to know.

"When I am with you I must pretend I am content to merely be in your presence. When, in fact, there is nothing I want more than to kiss you, to touch you. To believe, if for only one moment, that you are truly mine. Not because you are bound to me by the laws of marriage, but because you desire me as much as I desire you." He made a feral sound—almost like an animal in pain. "Even now, I must hold on to this chair. A flimsy piece of furniture, but it reminds me to be civilized. Because if I were not—God knows, neither your hatred nor your disgust would keep me from you."

She clutched at the edges of her wrap, fought to calm her racing heart. "I shouldn't have asked you," she whispered.

"I suggest you go to your bedchamber and dress yourself properly." His lips thinned somewhere between a leer and a snarl. "Lest I forget myself and all of my ducal proprieties."

She ignored his sarcasm and bitterness, his threat to ravish her, and instead focused on the quiet desperation lacing his voice. The wildness of that emotion intrigued her, fascinated her, and terrified her all at once. "I shouldn't have asked you," she repeated, as if saying it would erase the fact that she had indeed done so. As if it would remove the echo of his passionate speech, the nakedness of his eyes.

His eyes. Dear God, how could she have ever thought they were cold and empty? They were a silver tempest, raging with pain and longing and—they showed everything. They showed too much.

Gasping, Charlotte looked away. She didn't want to see it. She didn't want to believe him. He couldn't love her.

"No, my darling. You shouldn't have asked." His voice, soft now, wrapped around her like a silken caress. It tugged at her, nearly swayed her to turn toward him, to forgive—

With an anguished cry, she fled the room.

Philip paced the hallways of Ruthven Manor, searching for Charlotte.

Ten more days. Ten more days. The silent litany played over and over in his mind as the tap of his boots echoed off the marble floor.

Yesterday had passed too quickly. She had studiously avoided him for the remainder of the day, and he couldn't blame her. If anything, he was relieved he'd not had to face her after that embarrassing scene in the breakfast room. He hadn't ravished her as he'd wanted upon seeing her in nothing but a nightgown and wrap, but he had lost control of his emotions. Allowed her to see his weakness.

He hadn't gone searching for her when she declined to join him for supper that evening. Nor had he ventured near the music room when he heard the playing of the harp afterward, but had contented himself with listening to the lilting melody, closing his eyes and imagining the curve of her neck as she rested her head against the instrument's column, the stroke of her slender hands across the strings.

Yes, they'd both had their reprieve. But no more.

At the sound of hurried footsteps behind him, Philip whirled. He scowled at the bent head of Charlotte's maid. "Yes?"

"Her bedchamber is empty, Your Grace."

"You saw her this morning. You helped her dress."

"Yes, Your Grace."

"And she said nothing to you? Spoke of no plans, no thoughts for the day?"

The maid's head sank even lower. "Forgive me, Your Grace, but Her Grace doesn't take me into her confidence."

Silently cursing, Philip spun on his heel, marched a few paces, and turned again. "Fetch Fallon at once. He was to stay near her."

If she had fled, Fallon would know. Surely it was a good sign that the butler hadn't yet come to inform him of her departure.

Yet the maid remained, her gaze glued to the floor. The fingers of her left hand twitched.

"Well?" Philip demanded.

"It is Mr. F-Fallon, Y-Your Grace. He has also disappeared."

The high trill of another servant's voice down the hall echoed harshly in the sudden silence.

"I see. You may go."

Only with the utmost discipline was he able to keep himself still as he watched the maid walk away, his expression void of the panic consuming him at the girl's stuttered words.

For if Fallon were nowhere to be found, it could only mean he had followed Charlotte—wherever she may have gone. That he had not had time to alert Philip to her escape. She'd left him after all.

Once the maid passed from sight, he turned and ran down the hall. The front entrance was empty—no footman attended the door in Fallon's absence.

He rushed outside and around the corner, his eyes fixed on the stable ahead. "Here," he called to the unseen stable boy. "Ready Argos!"

It was a windy day, the sky threatening another rainstorm. The breeze whipped across his face, stealing his words.

"Here," he called again as he neared the doors. Yet no one answered, and no one appeared.

He made himself walk calmly down the row of stalls, careful not to frighten the horses. And with every step he cursed his missing servants, cursed Charlotte for leaving him, and cursed himself for driving her away.

Argos nickered and stomped as he neared.

"Easy, boy." He lifted his hand to stroke the stallion's forehead. He reached to unlatch the stall door with the other, but froze at the sound of laughter.

*Her* laughter.

As if he doubted his own hearing, or was afraid of scaring her away if he made too much noise, Philip crept silently toward the sound.

The door to the tack room was wide open, and every chair around the table in the center was occupied, every pair of eyes focused on the play of cards in front of them.

He immediately dismissed the others as unworthy of his attention. He cared only about Charlotte.

She hadn't left him.

He recognized the dress she wore as one of the many he had purchased for her. The neckline was appropriately high, the cuffs of the sleeves reaching to her wrists. A dress befitting a duchess.

Though the green muslin didn't cling to her curves or reveal a lavish expanse of bare skin, when she smiled, and as she turned her head just so, she appeared as alluring as if she'd worn one of her scandalous silk gowns.

And Philip realized that no matter how decorous

her attire, no matter even if he was able to convince her to wear sackcloth every day, nothing would lessen this need for her, this weakness in his character.

She would always tempt him.

"Charlotte," he murmured, uncertain whether he spoke because he wanted her attention or for the simple pleasure of saying her name aloud.

At once the play at hand ceased. A chair crashed backward as the man to Charlotte's right stumbled to his feet. "Your Grace!" Even shocked, Fallon managed an exclamation in monotone.

Philip stared at the frozen tableau of his butler, the stable boy, two groomsmen, the housekeeper, one of the cook's maids, and Charlotte in turn.

The smirk on her lips dared him to reprimand her, mocking him as always. But it was the slide of her gaze to the cards in her hand that momentarily stilled his breath.

She refused to meet his eyes.

How . . . interesting.

The Charlotte he knew, his shameless and wicked wife, would never have shown such vulnerability.

He retrieved the fallen chair and set it upright, careful to brush against her shoulder as he sat down. She wriggled her own seat to the left.

Philip casually draped an arm across the back of her chair and nodded to one of the groomsmen. "Deal me in."

"I believe," Charlotte said, her shoulders stiffening as he stroked the back of her neck, "you must wait your turn. Fallon is—"

"Leaving," the butler interjected behind them. "I—I mean, *we* must return to our duties at once. Thank you for the lovely diversion, Your Grace."

At his cue, the other servants bowed and curtsied and scurried away, knocking into one another in their haste to exit the tack room.

"No, you must stay," Charlotte called, half rising from her seat. "Fallon, you still owe me—"

The dull thud of the stable doors slamming shut cut off the rest of her plea.

Sinking back into her chair, Charlotte sighed heavily and flung her cards on the table.

"You seem rather desperate not to be alone with me, my dear," he drawled.

"Charlotte," she corrected immediately.

"Hmm?" He removed his gloves, his fingers aching to touch the velvet softness of her skin.

"I asked you to call me—" She jerked away as he caressed the curve of her jaw.

The heavy, dark heat of desire sharpened his senses, all of his nerves attuned to her scent, the unsteady rise and fall of her chest, the ragged sound of her soft breath as it escaped her lips.

"Very well. I shall do as you ask. Charlotte."

"Thank you."

He watched her long, slender hands reach out to gather the cards. Her fingers fumbled as she shuffled, and she cursed when one after another they slid across the table, some falling to the floor below.

She hastened to pick them up, but he halted her with a touch of his hand.

"Allow me."

Nodding warily, still refusing to look at him, she sat down.

It was an odd thing, really. She obviously didn't know how to act around him now. Was it his barbaric confession of his need to ravish her, he wondered, or his continued declaration of love?

He had been prepared for her to leave; he had anticipated her scorn, her hatred, her laughter at his desperation—all of these were expected and justified.

But for her to show even a sign of vulnerability, of uncertainty . . .

Not just to feel them, but to allow him to see her weakness . . .

Ten days to convince her to love him again no longer seemed such an impossible task.

Philip bent to collect the fallen cards. He spied one which had drifted to the ground near her skirts, and he fisted his hands, tempted to reach beneath her hem and stroke the delicate line of her ankle.

As if aware of the wayward hunger of his thoughts, her legs shifted to the left. "Ah, here is the last one," she announced, her voice a husky murmur in his ear.

Philip lifted his head to find her bent over, her face tantalizingly near. Gone was any hint of vulnerability, a spark of laughter instead brightening her eyes. It was almost as if he'd imagined her timidity a moment before.

With a slow wink, she scooped up the remaining card and motioned for him to hand over the rest of the deck.

"Sit down, Your Grace." This time she shuffled neatly, the cards a blur of precision beneath her fingers. "Now that you have scared away the other players, I demand a new game."

Determined to win back the ground he had lost, to set her off balance once again, Philip reclined lazily in his chair. Letting his thigh rest heavily against hers, he traced his fingers along the nape of her neck. "A new game? Of course. Although I must confess I didn't bring any coins along."

He replaced his fingers with his lips, brushing the sensitive skin below her hairline. "Perhaps we could play for"—he smiled against her skin as he felt her shudder—"other, more pleasurable prizes?"

"Mmm. Such as?" She arched her neck to the side.

Philip leaned away, his breathing not as controlled as

he might have wished. He stared at her unspoken invitation. He could imagine himself touching her, tasting her, the fragrance of her skin branding his senses as his lips made love to the elegant, creamy white column of her throat.

And he knew he wouldn't be able to stop there.

She offered herself so easily, yet it wasn't enough for him. He didn't want pieces of her, but everything—her body, yes, but also her heart, her soul.

Charlotte played the game of seduction well—too well. Yet he had only seen her react to his own overtures; never had she been the one to approach him.

Very well. Let her come to him. Only then would he know that it was because she truly desired him, and not because she felt she must act the role of temptress in response to his carnal pursuit.

"Philip?" She turned at his silence, her lips parted provocatively.

And as quickly as he'd resolved to endure her enticements, he found he didn't have the strength to deny himself entirely.

"A kiss," he said, unable to tear his gaze away from the soft ripeness of her mouth.

"Is that your wager, then?"

"Yes."

Charlotte pursed her lips, and he almost groaned. Dragging his eyes away from her, he focused on the tip of her fingernail, tapping against the cards.

"Have you ever swam in the nude?" she asked at length.

*Good God.*

"No," he answered, proud of himself for being able to even utter that short syllable. He stared across the tack room, willing the sight of saddles neatly hung upon the wooden wall to imprint itself into his mind. Anything to erase the unbidden image of Charlotte, splashing naked in the pond. Of Charlotte, her nipples peaked and hardened. "I'm not certain that's such a good idea. It is October, and the water will be quite cold."

She remained silent, as if mulling over the point. Then, just as Philip managed to fix the saddle to the lower right side firmly in his mind, she said softly, "Perhaps there are ways to make it warm."

Philip cursed silently, the saddle quickly giving way to a dozen flashing images showing precisely how he and Charlotte could warm themselves. Together.

"Is it settled then?" she asked, dealing out the cards. "The winning player will have their wager granted. If you win, it's a kiss. If I win, it's a swim in the nude. Do you agree?"

Philip grunted his assent. He knew he should hope, for the sake of his sanity, that he might win the wager. Yet as he leaned forward to pick up his hand from the table, he couldn't help but pray for Charlotte's victory.

# Chapter 16

*I*t was a very clever wager.

And a very foolish one, to tempt her indifference and her discipline.

"I seem to remember we were supposed to swim together," Philip called from the edge of the small pond.

"No, I merely said it would be a swim in the nude." The bark of the oak tree scraped roughly against Charlotte's palms as she leaned back. She forced a laugh to her lips, the sound of it hoarse from the dryness in her throat. "I never said I would join you."

He gave her a rueful grin over his shoulder, then planted his foot in the water. "It's freezing."

"I'm sure it will get better once you go in all the way." She, on the other hand, felt as if she were being consumed by fire. The muslin was suffocating, pressing down on her chest, restricting her breath. Even if she wanted to, she couldn't turn away. She was supposed to be accustomed to the naked male physique. And although it had been three long years since she had seen a man without any clothes, Philip couldn't know that. She must act as if she weren't in the least affected by his nudity.

But though she tried, she couldn't pretend to herself. Not when the fading autumn sunlight poured over his skin like the sweep of a lover's hand, painting the lines of his body in golden contrast to the shadows of dusk. Not when her heart betrayed her by beating so furiously, or her mind by imagining what it would be like to have her hands caress his skin, her mouth touch the warmth of his chest.

To be fair, she hadn't actually thought he'd go through with it, not with the chance that one of his servants or Joanna might see him in all of his ducal glory. But he had surprised her yet again.

"You do realize I shall be ruthless in my revenge, don't you?" Philip waded into the water, creating small waves which lapped at the sculpted muscles of his thighs.

Charlotte prayed she wouldn't faint.

His body jerked as the water reached his waist, and a low muttered curse drifted to her ears. "A-are you certain y-you won't come in?"

"Yes."

He turned around, and Charlotte was helpless to look away from the broad expanse of his shoulders, his chest, the lovely line of hair trailing over his abdomen and down, down—

"What if I drown?"

Her gaze snapped to his. "I shall fetch Fallon."

"Surely you will cry?"

"Copiously. A torrent of tears."

He smiled, his mouth curving in a luscious grin marred only by the clatter of his teeth.

How was it possible that he could make even goose-flesh appear attractive? "Is it truly very cold?" she asked.

He gave her an arch look. "You kn-know it is."

With a slight bow, he dove into the water, only to appear a moment later with long, even strokes as he swam toward the opposite edge.

Charlotte sighed. And for the first time, she was brave enough to admit to herself that it was with longing.

She wanted him.

Yes, she loved him. She had never stopped.

And she hated him. Or at least, she should, after all the pain he'd caused her.

But oh, how she wanted him.

So much, in fact, that she was tempted to forget that pain, to see if his love could heal her now, when the promise of it had almost destroyed her before.

As he reached the other side of the pond and dove again, loneliness taunted her. Her constant companion, it kept her safe in isolation, but a prisoner of her own fear.

Why could she not trust again? Why could she not believe him?

Would it truly be so terrible to allow herself to be happy with him?

Tormented by her thoughts, Charlotte idly scanned the pond, searching for Philip. Her eyes found only the calm surface of the water.

She surged forward. "No."

She clutched her skirts and ran, but they were so heavy, and then her shoes sank into the softened soil as she neared the water, slowing her pace even more.

"Philip!"

She would kill him if he was playing a jest. If he weren't already dead, if he hadn't drowned from the cold, she would kill him—

"Philip!" She wrenched his name from her throat, past the lump of panic that lay lodged there.

Toward the middle of the pond, a circle of concentric ripples fluttered over the water. Charlotte held her breath, her gaze glued to the spot.

As seconds passed and the water smoothed again, the

surface reflecting the darkening sky above with the clarity of a looking glass, something broke inside her.

Seized with a sort of madness, she kicked off her shoes. Then, as she twisted her torso in an attempt to reach the line of buttons at the back of her dress, she saw him.

Walking. Along the edge of the pond. Toward her.

"It was far too cold to swim back," he said with a sheepish shrug.

Frozen in place, torn between relief and embarrassment, Charlotte could only stare as he came closer.

When she didn't speak, his gaze drifted to her discarded shoes and then her arms, stretched at an awkward angle behind her. She could only hope he hadn't seen the fear on her face.

"You thought I had drowned, didn't you? You were going to rescue me."

The softness of his tone and the nearness of his large, naked body sent heat coursing to her cheeks. She dropped her arms and studied the sky. "No, I—I decided to go for a swim after all."

"Liar."

"No, it's the truth. You appeared to be enjoying yourself, and— What are you doing?" His hand enveloped hers, his touch somehow warm beneath the cold moisture still clinging in droplets to his skin. He lifted her fingers to his lips.

"Thank you." His eyes twinkled at her over their joined hands. "It warms my heart to know you don't truly wish to see me die."

"Humph." It was, really, the only appropriate response. Or, at least, the only response she deemed appropriate. The other urged her to hurl herself into his arms. "I think you should put your clothes back on now."

He kissed her hand again before slowly lowering it.

But he didn't release her, instead intertwining their fingers. For some reason, that simple gesture sparked another blush.

"Afraid you'll not be able to control yourself, are you?" he teased as they turned to walk back toward the oak tree.

"Quite so." Approximately thirty more seconds until they reached his discarded clothing, and then perhaps another two minutes while he dressed himself. All she had to do was continue to look straight ahead and count the time. Soon this weakness would pass.

One ... two ... three ...

"There is still the matter of my revenge to discuss," Philip said. "Clearly you intended to trick me. If I weren't a gentleman, I might be inclined to voice my suspicions as to the likelihood of you possessing the queen of clubs at the exact moment when it appeared I would win our little wager."

Would he question her if she insisted he not talk? Because when he spoke, the sound of his voice dragged her gaze toward his mouth. And then all she could do was stare at him, watching with avid fascination as his lips moved and curved and drew a hint of a smile to the corners.

She cursed and glanced away.

"Charlotte? The queen?"

"On the chair, under my skirts. I picked it up when the cards fell."

A moment of silence. "Ah."

They had arrived at the tree. Charlotte glanced down at the neatly folded stack on the ground: cravat, shirt, waistcoat ...

Confounded elaborate fashions. It would take him forever to dress, certainly longer than the two minutes she had promised her self-restraint.

Deciding it best to continue to the manor alone,

Charlotte gave a short wave. "I shall see you at supper. I just remembered I have to—"

She was whirled around, her back pressed against the oak, the dampness of Philip's skin wetting the bodice of her dress.

His breath was hot against her ear. "I believe you owe me a kiss." A drop of water fell from his hair to trickle over her collarbone and down her chest.

Charlotte shivered.

"Unfortunately," he murmured, his thumbs stroking the pulse points at her wrists, "the unbridled joy of having my nether parts exposed for all the world to see has disappeared, and I must keep it brief."

Then, with a gentleness she didn't know he could possess, he turned his head and placed a lingering kiss against her temple.

"I love you."

She didn't say anything. She didn't pretend she hadn't heard him, and she didn't deny his words or argue with him.

Instead, she simply closed her eyes and breathed. And in the silence which followed, as the darkness wrapped around them and the heat of his body seeped into her bones, she allowed herself to believe it was true.

Supper was a quiet affair, the mood far less volatile than usual.

It was, Charlotte decided, almost intimate in nature.

Philip questioned her about her opinions and preferences: her thoughts on industrialization and what it meant for the nobility as well as commoners; whether she preferred chocolate with or without sugar; and if she liked to read Austen more than Shelley.

He attempted to convince her that William Macready was a far better actor than Edmund Kean, then expressed his shock when she informed him that she hated not only the theater, but opera as well. She laughed at the way his jaw gaped open, but quickly quieted, her interest piqued, when he began to teach her how to curse in Italian.

It reminded her of the conversations they'd had years ago, when he would sneak her out of her parents' house to stroll with him through the woods separating the estates. Sometimes their words were mingled with stolen kisses and long embraces, but he always listened when she spoke, and acted as if everything she had to say was important. He'd been the only person besides Ethan to treat her so.

After dessert was finished and Charlotte announced her intent to retire for the night, he escorted her to the stairway.

"Nine more days," he said as she began to climb the steps.

Charlotte paused and turned to him. His hands were clasped behind his back, his shoulders rigid with tension. What did he expect her to do, to say? Her heart was still too fragile; even she was hesitant to take it out of the shadows and examine its scars, let alone voice her longing and desires to the man who had created the wounds.

Tilting her head, she gave a long, sly grin. "Take heart, Your Grace. Only a few weeks ago I would have gladly watched you drown."

His eyes followed the curve of her neck and lingered upon her lips before lifting to meet her gaze. Charlotte's fragile and scarred heart trembled.

"Then I have made progress," he said.

"So it would seem."

"And yet I couldn't help but notice how you didn't immediately come to my rescue this evening. I had time to swim to the far end and walk halfway back to you before you even removed your shoes."

Charlotte lifted her shoulder in a shrug—a gesture subtle and elegant, meant to draw attention to the fit of her bodice. As his eyes once again followed her movement, she scolded herself for provoking him. She knew he desired her, and her body's response to the heat in his silver gaze proved she was playing a dangerous game.

Grasping her skirts in one hand and the banister in the other, she continued to climb backward up the stairs. "You are the ninth Duke of Rutherford, all that is just and true and wonderful. Surely God would not dare allow you to die. But if it eases your mind, I will tell you the truth—it was the dress."

Philip's brow furrowed. "The dress?"

She turned when she reached the landing, sending him an innocent glance over her shoulder as she said, "Yes, the green muslin, the one you bought for me. Mud and grass stains are impossible to remove. It would have been a terrible waste."

His laughter followed her as she disappeared around the corner and entered her bedchamber. The rich sound lit a smile on her face as she closed the door and leaned against it, the wood smooth beneath her cheek and hands.

She sighed, wondering at her hope to hear his footsteps chasing after her, helpless to understand the extent of this longing for him.

All she knew was that each minute with Philip made it more difficult to maintain her pretense of indifference. At the same time she worked so hard to hold on to her facade of the seductive temptress, she feared he would see through her at any moment. And when he realized her deceit, that she still loved him, had never stopped loving him, and that she had always loved him and *only* him, she would be helpless.

*But,* whispered her bruised heart, *perhaps it would be worth it.*

If he had changed.

If only he hadn't said he loved her three years ago and made her believe him, then maybe she wouldn't have these doubts now.

Charlotte closed her eyes. She was tired of going around and around in her head and trying to convince herself of reasons why she should give him another chance when she knew that path would lead to her own destruction.

It was simple. She couldn't keep herself from loving Philip; she had long ago resigned herself to that inevitability. But willingly giving him power over her by letting down her defenses was inexcusable.

Straightening, she pushed away from the door. He wasn't coming after her, and she was glad.

Then she turned, and a disbelieving breath of laughter escaped her.

The wall to her right was blatantly stark, the portrait of the eighth duke, Philip's grandfather, absent. Where it had once hung proudly displayed, now only the discoloration of age remained to be seen.

Her stockings and scarves no longer served as irreverent decorations to conceal the last duke's disapproving sneer, but were folded neatly and arranged at the edge of her bed.

On top of the stack lay a folded note.

How unpredictable her husband had become. He must have ordered the portrait removed while they were having supper.

Charlotte moved halfway to the bed before she realized she was tiptoeing, as if the note were a secret and might be taken away at any moment before she could read the words within.

With trembling fingers she snatched the parchment and hastily unfolded it.

*I'd rather you wear these instead. I especially prefer the red lace stockings. —Philip*

Pressing the letter to her lips, she sank upon the counterpane. How could she resist his challenge? For though subtle, the invitation was clear.

The question, however, was whether she could indulge her desires and yet remain in control.

Charlotte reached out and sifted through the pile of silks and satins until she found the pair of red lace. They had always been one of her favorites, chosen for their decadence, their symbolic rebellion of everything Philip respected, everything he expected from a proper duchess.

How interesting that, above all others, he would favor these.

The note fell to her lap and an eternity seemed to pass away as she fingered the lace edges of the stockings, her chest rising and falling unevenly.

She feared she'd asked the wrong question of herself. It wasn't whether she could remain in control, but whether she wanted to.

Philip glared at the parchment lying on the desk before him.

No matter how much he tried, he couldn't seem to find the words to adequately express his thoughts.

The wastebasket near his chair was gorged with his many attempts. His fingers appeared tarred and feathered from stroking the quill from tip to end repeatedly as he sought the perfect phrase.

Should he change the fifth line from *soft with light* to *soft as night*? But no, he couldn't very well repeat the same word from the beginning of the poem.

Philip looked from his hands to the paper and back again. Snarling, he broke the quill with a satisfying crack.

Byron could go to hell.

Philip knew he should leave well enough alone. The

harp had gone over perfectly well; there was no need to continue torturing himself by endeavoring to write a poem for Charlotte.

But he knew he would, no matter how many hours he spent laboring in vain or fantasizing about the resurrection of Byron just so he could strangle him to the grave again.

It had been two months since he'd found the slim volume of Byron's poetry in the empty sitting room of their London town house.

No depression in the sofa had marked her presence; no perfume lingered on the pages. Yet as Philip had opened the book, he imagined he could see her face light with pleasure as she recited the verses, could see how the morning sun must have touched upon her skin and turned her dawn blue eyes to sparkling sapphires. It was as if she'd left an imprint in the air around her.

Since that time, for some inexplicable reason, the completion of the poem had become a symbol of hope that Charlotte would love him again. He'd burned his first epic attempt, and yet he continued to work on it. For even if it were terrible—and God, it was, really and truly awful—perhaps she would read it and finally believe he loved her.

If attempting to write the bloody thing had taught him nothing else, it was that only a lovesick fool could lament over the fact that the only English word which rhymed with "noble" was the most decidedly unromantic "global."

Philip lowered his head into his hands, then froze. With a muttered oath, he withdrew a linen kerchief from his pocket and methodically wiped at the ink on his face and hands.

He should be happy. The day had been quite successful, and Charlotte was slowly lowering her defenses.

When she spoke to him now, there was a softness in her tone that hadn't been there before.

But there was also the look—that uncertain, confused, almost wounded look which crossed her expression at times. Perhaps she thought she was hiding it well, or that he wouldn't see, but he did. And it tore him apart.

He was the one who had put it there.

Philip thought he had changed. Indeed, he knew he had—one could not love Charlotte without being transformed by her.

Yet he couldn't deny that he was still manipulating her. Putting his need to have her over her desire for freedom. He'd counted on winning her love, refused to consider the alternate possibility. He'd been convinced that the end would justify the means.

But now he had to realize that despite his best attempts, he might lose her.

How could he divorce her? How could he let her go?

But if he did not, if he reneged on the promise he'd never intended to keep, could he live with her hatred? The contempt she'd felt for him these past three years would be nothing compared to what it would be if he betrayed her trust yet again.

God, he was a selfish beast.

How could nine more days with her suffice? He needed a lifetime, an eternity of her laughter, her irreverent teasing and uninhibited passion.

To see her, to hear her, to have some part of her—even if none of her smiles were directed at him and he could never possess her heart.

Philip set the kerchief aside. He stared at his left hand, at the wedding band he had once scorned. A blackened web of ink stained the flesh around it, emphasizing the bright golden gleam.

He would not yet give up hope. Despite these inconvenient little bouts of doubt and despair, he knew Charlotte's resistance was fading.

He picked up the scattered pieces of the broken quill and the ruined kerchief, then tossed them into the wastebasket where so many of his failed attempts at poetry mocked him.

Steeling his thoughts against the possibility of defeat, he opened his desk drawer and drew out another piece of parchment and a new quill. The first lines of the poem were committed to memory, and the words flowed easily onto the paper.

He dipped the tip into the inkwell and paused, pen poised over the page as he fought for the next line.

"Her soul . . . No, the bright light of her soul—"

A knock sounded at the door of the study, Fallon come to stir the fire.

"Enter," he called, then bent his head over the paper as he wrote.

*The fierce light of her soul, it beckons me.*

"I've always wondered what it is that keeps you so busy in here," came a low, seductive voice.

The quill jerked across the paper, leaving a thin, uneven scratch.

Philip stared at the line. His pulse raced as he schooled his features into impassivity. He glanced up. "Estate business, my dear—"

The last syllable caught in his throat.

Cloaked in a red satin robe, Charlotte strolled across the room, her hips swaying in a gentle, undulating rhythm. She lifted her hands to her head and began to pluck the pins loose from her hair.

He watched, mesmerized, at the movement of her slender wrists, the deliberate flick of her fingers as she sent the pins scattering to the carpet below.

Her hair swept over her shoulders and cascaded past

her breasts, a heavy veil which was enough in itself to tempt him past the edge of reason.

"You said it again," she reprimanded. She halted in the middle of the room, the glow from the fire a backlight to the fullness of her curves.

"Pardon?"

"'My dear.' You said 'my dear.' You're only to call me—"

"Charlotte." Her name rushed roughly from his lips.

How could she not know it was her name that was the endearment, that he'd used those other words to protect himself from revealing too much? It was her name that was sacred, her name which he repeated over and over again to the silent evening shadows and the dawning sun, when his empty arms ached with want of her.

"Charlotte," he said again, uncaring now if his tone should disclose the extent of his affection. His need for her. "What are you doing here?"

She stared at him solemnly, her hands fiddling with the sash tied at her waist.

"Do you love me?" she asked.

Philip's heart clenched, a burning deep in his chest. They would never move past this doubt. She would never forgive him.

He sighed. "Yes, of course—"

"Say it," she demanded, her eyes fierce. "Say you love me."

His fingers gripped the quill. "I love you."

Her chest fell sharply, as if she'd been holding her breath, and she looked away. Then, with a slow nod, she met his gaze again.

Every muscle in Philip's body tightened at the provocative smile she gave him. He couldn't understand her. One minute the uncertain innocent, next the alluring siren—he couldn't decipher which one was the mask. Perhaps she was both, and he was destined for eternal torment as he fought this desire to protect and ravish her at the same time.

"Charlotte," he repeated, "why are you here?" His breath stuttered to a halt at a sudden thought. "I assume you found that I removed my grandfather's portrait? Your scarves and stockings—"

"Yes, and I found your note." Her eyes darkened to a devilish midnight gleam, her hands moving with a steady grace to untie the robe's sash. The satin folds parted, and Philip flinched at the loud crack of his quill as it snapped in two. He glanced down, tried to focus on the pieces as they fell from his fingers, but couldn't keep his gaze from seeking Charlotte.

He felt as a beggar might as he stared at the lure of a shiny gold coin—bewildered, almost weak from desire.

The matching red night rail's neckline plunged to reveal the swells of her breasts. The hem skimmed the tops of her thighs, her skin gleaming smooth and ivory white in contrast to the darkness of the shadows behind her.

Not far below the hem, two black garters held those glorious red lace stockings in place.

Unbalanced, Philip gripped the edge of his desk as he half rose from his chair. "God, Charlotte—"

She strolled forward and planted her hands on the opposite side, leaning in until their lips were scant inches apart. "I've come to give you the prize you lost, Philip. A kiss."

# Chapter 17

*N*othing had ever made Charlotte feel as powerful, as beautiful, as the flare of desire in Philip's eyes. The heat in their silver depths sent a flush of pleasure coursing along her skin. Although he hadn't yet laid a finger on her, she felt as if he had branded her with his gaze alone.

His stare followed her motions as she lifted a hand to his face. The curve of his jaw scraped her palm, and she gloried in its coarse texture, in the sudden need to feel the contrast of his stubble-roughened skin against the smoothness of her own.

Against her shoulders, her breasts, her belly, her thighs . . .

"A kiss," she repeated in a whisper.

Before the syllable could fade into silence, his mouth was upon hers, his lips firm and tender and wild. She met his touch eagerly, the desk pressing hard across her thighs as she balanced on her toes.

He tasted like darkness, like red wine and something indefinable, something singularly Philip. A moan rose in her throat and her hand fell to clutch at the broad strength of his shoulder.

A simple kiss, yet it made a mockery of all her rehearsed methods of enticement.

She turned her head away, wondering at the sudden urge to weep. Perhaps because she knew, if she listened to her head and not her heart, she would never find anyone else who could elicit this same violence of feeling, this overwhelming sense of belonging.

Only Philip.

His breath came harshly at her ear, and she pulled back to look at him.

She hadn't noticed it before, but faint black streaks marred either temple, one trailing to the outer corner of his eye.

He appeared mussed and boyish and oh so wonderful.

Charlotte smiled and reached out to trace the crooked line. "You have something . . ."

He touched his hand to his face where she lingered, then scowled. "The damned ink. I suppose I didn't get it all."

She pulled her finger back to show him the dark smudge staining its tip. "Not quite." Glancing at the paper on the desk, she asked, "What were you writing?"

Philip's hand slapped over the parchment, covering it from her scrutiny. "Estate business, as I said."

She lifted a brow. "Estate business?"

"Yes."

"And that's why you're hiding it from me?"

With one hand still concealing the contents, he pulled out a drawer with the other, then quickly placed the paper inside and shut the drawer.

"It's confidential," he explained as he moved around the desk.

"Mmm-hmm."

She waited until he was almost to her side, then sprinted in the other direction.

He was right behind her, but too slow. She yanked the paper out and danced away.

He stalked her around the sofa.

"Charlotte," he ground out.

She grinned. It truly was delightful when he used his deep warning voice.

Holding the paper aloft, she meandered backward through a cluster of chairs. "Tell me why you don't want me to read it, and I may oblige you."

"It's private."

"Is it truly estate business?"

He paused in the middle of the chairs and scowled at her. "No."

She lowered the paper, then shrieked as he lunged toward her. He caught her around the waist, but she extended her arm away from his grasp and read quickly.

"She walks in beauty, like the night, of cloudless climes and starry skies. And all that's best of dark and . . ." She frowned and looked over her shoulder at Philip. "A Byron poem? Why have you—?"

"I only used the first few lines," he retorted, his arms stiffening around her. "As inspiration."

"Inspiration? But I don't . . ." She lowered her eyes again to the paper and scanned the next lines, her breath quickening. "Philip, I—"

"May I have it back now?" he asked in a flat tone.

"You wrote a poem for me." Somehow it came out sounding more accusatory than she intended.

He released her abruptly and strode to stand in front of the fire, his back to her. "It's not finished. The ending is still rough, and I've been reworking some of the other lines. I asked you not to read it, but you—"

"It's wonderful."

She watched as his shoulders tensed, his hands clasping tightly behind his back.

Clutching the paper to her chest, she walked toward him. "I never thought—no one has ever—"

His laughter cut her off, a low chuckle that reverberated harshly around the room. He'd never looked more like the devil as he turned to face her, the flames behind him casting his features deep in shadow—all except the unholy gleam of his silver eyes.

Charlotte flinched, taking an involuntary step backward.

A corner of his mouth curled at her movement. He advanced toward her, his voice a velvet caress as he spoke. "Were you going to say that none of your lovers had ever written poetry for you?"

Her feet were rooted in place, unable to retreat.

Yes, she'd received poetry, but none of it had ever mattered. None of it had been from Philip.

His hand lifted to her cheek. She closed her eyes, shivering as he trailed a finger along the edge of her jaw, down her throat.

"Of course they did," he murmured, his thumb stroking along her collarbone. "How could they not? How could I not? We are all fools for you, Charlotte."

She hated how her breath came in short, shallow gasps. She sounded weak, when she wanted to be strong. But his touch and his nearness and his scent overwhelmed her, filled her lungs until there was no room for air, for nothing but him. "I don't think you're a fool."

"Oh, but I am, my darling. How else could I have hurt you, have let you go?"

He swept her hair back over her shoulder. She shuddered at the warm press of his lips against her neck.

"Let me love you now, Charlotte. Let me show you how much I love you."

Now was the time to leave, her chance to escape. Or

she could stay, and follow through with the decision she'd made in her bedchamber.

Hesitation seized her for only a moment. Opening her eyes, she stepped aside to place the poem on one of the chairs, then faced him.

He stood rigid, dark, and imposing, his features once again arranged into that stoic mask he favored. Yet this time she was achingly aware of the way it could not conceal the hunger in his eyes, the burning intensity of his gaze.

Her body reacted as if it were his hands which trailed over her skin, his mouth which lingered at the edge of her bodice. The sound of her own heartbeat filled her ears, and when his eyes lowered further, she knew he could see the aroused peaks of her nipples as they pressed against her night rail.

"Philip." In two syllables she yielded to him. Silently, she told him of her love, asked him to be gentle with her heart. She gave him the power to destroy her once again.

Wrapping her arms around his neck, she leaned into him.

If only for one night, she would forsake her fears. In the morning . . .

She wouldn't think of the morning, or the day after, or any other time in the future.

All that mattered was this, the sigh of his breath against her cheek, the fierce meeting of his lips to hers. For one night, she would lose herself in his arms.

He whispered her name while he drew her robe over her shoulders and down her arms. No other words were spoken as they undressed each other, their movements feverish, sometimes fumbling, in their haste.

She couldn't keep from touching nearly every inch of skin she uncovered, determined to see if her memory had been accurate.

It hadn't.

His skin was hotter, his muscles harder. They quivered as she skimmed her fingers over his stomach and back up to his chest, unable to yet venture lower.

It was almost laughable, how someone as sophisticated as she, someone rumored to have dozens of lovers, could still be hesitant about touching him so intimately. Even their past lovemaking and the sight of him nude earlier couldn't give her courage. Instead, some enduring sense of modesty, buried so deep that she hadn't been aware it even existed any longer, caused heat to rush to her cheeks at the thought of caressing him there.

He captured her hands and drew them to his lips, his mouth warm and firm as he kissed the back of each finger. She watched, her chest heaving, as he turned her hands and scorched the pulse point at either wrist with the hot press of his lips and tongue.

Somehow their roles had reversed. No longer the seducer, she had become his willing prey.

"You have beautiful hands," he murmured, stroking her palms with his thumbs. "Slender, elegant." His gaze fixed to hers, he kissed her wedding ring. "Thank you," he said.

Her eyes, heavy with desire, followed his movements as he knelt on the floor. "For what?"

"For not removing it," he explained, and tugged her down beside him.

If he only knew of the number of times she'd actually tried to dislodge it over the years, how she'd tried to pull it off, suck it off, how she'd used water, butter, and oil, all to no avail. She didn't tell him how she'd even gone to a jeweler, nearly crying with frustration and anger, convinced that Philip had somehow put a curse on her. She'd balked when the jeweler pulled out a vicious-looking file. But even then she was tempted, so desperate was she to remove the symbol of his ownership, the dream of a marriage that had turned into a nightmare.

But that was the past, and she didn't need to disturb the moment by correcting his assumption. Besides, she hadn't tried to remove it in a long time—several days, at least.

Instead, she gave him a saucy grin. "A proper duchess would never remove her wedding ring."

His answering smile, slow and wicked, set a fever racing through her veins. "Ah. But we both know you aren't very proper, do we not?"

As if to demonstrate the point, he bent his head and captured her nipple in his mouth. She moaned, threading her fingers through his hair. She urged him closer, arching her back to press more fully against the pain-pleasure of his suckling, the pull of his teeth and tongue all at once too much and not enough.

He pushed her backward onto the carpet and moved over her, his knee between her thighs. All the while, still his mouth laved her breast, his hand roaming to caress her other nipple to a peak. She writhed beneath him, the feeling of the lush carpet a decadent contrast to the warmth of his skin, the rough sensation of his stubbled jaw against her flesh.

Sighing his name, she placed her hands on either side of his face and pulled him up. She needed to kiss him, needed the intimacy of his lips on hers. Perhaps to remind him—and herself—that this was not merely a mindless meeting of bodies, but something more meaningful.

Though she wouldn't speak it, she wanted him to know her heart.

And perhaps he did know, for when his mouth covered hers, his touch turned gentle. Delicate. He slid his lips along hers from corner to corner, pausing to nibble at her lower lip, then kissing it as if in apology before moving on.

Never had Charlotte felt more cherished as he continued to tenderly ravage her mouth. Yet even that could not describe the feeling well enough.

She felt . . . *loved*.

Strange to realize it was Philip who was finally able to ease the loneliness which had consumed her for so long. Each press of his lips seemed to fill the emptiness in her soul, more and more until it overwhelmed her and she broke the kiss.

She opened her eyes, gasping. His gaze bored into her, as if he could see her every secret, her every fear and hope and desire.

"Don't cry," he admonished gently, and bent his head to brush his mouth across her cheek.

Only then did she feel the wetness on her lashes and on her face, where a tear had already traced its way to the curve of her jaw.

He stroked the hair at her temple. "Why—"

She kissed him again.

She wouldn't allow any questions when even she didn't know the answers. She didn't know why she cried, only that it was the first time she'd let the tears fall in front of him in three years.

Needing to distract him from her weakness, she pushed on his shoulders until he rose to his knees.

When he opened his mouth, she pressed a finger to his lips. "Shh. On your back."

He leaned back on his elbows and stretched his legs out alongside her hips, drawing her attention to the sleek muscles of his shoulders and biceps, his chest and stomach. A half smirk played at the corner of his lips when she lifted her eyes to his face, the knowing gleam in his silver eyes causing her throat to go dry.

"All the way," she ordered hoarsely.

How she wanted to make him beg, to lose control the way he made her lose all sense of time and reasoning.

Inhaling deeply, she moved to kneel beside him. She placed a kiss at the base of his throat, her hair swinging forward to cast a veil around them.

His hands came up to stroke her shoulder, her back, the length of her arm.

"No." She placed her palm over his hand as it trailed along her collarbone. "Let me seduce you."

He gave a low laugh. "Everything you do seduces me. All you need do is to breathe, and I would do anything for you."

Her chest ached at his words, but she somehow managed to send him a provocative glance through her lashes, her lips carefully arranged in a sultry pout. "Then be still, and let me do as I like."

"As you wish," he agreed. Then, folding his arms beneath his head, he whispered, so quietly she almost didn't hear it, "Charlotte."

Heart pounding, she leaned across him. The flickering shadows of the fire dared her to follow their path over every ridge and hollow of his body. With one hand on the carpet and one balanced on his chest, she took the lobe of his ear between her teeth.

He stiffened beneath her touch, and she drew her fingertips over his chest in figure eights, the pads of her fingers whispering across his skin.

Though she could feel him drawn tight like a bow beneath her, he gave no other indication that what she did pleased him.

She traced her way from his ear to his jawline, then continued on, replacing the teasing circles of her hand with her mouth. From the corner of her eye, she saw his arms jerk in response, then relax again. Beneath her, his chest rose and fell heavily.

A flush of arousal heated her skin at the evidence of his pleasure. It was a heady feeling, to be able to affect him so.

Once again, she used her hand to make the next bold foray, caressing the sculpted planes of his abdomen. She trailed back and forth from side to side, over the arrow of hair tempting her to go lower.

As her fingers grazed his navel, they brushed against his shaft, hot and smooth. She froze, then lifted her head to see his reaction. He stared back at her, hooded eyes glittering, his nostrils flaring with each breath.

It was that same sense of carefully leashed control he always had, the hint that beneath his polished exterior lay a man desperate to be released from his own model of propriety and civility.

How she wanted to make him uncivilized. To hear him groan and cry out, to feel him tremble beneath her touch, unable to contain his response.

For once, to surrender to her.

Philip began to sit up, reaching for her arm. "I believe," he rasped, "I have been well and thoroughly seduced."

Before she could convince herself otherwise, she wrapped her hand around the hard length of him, his flesh pulsing against her palm.

"Not quite yet," she murmured, and lowered her head.

"Oh, God."

Philip clenched his hand into a fist as he watched Charlotte take him into her mouth. He hovered over her hair for a long moment before finally sinking his fingers into the carpet behind him, digging and twisting the fibers viciously.

The pleasure was nearly unbearable, the lush velvet of her mouth tight around him, moving up and down in slow, exquisite torture.

He called out her name, called upon God and the devil and all the saints he could remember as he fought to keep control.

Then she flicked her tongue, and the next moment she was on her back and his body covered hers, his lips and hands raging over her every curve with fevered intent. He was helpless, mindless to everything except the hoarse cries issuing from her throat, the need to please her, to feel her writhe beneath him.

Her legs wrapped around his waist. Her hands clutched at his hair, then lower, her nails scraping against his back. The biting pain awakened something fierce inside him, dark and heavy, and though he had meant to wait, to pleasure her with his mouth the same way she had done to him, he could not.

Her head tossed from side to side, her eyes closed as she pleaded with him to stop, to continue.

He braced his arms on either side of her head. "Look at me," he demanded.

Her eyes glowed brightly as she met his gaze, her mouth parted in soft, heaving gasps.

She was beautiful. Glorious.

His.

He thrust into her, watched as she arched beneath him. He wasn't gentle or considerate, driving into her over and over again, moving them inch by inch across the carpet.

He ground his teeth at the heat of her flesh, a tight glove around him. Darkness tunneled his vision until all he could see was Charlotte, her hair tumbled around her face, the sweet dew of passion beaded across her forehead.

He sank into her again, and she bowed beneath him, clinging to his shoulders.

"I love you," she cried. Then she buried her face in his neck, her moan muffled as her body convulsed in short, jerking shudders.

Hearing those words, feeling her clenching tightly about him—it was too much. A harsh, guttural shout ripped from his throat as he poured himself into her, emptying not only his body but also his soul into her keeping.

They were quiet afterward, the absence of sound almost deafening. He held himself above her, his fingers tangling idly in the softness of her hair as they lay joined together. Only their breathing broke the silence, labored gasps gradually easing to slower, steady inhalations.

She'd turned her head to gaze at the fire, and he lowered his lips to follow the elegant line of her neck. Her skin was warm, damp, the flavor of salt and woman faint on his tongue.

She sighed. She stroked his back lightly, then stilled.

Philip lifted his head in question. A frown marred the smooth perfection of her forehead.

"Did my fingernails hurt you?" she asked quietly.

"No."

Nodding, she resumed her caress, but halted again when he asked, "Did you mean it?"

His chest seemed too tight as he waited for her reply, his heart beating faster and faster at her prolonged silence, until he thought she would refuse to answer.

Finally, with a whispered breath, she said, "Yes."

"You love me."

"I love you."

Her voice was hesitant, uncertain, and Philip wondered if she'd not meant to say it before, if her confession had been unintentional, a passionate declaration which had caught even her by surprise.

Either way, he wouldn't allow her to regret it.

He pressed a fervent kiss to her lips. "You love me. Tell me, Charlotte. Say it, my love, my life, my darling."

"I love you."

He kissed her brow. "Again."

"I love you."

He kissed her cheeks, her chin, her nose. "Again."

She wrapped her arms around him, laughing. "I love you, I love you, I love you."

He stared down at her. "And I love you." He kissed her again, his lips plying hers with a tenderness that only she could evoke.

She opened to him with a soft sigh, her arms and legs clutching him tightly. Philip hardened inside her again.

This time he made love to her gently, slowly. He lingered over the slope of her breasts, the hollow of her navel, the curve of her waist. He treated her as though she were the finest porcelain beneath his hands, his hands and mouth reverent as he touched her, drawing out sweet keening moans from her lips with each careful caress.

When he kissed the folds between her thighs, her moans turned to restless cries. He parted them, laving his tongue across the peaked bud of her flesh with light, flicking strokes until her hips writhed beneath him and he had to hold her in place with his hands. She was the angel that inspired him to be a man who could deserve her love, the demon that drove him to do whatever was necessary to keep her, and he worshiped her.

Her fingers grabbed at his hair, pushing him closer, then trying to pull him away. He murmured soothing noises, meaningless words intended to calm even as his fingers stroked with ruthless determination.

She was so soft, and wet. His muscles quivered with the urge to rise up and sink himself deeply inside.

Her scent, sweet and salty, was heavy in his nostrils, a tart blend on his tongue. As he languidly licked from her core to the stiff bud of her pleasure, her body began to shudder and low whimpers escaped her lips in short, gasping breaths.

At last, when her hands fell away from his hair to land limply on the floor, he rose over her. Cradling her in the shelter of his arms, he knelt between her thighs.

She lifted her head to kiss him.

"Charlotte," he whispered, and entered her with a fierce stroke.

As he possessed her in a slow, deliberately measured cadence, she seduced him with her mouth. Her lips invited him in, her velvet tongue a teasing contrast to the silken heat of her flesh below.

He was lost again, driven to the brink of madness. She surrounded him—silk, velvet, sweetness, salt. Hot, supple flesh and the darkness of pleasure spiraling higher and higher.

With a loud cry, he came inside her, his thrusts lifting her hips off the ground.

And through it all, she held on to him. She never let go.

She had come to him.

It was the first thought in Philip's mind once he was coherent again.

They lay tumbled together on the floor, her back warm against his chest, her legs tangled with his. His coat and her robe served as blankets—actually fairly useless as far as covers went, since his entire backside had become quite chilled.

But he dared not move for fear of disturbing Charlotte, fast asleep within his embrace. If he propped himself up on his elbow and turned his head just so, he could see the softness of her profile, outlined in firelight and shadows. He was unable to look away, transfixed by the lush crescents of her lashes, the slight parting of her lips, even the tiny birthmark low on her left cheek.

She had come to him, offering herself. She'd said she loved him, though she knew who he was, what he had done.

Did she suspect what he was still capable of doing?

Deceiving her, manipulating her, using her own desires against her in a plot to keep her as his duchess?

She must not, or she would never have trusted him enough to allow him to make love to her.

But it no longer mattered.

She was his. He would never again give her reason to speak of leaving him. He would continue to change, to earn the trust she had given him.

And, he vowed, pressing a kiss to her temple, she would never again regret loving him.

# Chapter 18

Charlotte awoke with a start.

Instead of waking in a cold, empty bed, she awoke to find a large male body draped over her.

Philip's large, *naked* male body.

She turned her head to study him, offering a silent prayer of thanks when she saw he was still asleep. The meager gray light that ushered in the dawn filtered through the curtains, softening the planes of his face, the angle of his stubble-darkened jaw.

He breathed deeply, his face composed even in sleep. Only the rise and fall of his chest indicated he was still alive.

That, and the wall of heat he seemed to give off like a furnace. It scorched her as she lay tucked beneath him, his arm laid across her stomach, his leg pinning hers to the floor.

It was cozy, and comforting, and all too wonderful.

She had to leave.

She'd known as soon as she donned those red lace stockings that there would be no turning back. She'd planned the seduction, had come to him with every intention of making love. It was what she'd wanted.

But she hadn't planned to give him more than her body. She'd never meant to say the words out loud. Even now, they taunted her, echoing in the back of her mind.

She stared at Philip, adoring the carved stubbornness of his lips, the aristocratic slope of his nose, the haughty line of his brow.

*I love you.*

Her fingers itched to touch him, a nearly uncontrollable desire which caused her hand to shake.

She began to reach out, then closed her eyes and turned away, hating herself for this uncertainty. If she stayed, she would be giving up the freedom she'd waited for. But it would mean nothing if all she thought about was Philip—wishing she could be with him, wondering if he was terrorizing the servants or sulking in his study.

A warm rush of air stirred the hair near her temple, and she tensed.

"Good morning," he drawled.

Apparently he had no compunction in touching her, for his hand soon found her breast, his palm molding and shaping the fullness as he trailed a line of kisses down her cheek to the corner of her lips.

Her body was traitorous, immediately responding with a delicious, pulsing ache between her thighs.

But then, she'd always done as he wanted, hadn't she?

He'd asked her to climb out the window of her bedchamber, to meet him behind her parents' house. He'd asked her to lie with him on the grass and gaze at the stars while he held her hand and told her of his dreams for their future. He'd told her he loved her and asked her to marry him.

"Don't." She shoved his hand away and surged to her feet.

"Charlotte?"

Snatching her robe from the floor, she turned her back and belted it tightly. Her fingers trembled as she tried to tie the ends.

He touched her shoulder. "Charlotte—"

She whirled, taking a step back. "I need to leave."

He attempted to follow her, his brow creased in a frown, but stilled when she held up her hand. "I don't understand."

"I need to think."

"What is there to think about? I love you. You love me—"

"I'm sorry. I . . ." She hurried to the door.

His voice halted her. "You said you would stay. We still have nine days."

She turned around. Her chest ached at the sight of him standing in the middle of the room. She could almost see the mask slowly sliding into place. One moment his eyes glittered with pain, the next they were flat gray mirrors, showing nothing of the emotion within.

"I can't," she whispered. She shook her head, unable to explain, unable to give him any more of herself. Perhaps in a few days, when she returned, she would be able to tell him. How she needed to be alone for just a little while, so she could—

"I won't let you go." His syllables were clipped. Harsh.

Her breath caught. "What?"

He began to dress, his movements abrupt as he fastened his trousers. "There will be no divorce."

The cold crept into her blood, traveled to her chest, and seized her heart with dread. The sound of her pulse filled her ears, the pounding so loud she could barely hear her own voice. He stared at her while he pulled on his coat. Perhaps she hadn't spoken, only thought she had. She cleared her throat and tried again. "The petition," she began. "You agreed—"

"I lied." He shrugged, then laughed hollowly. "I thought if I could make you love me again, then you wouldn't want the divorce any longer."

She shook all over. Her arms. Her legs. Even her teeth chattered inside her head. She tried wrapping her arms around her waist to get warm, but it didn't work.

Nothing had changed. Everything he'd said—they were just words.

She had known better, but she had let herself believe him. And now she was twice the fool.

She heard herself speak as if from far away, the tone devoid of emotion, empty. Exactly like her. "I love you, Philip. I loved you when I was a little girl. I loved you when you took revenge on Ethan by marrying me. I loved you all these years when you ignored me. And I love you still. But, *God*—"

Her voice broke, and a tear splashed onto her cheek. She dashed it away. Straightening, she looked him in the eye. So familiar, and yet a stranger. "I love you. But I hate you so much more."

She glanced past his shoulder, at the sunlight beginning to stream through the curtains. Somehow it seemed fitting that the world should continue merrily along while her heart was breaking.

"Good-bye, Your Grace."

Letting Charlotte walk out the door should have been the most difficult thing he'd ever done.

Instead, it was frighteningly easy.

After all, he was a duke. A duke did not create scenes. A duke did not behave improperly or act on the will of his emotions.

Philip had forgotten this before. He would do well not to do so again.

All he had to do was act according to the standards to which he was raised, as if nothing could affect him. It was the perfect solution to any situation.

And so Philip stood in his study for a long while after Charlotte left, unmoving. Statue still.

He forced himself to breathe, to inhale the faint scent of jasmine, a lingering impression of her presence. If he stared at the carved-wood door long enough, he imagined he could see her again, standing there. Dark hair tousled, eyes wide with hurt, then disbelief, anger, and finally . . . nothing.

No, that wasn't quite true. He'd seen plenty of loathing in her eyes. She'd never become as adept as he at hiding her emotions.

Unfortunately for him.

If only she knew how unnecessary it was; he possessed enough self-loathing to compensate for any lack on her part.

He listened to the floor creak above him, the sound of swift footsteps pattering across—Charlotte's maid, no doubt, hurrying to do her bidding.

He might have half an hour before she departed, back to London and her throng of admirers. How they would welcome her, inviting her to their debauched gatherings, spouting praise for her beauty, daring to touch her hand, her shoulder—

Philip strode from the room and marched up the stairs, smiling grimly as he imagined smashing his fist into the face of every man who had ever made the mistake of being seen with Charlotte. She was still his. And she mattered more than a litany of phrases about what dukes should or should not do.

He would begin with Denby. He had enjoyed having Charlotte sit in his lap far too much. The portly sod.

Philip rapped on the door of Charlotte's bedchamber. When no answer was forthcoming, he pressed his ear to the wood. He heard her clipped tones, then the soft response of a servant.

"Charlotte," he called.

The voices grew silent, then began again as loud as before.

So she thought to ignore him, did she?

He turned the knob. It was his house, after all, and he would enter as he pleased. The knock had been a mere courtesy.

Except that the door was locked.

Grumbling, he walked through his own bedchamber and headed for the door between their rooms. When he twisted the knob and found that it, too, was locked, Denby earned another blackened eye in his imagination.

He retrieved the door's key, remembering with acute clarity how the man's gaze had been firmly attached to the expanse of Charlotte's bosom.

The key clicked loudly, and although it was probably entirely unnecessary to announce his presence, Philip still sent the door crashing into the wall.

She had dressed quickly. It was one of her old dresses—had she hidden it away?—a buttery yellow color which accented the smooth white gleam of her skin. A great amount of which was exposed by the low neckline and short sleeves.

At Charlotte's startled curse, he arched a brow and dangled the key from his fingertips. Her lips pursed, but all she did was turn back to her maid and the open valise before her.

"Leave us," he ordered.

The maid didn't hesitate before scurrying away through the open door.

Charlotte rounded on him, her hands on her hips, her eyes flashing. "Can you not leave me be?"

"I should think that answer would be obvious."

Scowling, she marched to the armoire and yanked it open.

"You will have no other lovers," he announced.

She paused in the middle of pulling out a dark blue gown. Then she began to laugh, a low chuckle that continued on and on, the sound almost maniacal.

"Why are you laughing?" he demanded.

Still she continued, the gown falling to pool on the floor by her feet.

Philip closed the distance between them, put his hand on her shoulder, and turned her around. "Charlotte—"

His hand dropped away at the cold scorn in her eyes.

She stopped laughing and lifted her chin. "Do not worry, Your Grace. There will be no other lovers. There has never been anyone but you. You see, unlike some, I understand faithfulness."

His stomach clenched. "I saw you. I saw you enter Lord Chalmsey's house. I watched from my carriage. You didn't leave until late the next morning."

She tilted her head and tapped her finger to her mouth. "Oh, yes, dear Chalmsey. He let me sleep on the sofa in the library when I claimed to be too ill from spirits to return home. Or to accompany him to his bed. He even threatened to call for a physician. Chalmsey's actually one of the more honorable ones. Lord Mayfield, however, once tried to force himself upon me when I pretended to be too drunk."

Denby was immediately lowered on Philip's mental list, replaced by Mayfield. No, that wouldn't do. Another list was needed, specifically for those he intended to disembowel.

"I trust he didn't succeed," Philip growled.

"Indeed not. I kneed him in the groin."

He growled again.

"It wasn't as difficult as you might think," she continued. "I merely confirmed a few rumors, and then any man who wanted others to think he had made a conquest of me began his own rumor. I simply never contradicted them. And I continued to act like a harlot, as if it were all true. So you would agree to a divorce."

She looked up at him then—a quick glance—then down again. "But none of it was true," she said softly. "And you didn't care, anyway."

"I *did* care," he countered fiercely. "I hated seeing you with one man after another. With any man but me. I wanted to kill each and every one of them for daring to dance with you, to touch you."

But there had been a time when he hadn't cared about anything she did, when he only scoffed at her attempts to provoke him. It had been easier to ignore her, just as it was easier to ignore his conscience.

Her silence told him that she remembered that time as well.

She gathered the gown into her arms. "I almost took a lover." She said it matter-of-factly, without the slightest hint of taunting in her tone.

He quickly forgot his transgressions as a black rage consumed him. "Who?"

She shook her head, went on as if he hadn't spoken. "But I couldn't. I was to send for him, but when the time came, I . . ."

"What, Charlotte?" he pressed. "Tell me."

"I could only think of you." She paused, staring ahead. "I hated you for that."

"Because you love me."

"Yes."

He was the only man she had ever known.

Realizing that he was the only man who had ever possessed her, slept with her in his embrace—it sent a primal thrill running through him, an uncivilized joy he'd known before only in her arms.

It was humbling to realize she loved him so deeply. That even after he had betrayed her in so many ways, she had remained faithful to him. He would never deserve her, no matter what he might do to try to atone for his deeds.

But surely, if they loved one another, he could convince her not to leave. He grasped Charlotte's elbow to help her stand again.

She tensed beneath his touch. "Release me." Her voice shook.

He withdrew his arm, but stepped toward her. "Stay, Charlotte. I love—"

She lurched away from him, crashing into the armoire. "Can't you see?" she cried. "It doesn't matter. I thought it would— God, how I wished all these years I could have been someone different, someone better— then you might have loved me."

He reached for her, needing somehow to bridge the distance she was trying to put between them. "I was blind. A fool. I—"

"Stop. Just stop, Philip." She skirted around him, laid the gown beside the valise.

He followed her movements, crisp and efficient, as she paired the sleeves together, then carefully began to fold the top over the skirts.

Something settled in his chest, something hard and heavy. "I will not beg," he said finally.

"I wouldn't expect you to."

And somehow he knew even if he did, it wouldn't make a difference. She would still leave.

A thick silence pervaded the room as she continued to pack. She took everything, filling one valise after another. An assortment of bandboxes, three trunks—all of her belongings, including everything he had bought for her, disappeared into their vast depths.

It was as if she didn't want to leave anything behind. As if she never planned to return.

"You must take the harp," he said.

She stilled. "It's too big."

"Then I will send another coach with you." He couldn't bear to have it here. Even if he didn't enter the music room, he would know it was there, untouched, unplayed. And he would believe she might come back to Ruthven. He would torment himself by imagining Charlotte as she sat at the harp, strumming the strings with her fingers, her head bent just so.

"If you don't take it, I shall have it destroyed."

She dipped her head. "Very well."

Philip breathed again.

Once she closed the last trunk, he walked to the door opening onto the corridor and unlocked it. Then he rang the servants' bell.

Her maid appeared immediately. The girl must have been waiting just outside. Hovering, no doubt. Hoping to overhear their conversation.

In the past, Philip would have dismissed a servant for such an offense. Now, he couldn't find the interest to care. "Have Fallon prepare the carriage and another coach. Send someone to carry Her Grace's baggage. She is ready to depart."

The maid curtsied, her eyes wide, and slipped away.

"She seems well mannered," he commented idly. "What is her name?"

"Anne. She's been my lady's maid for two years." Her tone implied he should have known this.

"Hmm. Is she the one who dresses your hair?"

"My hair?"

"Yes." He made a whirling motion at the back of his head. "I like when she does this."

Charlotte looked at him as if he had momentarily lost

his mind, her brow wrinkling. "A bun. You like when she puts my hair into a bun."

"Yes. It's very pretty."

"Oh." She lifted her hand as if she would pat her hair, then slowly lowered it. "Thank you."

"You're welcome."

And that was the extent of the only conversation they had until the footmen came to carry her belongings outside.

There was nothing left to say.

They watched together as the footmen trekked in and out of the bedchamber. The valises, bandboxes, and trunks disappeared. Philip counted each of them in his head. He memorized their shapes, their colors, the small details which distinguished each from the other—the stripes of red on one bandbox, a pattern of leaves on another.

Somehow it seemed important to be able to remember this moment clearly.

As the last piece of luggage—a trunk with a sovereign-sized dent near the latch—was carted away, Charlotte turned to him.

"Once again, I bid you farewell."

"Charlotte—"

She disappeared, exiting the room and rounding the corner before he could finish his reply.

He ought to be grateful. Although he'd said he wouldn't, he knew he would have begged her to stay.

Her slippers made no noise on the stairs, so he imagined her flying down them. Fallon would be standing at the open door, would bow as she passed by him. He imagined her entering the carriage, settling her skirts for the long ride back to London.

Philip heard the shout of the coachman outside, the rumble of wheels.

She would part the curtain at the window. Perhaps

her fingers would tremble as she did so. She would look out, try to glimpse him at the window of her bedchamber, remember when she couldn't find him that her window overlooked the garden.

Philip started toward the corridor.

Perhaps she would panic and change her mind, pound on the carriage roof, order the coachman to stop—

He halted on the stairway landing, his left foot hovering above the first step down.

The rumbling of the carriage wheels continued, gradually fading away.

Philip lifted his foot next to the other. He stood that way for a long time, staring at the marbled tile down below, straining to hear the rumble return.

It never did.

# Chapter 19

Fallon set the breakfast tray on Philip's desk.

"Shall I open the curtains, Your Grace?"

"No."

Philip blinked wearily at a point beyond the butler's head. Sometime during the night the shadows on the wall had transformed into grotesque faces.

Thank God, he had yet to begin to talk to them.

"I hope you won't think me impertinent, Your Grace . . ."

Philip blinked again, this time trying to focus on the gray blur where Fallon's face should have been. This could prove to be an interesting diversion. He waved his arm in a magnanimous gesture.

"I wonder if I shouldn't send for Dr. Barrow."

"I'm not ill," Philip replied, scowling.

"Of course not, Your Grace," the butler quickly agreed.

"Do you hear me coughing?"

"No, Your Grace."

"Do I appear sickly to you?"

Fallon remained silent.

Philip tapped his fingers on the desk. To be honest, he felt ill. Weak.

Over the past three days, he'd rarely moved from this chair and when he did he'd stumbled, the muscles in his legs quivering with each step.

Fallon opened his mouth, paused, and closed it.

"Speak," Philip commanded.

"Perhaps Dr. Barrow will be able to provide a tonic to help you sleep."

He didn't have trouble sleeping. It was the dreams he needed a cure for. The dreams which had kept him in his study for the past three nights, determined to stay awake. Or to exhaust himself to the point where he fell into a sleep so deep he would be unable to dream.

But he'd failed at both. Despite his efforts, he continued to doze off—intermittent naps that kept him just short of becoming delusional. Yet it was still a state where his mind was free to torture him with images of Charlotte.

Sometimes she was laughing, her arms spread wide as she twirled beneath the sky. Or she would moan as he kissed her, caressed her, undressed her. And she would lead him to her bed, her eyes dark and sultry as she glanced at him over her shoulder.

But it was worst when she was silent. She just stared. Her mouth never moved, but still he could hear her voice softly accusing him, reciting all the ways he'd wronged her.

He always managed to wake himself up before she began to cry. He didn't understand how he knew she was about to, but he did.

No, a sleep tonic would be of no use to him. He needed something to help him stay awake.

"Sending for Dr. Barrow would be unnecessary."

Fallon inclined his head, then motioned toward the windows. "Please, Your Grace, at least allow me to draw the curtains. You are far too pale—"

"That will be all, Fallon," Philip said, his syllables clipped.

The butler froze, then executed a sharp bow. "Your Grace." He exited the room, pulling the door closed behind him.

Philip glared at the shadowed faces on the opposite wall. Then, reluctantly, his gaze shifted to the bank of windows. Try as he might, he couldn't keep from seeking them out. As if he could see through them to the path a carriage would take in coming to Ruthven Manor.

He'd ordered the curtains to remain closed so he wouldn't be tempted to watch for her return, and yet he kept opening them, stealing glances at the drive beyond.

It was pathetic, really.

He'd thought it had been the worst sort of hell to love her before, when he believed she hated him.

But this—knowing she might be with him now if it hadn't been for his own bloody pride—it was unbearable.

With a low curse, Philip planted his hands on the desk and stood from his chair. He grunted, satisfied when he wobbled only a little.

The pungent smell of kippers and poached eggs wafted through the air, and he curled his lip in disgust at the sight of the covered breakfast tray.

The less he slept, the more the sight and smell of food seemed to turn his stomach.

Surely Fallon had noticed that each tray he returned to the kitchen was mostly untouched. And yet the man continued to deliver Philip's meals at regular intervals. Yesterday he had even brought a tea tray.

A *tea* tray, replete with sugar and milk and an array of biscuits, scones, and tarts. As if Philip had ever taken tea unless the rituals of polite society required him to do so.

The entire household was coddling him, treating him like an invalid. Even his valet had entered once, asking if he would like for him to bring a change of clothing to the study.

He would change his clothes when he damned well liked.

Perhaps he would run through the entire house naked, even.

He could do as he pleased. He was the bloody ninth Duke of Rutherford.

Shuffling around the desk, he caught sight of his grandfather's portrait. Philip returned the old man's imperious stare with a glower of his own.

"You wouldn't like that very much, would you? No, of course not. It wouldn't be *proper*."

He was still lucid enough not to expect a response from the inanimate object, so he continued toward the door, his arms spread to either side for balance.

He turned around. "I wasn't proper the day I took off my clothes and swam nude in the pond. Anyone could have seen me. The servants or Joanna or anyone in the whole bloody world could have seen me in all of my bare-assed ducal glory."

His gaze drifted to the windows, and when he began to shake, it wasn't from weakness but from rage. He narrowed his eyes at the portrait again. "Damn you," he muttered low.

It bore repeating.

"Damn you."

He shouldn't have stopped with Charlotte's bedchamber. He should have taken down every last painting of the old duke.

His grandfather didn't deserve to be recognized or honored. He had never done anything to merit Philip's respect or love. Everything he'd done had been to manipulate him, to control him.

Philip wove his way back to the desk and flung aside the domed cover of the breakfast tray. It bounced and rolled across the carpet, finally careening into the leg of the sofa. Steadying himself with one hand, he speared a kipper with the fork and crammed it in his mouth, glowering at his grandfather's silent sneer as he chewed.

At length, once he'd cleared away all of the kippers and eggs, he sank back into his chair and waited. Tapping his fingers together, he contemplated the portrait.

Hanging it in the gallery wouldn't be sufficient. Neither would moving it to the attic, to be tucked in some dark, hidden corner.

Minutes passed. He could feel his strength returning, his mind clearing as if a fog had been swept away.

Standing up, he walked to the portrait and removed it from the wall. It was large, and heavy, and though he tried to carry it, he wasn't yet strong enough.

He ended up dragging the portrait to the door, where he leaned it against the wall. He would have a footman put it somewhere out of sight until he could determine what to do with it.

His face itched, and he rubbed his jaw. The thick stubble didn't scrape his palm, but tickled softly. He needed a shave. And a bath.

*And* a change of clothes, though he might dismiss his valet if the man so much as smirked.

He made his way along the corridor toward the stairway, halting only a few times to steady himself.

He would find Charlotte. If she wouldn't return to him, then he would go to her. He wasn't certain what he would do then, but at least she would be near.

She wouldn't welcome him, of course. She'd made that clear. But perhaps if they crossed each other's path—not too frequently, and never for too long—she might begin to detest him just a little less.

As he passed the library, his grandfather's bust caught

his attention. He'd never before realized how very arrogant a man the old duke must have been, to have commissioned an artist to sculpt his likeness.

But then again, he had also hung countless portraits of himself throughout the house.

"Arrogant" might not be a strong enough word.

Philip stopped in front of the bust, surprised at how much it resembled the actual man. He reached out to smooth his hand over the wig, the grooved texture of the clay cool beneath his palm. The nose was too short, the slight hook at the end noticeably absent. But the mouth and the eyes were the same. Thin lips, though not curled, still somehow gave the appearance of a sneer. Narrowed eyes, the gray clay as cold as the silver ones they were meant to duplicate.

Philip dropped his hand.

Except for the wig, it could have been a bust of himself.

Was this what Charlotte saw when she looked at him?

Once again he studied the replica of the man he had feared but never loved. He had the same haughty arch to his right brow, the one Philip used when a condescending stare didn't send London's fops scurrying away fast enough.

His grandfather had raised him to be a proper duke. Observing all social niceties to a fault. Scorning those who deemed themselves his equal.

Arrogant. Callous. A man to despise.

Philip began to breathe faster, the air rushing in and out of his nostrils. The darkness of his childhood, the pain he'd thought had disappeared, returned to grip him.

With a low oath, he clutched the bust between both hands and lifted it above his head. Hurling it to the ground, he watched it shatter into pieces against the tile. Although a shard ricocheted, slashing across his cheek, he didn't flinch.

He was not the same man as his grandfather.

He never would be.

"You are a horrible friend," Charlotte muttered to Lady Emma Whitlock.

"I only introduced you." Emma stared after Lord Forshaw, a frown drawing her blond brows together. "I still don't understand how he could step upon your toes so many times. It was a *quadrille*, for heaven's sake."

"Yes," Charlotte said drily. "Apparently my bosom is most distracting."

Emma looked down at her own bodice and sighed. "I should like to be distracting." She glanced up quickly. "Not for the sake of any suitor, of course, but simply for my own vanity."

And that was why she and Charlotte were friends. The earl's daughter was the only woman in London who didn't suspect Charlotte of trying to steal her beau, fiancé, or husband. Emma far preferred her own imaginary heroes and villains to any of the men of the *ton*.

"Your bosom is delightful," Charlotte said. "There, now that your vanity is appeased, you may either go with me or I will leave you stranded here."

Emma rolled her eyes. "You must admit, the evening hasn't gone as poorly as you thought—"

"Everyone is staring at me."

"Everyone always stares at you," Emma pointed out. "And besides, he did kidnap you. If I weren't looking at you already, I'd stare at you now. You are far more interesting than I."

Charlotte's laughter stuck in her throat as a tall man with dark hair walked across the room beyond Emma. Her heart raced.

But no, it wasn't Philip. His shoulders were too narrow.

He was only one of many tall men with dark hair who

had caught her eye that evening. She'd never noticed it before tonight, but it seemed England's aristocrats bred mostly tall and dark men.

It was quite frustrating, especially when one was trying desperately to forget one specific tall man with dark hair. And failing miserably. Damn him.

"Charlotte?" Emma waved her hand in front of Charlotte's face.

"Yes?" She focused on her friend again, fixing a bright grin on her face.

"No, don't give me that fake smile. You were thinking of him again, weren't you?"

"Certainly not," Charlotte replied, searching the crowd for more tall, dark gentlemen. She couldn't shake the feeling that he was here. The sense that always alerted her to his presence teased her nerves, prickling her skin with awareness.

"Aha! Then how do you know which 'him' I referred to?"

"I—" Charlotte snapped her mouth shut.

"He isn't worth your thoughts, the wretch," Emma declared loyally. "I cannot believe he lied to . . ."

Charlotte looked at her when she didn't finish the sentence. Emma raised her eyebrows meaningfully, then darted her eyes back and forth from Charlotte to a space over her left shoulder.

Turning her head, Charlotte attempted to glance behind her without being too obvious.

Her breath seized in her chest. Philip stood not two feet away.

As their eyes met, he inclined his head and stepped forward. "Good evening, Charlotte," he greeted her, his voice low and intimate.

She swallowed and lifted her chin. "Your Grace."

His eyes searched hers, and she looked away, her pulse pounding in her ears. Taking a deep breath, she reminded herself that her response to him was normal. Anger could provoke a physical reaction more quickly than any other emotion.

Speaking brusquely, she motioned to Emma. "Perhaps you remember Lady Emma Whitlock, Lord Severly's daughter."

He bowed. "Lady Emma."

"Your Grace." Emma's shallow curtsy was nothing more than a creak of the knees.

Dear, loyal Emma.

Philip turned to Charlotte. "May I have the next dance?"

She glanced at Emma. "Actually, we were about to leave."

Emma nodded weakly, clutching a hand to her stomach. "I feel quite ill, I'm afraid. The punch, I think."

Philip's eyes narrowed. "Perhaps I should alert the hostess."

Charlotte opened her mouth at the same time Emma exclaimed, "Oh, no!"

He arched a brow. Then, strangely, lowered it slowly, as if he didn't *want* to arch his brow. It was rather an odd thing to see.

"I mean"—Emma clasped her hands behind her back, then brought her hand to her stomach again—"I'm not sure the punch is the culprit. I shouldn't want Lady Hysell to worry for nothing."

Charlotte glanced at Philip, who nodded as if this made perfect sense and wasn't in any way the least suspicious.

"I found your note. You are staying with Lady Emma?" he asked her quietly.

She nodded.

"Then it's settled. I will take you to her house after our dance." He held out his hand. "I believe the music is starting now."

And it was. Rising over the steady murmur of gossip and laughter around them were the lilting first notes of a violin. Couples separated in the middle of the ballroom to form the squares for another quadrille.

"No," Charlotte said.

To her right, she could see Emma give an encouraging nod.

"Come now, Charlotte," he taunted softly. "You're not afraid, are you?"

Emma coughed loudly, so much so that a few people standing nearby edged away. "My throat," she rasped. "It cannot be the punch, after all."

Charlotte glanced from Philip to Emma, then back again. She could feel the other guests watching them, waiting to see whether she would take his hand. If only to subdue the speculative whispers, she should dance with him. Besides, she wasn't a coward.

Yes, those were two very good reasons why she should accept his offer.

And the flush that burned in her cheeks as she placed her gloved hand in his had absolutely nothing to do with his nearness, but rather the close confines of the overcrowded ballroom.

"One dance," she said, "Then Emma and I must leave."

"But—"

Emma's protest faded as Philip escorted her away.

Charlotte studiously avoided looking at him as she waited for the quadrille to commence, instead murmuring a greeting to the other couples.

The cue sounded, and they were the first to dance.

Charlotte held her breath, waiting for Philip to speak so she could set him in his place. She had imagined many times what she would do when he came to London, and she already had several prepared responses for any apology or explanation he might attempt. Each one was sure to show him how little he meant to her now, how strong she'd become in the two weeks they'd been apart.

Yet through the entire *L'été* figure he never once spoke; neither did he say anything as their part ended and the next couple began.

Charlotte slid a sidelong glance at him through her lashes and nearly gasped. He was staring at her without any form of pretense, his gaze direct and smoldering.

She looked quickly away, mentally flipping through her previously approved list of retorts and quips. When she found none to suit, she instead hissed, "Stop staring at me."

"As you wish," he murmured in return, and was silent.

She tapped her toes as the couple in the opposite corner of the square performed the figure, her fingers twisting in her skirts.

He wasn't supposed to be silent or do as she asked.

She snuck a peek at Philip out of the corner of her eye to see if he was looking at her again, or—better yet—opening his mouth to speak.

But his profile was to her, his eyes focused straight ahead, his mouth woefully shut.

As the last couple danced, Charlotte fought back a wave of disappointment. She should be glad of his sudden decision to ignore her; it would make pretending as if he didn't exist even easier.

The music ended, and she too stared straight ahead as she placed her arm over Philip's. He guided her back to Emma, who launched into a coughing fit as they approached.

Charlotte turned her head toward Philip and smiled woodenly. "Your Grace—"

"Thank you for the dance," he said, lifting her hand before she could remove it and placing a kiss on the back. Then, as his eyes captured hers with that same smoldering intensity, he withdrew a folded piece of paper from his pocket. He turned her hand over and placed it within her palm.

"I'm sorry," he whispered, then nodded once at Emma and walked away.

Charlotte's fingers curled tightly around the paper as she watched him leave, realizing only once he was out of sight that he'd apologized and she'd said nothing.

"Are you certain you want to leave?" Emma asked as they stepped outside, the noise and light of the Hysell ball receding behind them.

Charlotte didn't bother to answer, her thoughts focused on the parchment in her hand, anxious to retire to her bedchamber at the Severlys' home and read Philip's note in privacy.

Besides, she'd already answered the same question from Emma two times as they wended their way through the throng of guests.

Emma sighed deeply. "And I had heard Lord Courtenay and Mr. Morrow were both to be present tonight."

"And that is interesting because . . ."

She swung her head around. "Why, because— Oh, I forgot you weren't here." Her eyes lit and she peeked furtively around before leaning in close to Charlotte. "Mr. Morrow publicly accused Lord Courtenay of seducing his wife."

Charlotte shrugged. "He probably did."

Emma nodded. "Yes, but Mrs. Morrow was there, and she stepped between them and begged Lord Courtenay to run away with her to France."

Charlotte halted and stared at her.

Emma's eyebrows wiggled. "Isn't it delicious? Of course, Lord Courtenay refused, and now both Morrows are furious with him—Mrs. Morrow for rejecting her and Mr. Morrow for insulting his wife." She glanced over her shoulder at the Hysell house. "Now you see why I wanted to stay. It is the perfect story for my new novel. Passion, jealousy, violence . . ."

"Violence?"

She turned back to Charlotte. "It's possible. It could happen tonight." She paused. "Are you certain you want to leave?"

Charlotte groaned. "I thought your stomach and throat hurt."

Emma made a face and rubbed at her throat. "You know very well I did that for your benefit."

"And that is why I love you dearly." Charlotte continued to walk toward where the Severlys' carriage awaited them at the curve of the drive, Emma trailing behind.

As they reached the carriage, Emma asked, "What did he say to you during the dance?"

The footman opened the door and Charlotte climbed in. She waited for Emma to sit across from her and the door to close before she answered. "Nothing."

Emma leaned forward, frowning. "Nothing?"

"Not one word."

"Then you weren't able to—"

"No," Charlotte said.

"After all that practicing—"

"I know. It was very disappointing."

Emma sat back and blew out a loud breath. "Well, we shall simply have to continue. Since he is back in London now, there will surely be plenty of opportunities for you to see him, and when you do, you will need to be ready. If ever a man deserved his comeuppance, it is the Duke of Rutherford."

Charlotte smiled. "I did like your suggestion for the comment about the tadpole."

"*Slimy* tadpole," Emma corrected.

"Of course."

They lapsed into silence as the carriage made its way east through Mayfair, to the older houses which weren't quite as fashionable as Philip's but still considered highly respectable.

Every ten seconds or so Charlotte glanced down at her hand where she clasped the folded note, then resolutely looked away.

"You're not going to wait until we get home to read it, are you?" Emma asked.

Which meant, of course, that Emma didn't want to wait to know the note's contents, either.

"It's dark," Charlotte said pointedly.

Ever resourceful, Emma reached over to where the lantern hung by the door and lit it.

"It's far too bumpy," Charlotte hedged, then scowled as Emma quirked a brow. The well-sprung carriage was anything but bumpy; the most irregular of cobbled streets or dirt roads would not have so much as jostled its passengers. "Oh, very well."

Fingers trembling only slightly, she unfolded the paper and angled it toward the light. Her chest began to ache as she read

> She walks in beauty, like the night
> Of cloudless climes and starry skies
> And all that's best of dark and bright
> Meet in her aspect and her eyes
> Eyes which shine with undimmed life
> A beauty to provoke angels' envy
> Too much for even heaven's great heights
> Cast to earth, a goddess among humanity
> The fierce light of her soul beckons me
> A brilliant, pure, and passionate flame
> Though she is good, and I unworthy
> I will love her beyond death's refrain

He'd finished it. He'd changed a few words and added a few lines, and it was . . . beautiful. True, the meter was off and some of the words didn't exactly rhyme, but still . . . it was quite simply the most wonderful thing she'd ever received.

"What does it say?" Emma asked.

Charlotte swallowed. "It's a poem."

There was a slight pause, and then: "I don't understand."

Charlotte nearly laughed, for it would have been the precise reaction of anyone else who had ever met Philip and then discovered that he read poetry. Or liked to give poems as gifts. She would have laughed, if she hadn't been so very close to crying.

"He wrote it. Well, not the first part—that he copied from Byron, but—"

"He *wrote* it?"

"Yes." Charlotte shook her head. "No, not all of it. Byron wrote the first part—"

"Byron?" Emma echoed.

Wordlessly, Charlotte gave the paper to Emma, who smoothed the page over her lap and bent her head.

"Oh," she breathed after a moment, her finger trailing along the edge of the paper as she read. Then, after what seemed an excruciatingly long period of time, she raised her head and stared at Charlotte, her eyes wide. *"Oh."*

"Indeed," Charlotte said. *"Oh."*

# Chapter 20

Philip held out his card to Lord Swinney's butler. "He's expecting me."

Whether the earl wished to see him was another matter entirely. Philip had sent a letter through his solicitor expressing his desire to purchase the last of Astley's nude sketches of Charlotte. The man had yet to make a reply even after three days, but Philip refused to wait any longer.

The butler's eyes widened upon reading his card; then he swept to the side to allow him entrance. "Do come in, Your Grace. I will see whether Lord Swinney is at home."

Philip stepped inside and pulled out his pocket watch. The cold autumn wind rushed through the closing door, threatening to tip his hat off. "Please inform Swinney I will give him precisely five minutes."

"Your Grace?"

"Five minutes, no more."

With a wary glance, the butler wandered away. Philip settled his hat more firmly on his head; he had no intention of staying long. It had been fairly easy to convince the other men to part with the sketches of Charlotte. Although Swinney seemed reticent to speak with him, Philip was prepared to increase his suggested purchase price to whatever number the man required. Buying the portraits would be worth any amount of money.

He considered his timepiece again. One minute remained. Like some of the others, Swinney had been rumored to be Charlotte's lover. Even though Philip now knew the truth and had no need to harm the earl, a certain violence pounded through his blood as he thought of Swinney looking upon Charlotte's nudity and lusting after her. As he spied the butler returning to the entrance hall, he almost wished he would have been late.

"This way, Your Grace. Lord Swinney will see you in his study."

The door to the room was open, and Philip waited until the butler had made his announcement before entering. Swinney stood behind his desk. He was a tall man, though an inch or so shorter than Philip, with light brown hair. Though a decade older, he'd kept himself physically fit. Philip could well imagine him flirting with Charlotte, attempting to seduce her into his bed. Once she was free, would he try to do so again? Would Philip be able to withstand knowing she was with someone else?

He must. He had to let her go. He might seethe with jealousy, but at least she would be happy.

Philip inclined his head in a polite nod. "Lord Swinney."

"Your Grace. I trust you are well?" He motioned to a chair near the desk. "Please, have a seat."

"Thank you for the pleasantries, but I prefer to stand. I've come about a sketch I believe you have in your possession. Of my wife."

It was slight, but Philip still saw the small tilt at the corner of Swinney's mouth. "I must admit, your letter was quite a surprise. I hadn't thought you cared."

Another sin of his, one that he would regret until his last breath. But hopefully, Charlotte would know very soon that he had spoken the truth when he said he loved her. "I do. I wish to buy the sketch for five hundred pounds."

It was a hefty sum, but he didn't want to waste time on negotiations. Sweeney would know he was serious.

The earl's fingers tapped at the edge of his desk. "Five hundred pounds," he repeated. "Perhaps I shouldn't sell it, if you think it's worth such a price."

Philip bared his teeth in a smile. "Do not mistake the generosity of my offer for weakness. I *will* have it, one way or another."

Sweeney arched a brow. "One thousand pounds."

"Done," Philip agreed swiftly, then gave Sweeney his solicitor's address where a draft would be waiting for him later in the day. "Now, where is the sketch?"

"Yes . . . If you don't mind, Your Grace, I believe I'll have Davies show you the way."

As Philip followed the butler a few minutes later into Sweeney's bedchamber, he understood why the earl had been reluctant to act as his guide. If he had been within reach, Philip would have killed him. The portrait of Charlotte hung on the wall opposite the bed, low enough that a person reclining would have been able to see it past the bed canopy. The bastard had pleasured himself with her likeness.

Philip growled and strode toward the sketch, then wrenched it off the wall. With a black glower at Davies, he made his own way through and out of the Swinney residence. Though tempted to step into the study, he was able to resist by focusing on his next goal, the one that had made each passing minute worthwhile over the last several days: he would see Charlotte.

*     *     *

Charlotte and Emma sat in a row of chairs at the Boughan musicale, awaiting the beginning of the performance.

"You're doing it again," Emma muttered.

Charlotte dragged her gaze toward Emma's face. "What?"

"You can pretend you don't know what I mean all you want, but I know you're looking for him."

Charlotte sighed and leaned back, crossing her arms over her chest. How was it possible to be so angry at him and yet want to be with him at the same time?

Though she'd continued to tell herself over the past week that she still wanted her freedom, she couldn't deny that she thought about divorce from Philip much less than she thought about *him*.

She could have blamed it on the poem, but no rhyming words—no matter how prettily phrased—had her staring at her bedchamber door at night, fighting the urge to go to their town house and see him.

He had lied to her and manipulated her, but she knew that the only control he had over her now was that which she gave him. And the problem was no longer that she *couldn't* stop loving him, but that she didn't *want* to stop loving him.

Bloody hell.

"What was that?" Emma bent her head to peer into Charlotte's face.

"What?" Charlotte asked, thinking about Philip—of course.

Emma motioned to her throat. "You groaned."

Charlotte shrugged. "I was, er, thinking about the musicale and wishing we weren't here." Which was true. She'd much rather be with Philip.

Emma narrowed her eyes. "Uh-huh," she said, before turning toward the impromptu stage created for the small gathering.

Aware of Emma's ever-watchful presence beside

her, Charlotte was trying to surreptitiously survey the room for Philip when she noticed a very particular thing.

She nudged Emma in the ribs. "We are alone."

Emma gave her a quizzical look. "There must be over a hundred people here."

Charlotte sighed. "Yes, but they are all sitting on the rows behind us and in front of us. Haven't you noticed no one is sitting beside you?"

Emma turned her head to the right, where at least five empty seats lay between her and the next guest. She peered past Charlotte, where perhaps a dozen seats were unoccupied, so that Charlotte was the last person sitting on that side of the row.

"Perhaps I have broken out in a rash?" Charlotte asked drily.

Emma grinned. "If so, then I have, too. Excuse me for a moment. I believe there is gossip to be had."

She stood up and scooted past Charlotte.

As Charlotte settled her skirts again, she saw that a woman with a long nose two rows ahead was watching her over her shoulder. When their eyes met, the woman jerked her chin and snapped her head around.

Charlotte smiled to herself.

She wasn't unaccustomed to being slighted or made to feel like an outcast. God knew her actions over the years had warranted such a response from society's self-righteous matrons and virgin debutantes, and her background as a squire's daughter left much to be desired. As the Duchess of Rutherford, however, she'd always been treated with a reluctant respect. Even if the stodgy members of the *ton* didn't quite meet her eyes, they still managed a proper greeting.

Now she was being given the cut direct, and she couldn't help but wonder what must have happened. Or, more to the point, what Philip had done.

As the musicians walked onto the stage and settled in their chairs, Charlotte decided to amuse herself.

Finding a face turned toward her out of the corner of her eye, she glanced in that direction and made eye contact with the blond young man. His eyes widened and his mouth parted, and then he spun around so fast in his chair that he knocked into the woman beside him. Who, in return, scolded him and peered behind her to see what he had been looking at.

Charlotte smiled and gave a small wave.

The woman froze, then slowly turned to face the stage.

The evening might prove to be far more interesting than she'd originally thought.

As the first strings of a Bach concerto vibrated through the air, Charlotte nodded at a portly man with bulging eyes and another woman who had her hair piled high on her head to divert attention from the prematurely balding sides. A few minutes later, in the midst of a violin solo, Charlotte had half of the audience turning red in the face as she waved, nodded, winked, and even blew a kiss.

The next piece, a Mozart piano sonata, was just beginning when Emma returned. She plopped down on the seat beside Charlotte, a flush high in her cheeks, her eyes gleaming bright. She reached out and gripped Charlotte's hands. *Tightly.*

"Ow," she said, tugging them free. "I need those—"

"A divorce," Emma said breathlessly. "His Grace petitioned the courts for a divorce." She grasped Charlotte's hands again. And this time, Charlotte didn't notice when she pressed the bones together.

Oh, God. He'd done it. He'd actually done it.

Emma cocked her head to one side, her lips pursing. "At least, that's the rumor."

"How do you—"

"Lady Fitzwilliam. She heard it from her husband, who heard it from their daughter's new husband—did you know they eloped to Greece? Not Scotland, but Greece. Is that not the most romantic thing you've ever heard?"

Charlotte opened her mouth to agree, then caught herself. "The rumor, Emma," she pressed.

Emma returned her gaze from the ceiling, where she had presumably been imagining two of her characters disappearing beyond a lovely Greek horizon.

"Yes, the rumor. As I was saying, the new husband heard it from Lord Rothmar, who heard it from Lord Ste—"

*"Shhh."*

They both turned to find the person who made the noise. All four people behind them—what appeared to be a mother with her three daughters—immediately blanched upon meeting Charlotte's gaze. One by one, they looked past her to the musicians.

Charlotte and Emma turned back around.

"Well, I couldn't hear the cello," they heard whispered behind them.

Charlotte squeezed Emma's hands. "Lord Rothmar?"

Emma nodded. "He heard it from Lord Stebbins."

She waited, but Emma just looked at her. Finally, she asked, "And how did Lord Stebbins hear?"

Emma blinked. Then she blinked again. "I don't know."

Charlotte stood up.

"Where are you going?" Emma asked, her voice rising to be heard above the chorus of voices protesting that they couldn't see.

"I need to go home."

"Why?"

Charlotte sat down again. It was a good question. What would she do? Ask Philip if the rumor was true?

And if it was, what then? Thank him? Congratulate him? Did one pull out a bottle of sherry to mark such an occasion?

Besides, she didn't really feel like celebrating.

She felt . . . odd. Lost, almost. Because if Philip finally granted her request and divorced her, she would no longer be the Duchess of Rutherford.

Which meant he would no longer be her husband.

An obvious result of divorce, of course, but one she wasn't prepared for in the least. She'd thought she was; she'd had dreams, many dreams of what she would do and who she would be when she was free.

Yet now she couldn't remember any of those dreams.

All she could think about was Philip, and what he would do if the courts approved his petition. It would take months, of course—possibly a year or more, even—but then . . .

Would he marry again? Would he love his new duchess? Would he look at her with hunger in his eyes and write her love poems that made her want to laugh and weep at the same time?

Emma leaned over. "Are you all right? You look . . . strange."

"I'm great. Wonderful. *Fantastic*." She said the last with such force that Emma recoiled.

Charlotte smiled brightly, and it somehow felt like her lips were detached from her body. The stares hadn't bothered her before, but they did now. They weren't looking at her because of who she was—society's darling harlot—but because of the divorce petition. And she hated them for their gossip. Hated that they had known before she did.

The musicians rose and bowed to the audience, marking the first intermission. Though Charlotte fixed her eyes on the harpist, she could still see several of the guests watching her. Her cheeks burned.

"I'm certain he would retract the petition if you asked," Emma said as they applauded.

"Why would I do that?" Charlotte murmured. "This is what I've always wanted."

Emma was silent for a moment. "Of course," she said at last, patting Charlotte's hand.

And for some reason, more than the judgmental stares, the haughty noses lifted in the air, and everything else, that made Charlotte feel the worst.

Although Emma suggested they leave during the intermission, Charlotte refused. She would stay through the entire musicale. The gossipmongers might say many things about her, but she wouldn't give them a reason to call her weak.

"It's not necessary to hover within six inches of me," she told Emma, sipping at the punch. She seemed to have developed a bit of masochism, for even though it tasted distinctly like cabbage, she kept drinking more and more.

"I like hovering," Emma said idly, her head tilted toward a pair of matrons and their daughters. Turning toward Charlotte, she huffed. "They say you've been to bed with half the men in London. As though you wouldn't have better taste. Maybe *two* of the men in London would be worthwhile, but . . ."

Charlotte sucked in a sharp breath. She'd heard his voice. Twisting around, she spied Philip moving through the crowds, his gaze fixed on her.

". . . and Blackwell, but even he has that glass eye from the war. Which, in a way, I suppose—"

Charlotte nudged her friend. "He's here."

Emma craned her neck toward all four corners of the room. "Blackwell's here? Where?"

"No, my hus—His Grace." Her cheeks burned as he approached, unable to imagine what his intention would be in seeking her here. Would he confirm the rumor, or deny it? Why must her pulse leap at the thought of the latter?

"Oh." Emma edged nearer. "Shall I pretend to be ill again?"

Before Charlotte could shake her head, he was there, standing before her, and although she had to tilt her head back to look at him, she emphasized it with a hike of her chin as well. "Your Grace."

"Charlotte." He smiled and reached for her hand. Lifting it to his mouth, his lips lingered against her gloved fingers. Her heart throbbed painfully with each second that passed.

*I hate him. I love him. I hate him. I love him.*

He lowered her hand, but didn't release her. "Smile, my love, so everyone can see."

Emma cleared her throat. "I will be nearby. Less than two feet away."

Charlotte watched Emma turn her back and inch to the side, close enough that she could still overhear everything they said. As if he were her force of gravity, Charlotte found her gaze being dragged back to Philip, her lips curving as he'd suggested. "Exactly why am I smiling?"

"A claim of adultery seemed the easiest way to win the petition, but I hate for them to think ill of you."

Her smile froze in place, achingly numb. "Then it's true? The divorce rumors?"

"Yes." Philip reached toward her, and for one breathless moment Charlotte thought he might stroke her cheek, but his arm fell away. His chest expanded as he inhaled deeply. "And I hope one day you can forgive me."

His silver eyes searched hers, and Charlotte forced herself to look away, smiling into the crowd. "What, no declaration of love? No demand to see how you've changed?"

His fingers tightened around hers, then eased. "I don't expect you to forgive me now. But . . ."

When he didn't speak for several seconds, Charlotte glanced at him.

He smiled, more charming than before, and released her hand. Bitterly, she realized he was continuing his performance for the musicale guests. "Ah, yes. I'd forgotten." He leaned toward her, his voice a low murmur in her ear. To the others, it must have appeared quite intimate and confusing, given the common knowledge of their relationship. "I recently acquired all of your nude sketches. I'm taking the liberty of delivering them to the Severly residence tonight. I thought you might like to have them."

"I—"

"Of course, if you want to sell them again, that's your decision. But considering the truth of your previous behavior, that you acted as you did only to provoke me, I assumed you would want the choice."

Why wouldn't he let her keep him assigned to the label "bastard"? Why must he tear her heart to pieces every time she decided to hate him? "You didn't want them?" she whispered, unable to stop the flush of pleasure at the thought of him looking at the sketches. She wanted him to desire her still, to lust after her.

He made a choked sound. "I think it would be better for both of us if you had them."

She nodded, her eyes halfway closing at the nearly tangible touch of his breath on her skin. "Thank you."

Straightening, Philip took her hand again. Although it appeared he tried to smile, the gesture didn't make it beyond a shallow indentation. He stared down at their joined hands and intertwined their fingers, and Charlotte drank him in. From the shining black crispness of his hair to the condescending wing of his brow, from the firm line of his mouth to the proud jut of his chin, she devoured him, both grateful for the opportunity and ashamed of her own indulgence.

Then he looked up, bent to kiss her cheek, and stepped away. "Good night, Your Grace," he said, bowing.

She curtsied, her lashes lowering lest he see her hunger and disappointment at his departure. "Your Grace."

"I love you."

Though she jerked her gaze up at his low words, he was already gone, striding away through the crowds.

Two weeks later, a knock sounded at the door of the drawing room. Philip turned away from the window overlooking the street.

"Enter."

Fallon appeared. Philip glanced at the ormolu clock on the mantel. It was thirteen minutes past eleven. Only three minutes had passed since he'd last looked.

"Well?"

Fallon inclined his head, then began to speak in the tone of a soldier reporting to his superior. "She hasn't strayed from the Severlys' house this evening."

"Are you certain? She might not be at any of the society events, but she could have gone to Fontaine's, or one of the other gambling dens she likes to visit."

"No, Your Grace. As you requested, I posted a groom across the street to watch for her departure. She hasn't left."

Philip looked back at the clock. If she was still at the Severlys' house, then it was unlikely she would leave for entertainment elsewhere at this hour.

"Very good," he said, moving to sit upon one of the wingback chairs before the hearth. "What of today?"

In a low monotone, Fallon reported Charlotte's actions throughout the day, pausing every so often in his telling to answer Philip's questions.

A walk in the park in the morning. Alone. A stroll

down Bond Street with Lady Emma Whitlock. No, Her Grace did not buy anything, but Lady Emma bought a rather large and frightening purple hat with pink feathers. They rode through Hyde Park in the late afternoon, and were seen at one point talking with Lord and Lady Fitzwilliam. Her Grace wore a frown.

"Why was she frowning?" Philip asked. She hadn't seemed upset at the Boughan musicale.

"I cannot say, Your Grace. The footman wasn't close enough to overhear their conversation."

Philip regarded him for a long moment. "Has she seemed happy otherwise?"

The butler's mouth parted, almost as if in surprise, and then promptly shut. It was the most emotion Philip had seen from him in a decade. That is, if one didn't count the night Philip had caught him playing cards in the stables with Charlotte.

"Forgive me, Your Grace. I did not ask him to report on Her Grace's facial expressions, only on her whereabouts and her actions. I will make the appropriate inquiry and return shortly."

"Very well." Philip began to wave him off, then thought better of it and called, "Fallon."

The butler executed a sharp turn. "Your Grace?"

"Thank you."

Fallon's eyes shifted to the door, then back again. "You're welcome," he said stiffly, then paused. "Is that all, Your Grace?"

"Yes." He moved to the desk, bending his head to the sheaf of papers before him. The sound of the door thudding followed Fallon's departure.

On Tuesday, Thursday, and Saturday morning of last week Charlotte had gone for a walk in the park by herself. That was nothing out of the ordinary. And she seemed to regularly go shopping with Lady Emma; last Wednesday indicated Lady Emma had also returned with a hat, only this one had been covered in red and yellow beads. But none of his notes since his return to London included the observance of Charlotte's expression—happy or otherwise. This was why the sudden mention of a frown was all the more concerning.

He wasn't stalking her, precisely. He was simply . . . observing. She might have no desire to be with him, but he had not lost his craving for her. And if he couldn't be with her, if he couldn't see her or talk to her—and he didn't trust himself to do any of these things, when he'd very nearly given in to the temptation to throw her over his shoulder and abduct her yet again the night of the musicale—then he could at least hear *about* her.

Philip sometimes wondered if this observing would be something he continued for the rest of his life, even after the courts approved his petition for a divorce. And he knew they would. He was, after all, the ninth Duke of Rutherford. He always got what he wanted. Except for Charlotte.

It was bloody ironic. Or perhaps, not ironic at all, but simply very, very sad.

But then he didn't like to think about the rest of his life, or about the divorce petition. For he knew himself well, and feared that if he dwelled upon it too much, he would try to revoke his appeal.

Apparently selfishness was a difficult habit to break. And he was trying not to be as selfish as he'd once been, to allow Charlotte the freedom she wished. If he'd learned anything since he'd abducted her, it was that he hadn't loved her nearly enough, that his plans had been centered on what he wanted and what he desired. Now, nothing mattered but her.

It was the knowledge that he would finally be the cause for some happiness in Charlotte's life, as well as the determination to distance himself from his grandfather's memory, which kept him from rescinding the petition.

A knock sounded again.

"Enter."

The door opened, and the butler stepped inside. "Your Grace," Fallon intoned.

"What did he say?"

"Although he didn't pay particular attention to Her Grace's expressions or mannerisms, he does remember thinking that she has appeared rather serious recently."

"Serious," Philip repeated.

"Yes, Your Grace."

"Did he mention whether she seemed happy or sad?"

"No, Your Grace. Only . . . serious."

Philip felt his throat tighten, and he repressed the urge to growl in frustration. "Serious" could mean she was thoughtful, or that she was simply being polite. Or that she was bored *because* she was being polite.

The footman should have watched her eyes. Then he would have known how she felt, because her eyes always gave her away. They would sparkle, or gleam, or twinkle. They would glitter with anger, or go soft with sadness. Philip had seen them empty of emotion only twice—once the morning after their wedding, when he'd told her he didn't love her, and the other the day when he told her he'd never intended to grant her a divorce. It was a look which would haunt him forever.

"Serious" was not sufficient for his curiosity. He needed to know more.

"Bring me ink and paper, Fallon. I have a letter to write."

The next day, Charlotte lay curled on the window seat of one of the guest bedchambers, reading the poem Philip had given her. It had become a guilty pleasure of hers, and she refused to keep count of the number of times she'd taken it out, her eyes scanning the lines in a per-functory movement as she recited it by heart.

"The fierce light of her soul beckons me . . ."

She paused, closing her eyes, her fingers crumpling the edges of the paper. She imagined Philip at his desk, his head bent as he penned the line, the tips of his fingers stained—

"What are you doing?"

Charlotte jerked, her head banging against the windowsill behind her. Rubbing her head, she glared at Emma. "Knocking, Emma. Is it too much to ask?"

Emma pushed Charlotte's feet aside and sat on the window seat beside her. "But by not knocking I often discover very interesting things. For example, three days ago I found one of the housemaids and a footman locked in a rather fervent embrace when I didn't knock upon entering the east parlor."

Charlotte drew her brows together. "Do you usually knock before you go into the parlor?"

"No, but it was an example, meant to illustrate my point. If I *had* knocked, they would most certainly have separated before I could have seen them so."

Charlotte just looked at her. "Don't you have a book to write?"

Swinging her feet, Emma peered carefully about the room. Charlotte wondered if perhaps she thought a footman might be hiding nearby.

At last she sighed. "I do, but I killed off my main character."

Charlotte tucked the poem beneath her skirts, hoping Emma wouldn't notice what she'd been reading. "I could see how that would be a problem."

"Actually, no. I meant to kill him off. The problem is, however, that I still have ninety pages to go."

"Perhaps you could resurrect him, and then kill him off again."

Emma's head swung about, her jaw agape. She leaned

forward and hugged Charlotte. "I adore you," she said. "Absolutely *adore* you."

She bounded—truly, there was no other word to describe the enthusiastic leap—off the window seat and hurried to the door.

"Oh," she exclaimed, turning around. "I forgot to tell you. There is a man downstairs waiting for you."

And with that rather vague statement, she left.

*A man.* Not *your estranged husband* or *one of your admirers* or even *a crazed chimney sweep who wandered in off the street*, but *a man*.

Of course, Charlotte immediately assumed it was Philip, her heart showing its agreement by ratcheting around in her chest.

But if it was Philip, wouldn't Emma have said so?

Nevertheless, Charlotte took a moment to glance at herself in the mirror and smooth her coiffure before going downstairs.

The man in the drawing room did not, in fact, turn out to be Philip. Swallowing her disappointment, Charlotte smiled in greeting. "Mr. Lesser! How wonderful to see you. Forgive me for asking, but . . . Why are you here?"

"Your Grace." The tutor bowed deeply, then adjusted his spectacles as he straightened. "His Grace sent me to continue your lessons."

"He . . ."

Charlotte considered herself quite rational, though she did have her moments. Yet she couldn't understand why Philip would bid the tutor to instruct her further when he had taken the first step to ending their relationship. If anything, he should be avoiding her, avoiding any thoughts of her. Just as she should be avoiding any thoughts of *him*.

"Shall we begin? His Grace told me you brought the harp with you?"

"Er . . . yes. Right this way." She led him from the drawing room to the Severlys' music room. "Although I must tell you I haven't played much recently," she said.

In truth, she hadn't touched the instrument at all since she'd left Ruthven Manor. She had tried to play. One night when she'd been unable to sleep, she had tiptoed downstairs and sat at the harp, positioned her hands as Mr. Lesser had showed her, and taken a deep breath.

And that's all she'd done. She couldn't make herself actually draw music from the strings. She'd just sat there for a long time—it might have been over an hour— thinking of Philip, and the petition, and of Philip again.

No matter how she tried to redirect her thoughts, somehow they always came back to him.

The early-afternoon sun spilled into the room in four neat little rectangles. It was a lovely room, royal blue and cream, trimmed with gold accents. Its beauty should have inspired her; instead, her stomach twisted into knots upon seeing the harp.

Mr. Lesser either didn't notice her discomfort or chose to ignore it, motioning her to take a seat. "First we shall begin with your scales. I trust you remember?"

Charlotte nodded and lifted her hands.

She haltingly made her way through the first scale, her fingers stumbling halfway through when she remembered how Philip had watched her at her lessons, prowling around the room, his gaze prickling her skin and causing her pulse to race.

She heard Mr. Lesser's exasperated sigh behind her.

"You aren't concentrating," he said.

"No," she admitted, letting her hands fall away to clasp together in her lap.

He paced toward the window, his head bent at a forty-five-degree angle, then spun on his heel and paced back to her. "Your Grace, I must ask you a question. Why do you wish to play the harp? Are you planning a grand recital where you would like to impress your friends?"

Charlotte stared at him. It was such a ludicrous idea. "No."

"Is it for your husband's pleasure, then?" Before she could answer, he shook his head. "Surely not, since you are here and he is"—he waved his hand toward the windows—"there."

She pressed her lips together.

Mr. Lesser continued, pacing away once more. "If it isn't for your friends, and not for your husband, then may I assume it is for yourself, Your Grace?" He pivoted toward her, his brows lifted high above the rims of his spectacles.

Charlotte arched a brow at him in return. "I believe I see your point, Mr. Lesser."

He inclined his head. "Very good, Your Grace. The scales. Again."

She strummed her fingers over the strings, back and forth, again and again, moving from one scale to the next. She was still not perfect, as she accidentally plucked the wrong note at times, but she took it as a sign of improvement that Mr. Lesser didn't halt her, nor did she hear his voice lifted in supplication to heaven.

And though she continued to think of Philip, she thought instead of the way his eyes lit with pleasure when he gave her the harp, of how he encouraged her to continue despite the blisters on her fingertips.

He'd asked her to forgive him at the Boughan musicale. But her defenses had begun crumbling even before he'd posed the question, and she feared she'd already forgiven him. It frightened her, how she couldn't hold on to her bitterness as easily as she had in the past when he'd been cruel and indifferent.

As she finished the last scale, she turned toward her

instructor. "Do you know why he sent you here? Did he tell you how much longer he wished you to teach me?"

Mr. Lesser shrugged, the sun glinting off his lenses. "I only received a note requesting that I come to you today. I am to see him tomorrow, when he returns to London."

Charlotte straightened. "You mean he isn't here now?"

"No, I believe he returned to the estate in Warwickshire." He hesitated for a long moment. "I heard a rumor he is intending to sell it off."

"Sell it? But why?"

Mr. Lesser averted his gaze, as if he regretted telling her. Finally, he said, "It's only speculation. As you must know, there are many rumors going around since he made his petition."

Charlotte exhaled. "Then it isn't true."

For some reason, the thought of Philip selling Ruthven Manor made everything seem more permanent, more settled. Besides the London town house, it was the only place they had ever lived together, never having visited any of the other estates strewn across the English countryside. Ruthven Manor contained memories of their history—playing as children, his courtship of her, that awful time after the wedding, and then his most recent betrayal. And if she were ever to completely reconcile with her parents, it would be strange to visit Sheffield House and realize Philip no longer lived on the other side of the woods.

Not that it mattered whether he sold it, in the end. A divorce was as permanent as one could get.

Mr. Lesser adjusted his spectacles. "However, there is also the rumor that he is planning to renounce the dukedom."

*"What?"* Charlotte surged to her feet. "Where did you hear this?"

"Lady Beatrice Pierson. I give lessons to her on the violin, and she said yesterday that she heard it from—"

"Oh, never mind." The exact chain of who had told whom was of little importance. Her mind raced, her heart thudded furiously as she strode to the door, stopping halfway only when she realized she had no idea where she was going. Philip wouldn't return to London until tomorrow.

Not only that, but she wasn't quite sure what she would say when she saw him.

She stared at the door.

"To be honest, Your Grace, I am surprised you haven't heard of it. No less than five people—"

The door crashed open, and Emma burst in. "Charlotte! You will not believe— Oh, hello." She made a proper curtsy to Mr. Lesser, then continued on in a lowered voice which nonetheless carried to every corner of the room. "Mother just told me that Lord Dabney was riding along Rotten Row this morning, and *he* told *her* that the Duke of Rutherford is planning to—"

"Renounce his title?" Charlotte finished for her, feeling as if all the air had been squeezed out of her lungs.

Emma's lips remained parted for a few seconds longer; then she wrinkled her brow. "How did you know?"

Charlotte gestured to Mr. Lesser wordlessly, not even bothering to introduce Emma, or to tell her she needn't have curtsied.

She looked toward the door again.

Even if the Severlys allowed her to borrow their carriage and she left now for Ruthven Manor, by the time she arrived Philip would probably have already departed again for London.

Tomorrow, however, she would see him and demand to know whether the rumors were true.

# Chapter 21

Charlotte stood upon the front steps to the Rutherford town house, her arms folded across her chest. Even though she wore gloves, her fingertips tingled from the early-November cold. A feathered snowflake floated down through her field of vision. She glanced up past the eaves of the house. The early-winter snow danced in the gray morning light, soft flurries whirling upon the air playfully as they fell.

As another snowflake dusted her cheek, Charlotte breathed a resolute sigh, the action forming a frothy white puff of air.

Lifting her hand, she grabbed the brass knocker and—

The door swung open, the knocker pulled from her grasp.

Fallon appeared in the entryway, his usual impassive countenance giving way to relief when he saw her. "Oh, thank God."

Charlotte blinked. "I beg your pardon?" she murmured. She couldn't have heard him correctly.

"Forgive me, Your Grace. It's just—it is so *good* to see you."

He stepped forward, and for an instant Charlotte thought he might try to hug her. Her arms rose slightly from her sides, her legs stiffening to prepare for his embrace—actions which she could only attribute to a momentary bewilderment. But he stuttered to a halt at the threshold and instead moved aside, sweeping his arm in a gesture for her to enter.

She edged past him, unable to find her voice. In three years, she had never heard the butler speak in anything but a monotone. To hear him speak otherwise now—and so freely—was tantamount to seeing the four horsemen of the apocalypse descending from heaven.

She cleared her throat, wondering if he might be ill. Consumed with a fever, perhaps. "Fallon, er . . . Yes, thank you." She allowed him to take her coat and hat.

He leaned in toward her, his voice a hoarse whisper. "I fear His Grace has gone mad. I considered writing and asking you to come, but I " He shook his head. "Ever since you left, he's not been the same. After you returned to London . . ."

Fallon's eyes gleamed brightly as he continued speaking, and though she tried to concentrate on what he said, the words "he's not been the same" kept echoing in her head.

She frowned. Philip had certainly seemed normal at the Hysell ball and the musicale. Contrite, perhaps, but otherwise as normal as he could be. He hadn't appeared tormented, mad, or ill. Then again, he had so many masks that sometimes even she was fooled.

". . . burned them all. Burned them! He wanted a great big bonfire, he said, to—"

"Wait." Charlotte held up her hand. "What did he burn?"

"The portraits of his grandfather, every last one. He'd already smashed the bust outside the library. And he ordered the portraits here to be taken down, too."

He pointed across the entryway, and Charlotte followed his gaze to a large blank rectangle on the wall.

"He removed the portrait from my bedchamber at Ruthven, but I thought that was only for my sake," she said, glancing back at Fallon.

"It was. He instructed me to have the footmen take it elsewhere so it wouldn't bother you. But then, when you left, he . . ." His voice trailed off, and he looked at Charlotte with a guarded expression before he continued. "He wasn't well."

Her heart thumped hard against her ribs. Was it cruel of her to be so happy at his words, to want to ask for each explicit detail of Philip's misery? She opened her mouth to ask what he meant, but he went on before she could speak.

"The day the bust was broken, he decided to take down the portraits—all forty-three of them—"

"Forty-three?" Charlotte repeated incredulously.

Fallon nodded. "It took us all night to locate all of them and move them to various storage closets. Then the next day His Grace decided to burn them."

"That is strange," she said softly. Indeed, it was wholly unlike Philip. Though he'd admitted being scared of his grandfather as a child, she'd thought he'd always loved the elderly duke. And it was certainly odd to burn them, when he could have just left them out of sight.

"But that isn't the strangest part," Fallon said. He peered down the corridor, as if to make sure Philip wasn't nearby.

Then he turned to Charlotte. "He's started thanking me, Your Grace." His beetled eyebrows pulled low. "When I iron the paper, he thanks me. When I announce a visitor, he thanks me. Why, he even thanked me the other day for opening the door. 'Thank you, Fallon,' he says."

His impression of Philip was spot-on, his voice deep and his syllables clipped, and Charlotte nearly smiled. But why would he be thanking his servants? It was almost as if he were still trying to change . . . Except he had already petitioned for the divorce. He knew she wouldn't return to him, so it couldn't be for her benefit.

Fallon stared at her, his expression deeply chagrined. "I've never been thanked before for doing my duties. Not by His Grace, and not by the old duke before him." He shook his head ruefully. "I don't know what to do, Your Grace."

Something flared inside her at that moment, something small and dim, but significant nonetheless. Hope. Immediately, Charlotte quashed the feeling. She might have forgiven him, but trusting him with her heart again was a much larger step, one she didn't know whether she would ever be prepared for.

"I'm not sure I can do anything," she said. "And truly, it doesn't seem that terrible. It seems he is acting better than ever before."

"That's just it, Your Grace," Fallon replied. "His Grace has never been *nice* before."

"I understand, but—"

At that moment, a door opened down the corridor, and Mr. Lesser emerged. As he neared, Fallon returned to the front door.

After she and Mr. Lesser exchanged greetings, Charlotte gestured past him to the corridor. "Did he tell you how much longer our lessons would go on, or why he bid you to continue them?"

Mr. Lesser's eyes shifted behind her, then back again. "Ah, no. I fear I neglected to ask . . ."

Charlotte inclined her head. "I will be sure to inquire,

then," she said. "Good day, Mr. Lesser. And don't worry," she added, "I am practicing."

He smiled. "Very good, Your Grace."

As she walked to Philip's study, she counted her steps, measuring her breath with each even footfall. The door was halfway open, but she knocked anyway, needing those last few moments.

"Enter."

He was standing at the window, his hands clasped behind his back. Before she could speak, she saw his shoulders tense. "Charlotte," he said, and turned around. His eyes raked her from head to toe, and she felt heat steal into her cheeks. It wasn't a seductive look, but it was intimate nonetheless, almost as if he could bind her to him with his gaze.

She inhaled deeply. "How did you know it was me?"

His mouth tipped up at the corner. "I just did."

She nodded. It shouldn't have made sense, but it did. She was the same way; every time he entered a room, she could feel it—almost as if the very air she breathed shifted with the force of his presence.

He moved toward her, then stopped. "How are you, Charlotte?"

Her mouth parted. She didn't know how to answer. He had never asked her such a question before, and in truth, she'd been reluctant to examine her feelings too deeply lately. It was easier that way.

"I'm fine, thank you," she finally said. Then, because it seemed polite: "How are you?"

"I've missed you."

They stared at one another for a long moment, and though neither of them moved, the space between them seemed to lessen in distance.

Charlotte took a step backward.

"I heard you planned to renounce the dukedom," she said, the words rushing out in a breathless stream.

His brow arched. "I'd not heard that one yet. Although I did like the rumor about me deciding to join the clergy."

"Then you're not planning to—"

"No." He paused. "Do you want me to?"

She shook her head. "No, of course not. I just . . ." She glanced away, then back. "I had hoped it was untrue. I know how much being a duke means to you."

"You mean more." He said it quietly, so convincingly, and Charlotte's heart wrenched inside her chest.

Deciding it was best to pretend she hadn't heard him, she walked past him to the window. She needed something to look at besides Philip. She watched her fingers trail along the dark wooden trim, then stared outside at the flurry of snowflakes. They were falling faster now, a frenzied white blur.

"What of selling Ruthven Manor? Is that also a rumor?"

"No, it's true. I have no wish to live there any longer. There are too many memories," he said, his voice coming closer as he moved to stand beside her.

She opened her mouth to ask if he meant memories of her, but thought better of it.

"I thought it was entailed," she said instead.

"It isn't. Ruthven Manor is the ducal seat only because the sixth duke decided he liked Warwickshire better than Cumberland," he said, then added wryly, "Too many Scots, I believe."

As he spoke, his breath fogged the window, and he wiped it away.

"But you did petition for the divorce," she said quietly.

"True."

He turned his head toward her, and, as a matter of course, she turned hers.

"Soon you will be free," he said. His lips curved

slightly, as though he couldn't quite manage a full smile.

"As will you." Her gaze met his steadily, searching for—something. "To find a new wife, a proper duchess."

His half smile faltered.

She turned to inspect the snow again. She'd seen enough. The pain and the longing were still there. "Fallon said you've been acting rather strangely of late."

He didn't answer her, though she waited for a long while. "Philip?"

"I need you to leave," he said, his voice hoarse.

"I—" The words stuck in her throat, and she put a hand there, trying to coax them out.

"Please. Go."

He shoved away from the window and moved to the door, still partially open. Only now he swung it wide, then stood beside it like a statue.

Charlotte walked toward him, her feet heavy. She tried to catch his eye, but he refused to look at her. She felt hollow inside, yet an aching pressure built in her chest at the same time, pushing and pulling and twisting.

Pausing before him, she tried to think of something to say. Something that would ease his pain. But the words she wanted most to say—*I love you*—were the same words she fought so desperately to leave unspoken.

At last she simply left. She walked out the door and down the corridor to the entryway, where she stopped. Fallon was gone from his post.

All she needed to do was open the next door and leave. If she liked, she could make sure she never saw Philip again. It would be easier that way. She could leave London—leave England, even. She could go someplace where no one knew her name, where they didn't know she'd once been a duchess, or that she'd played the role of a harlot. It wouldn't matter where, as long as she was far away from Philip. She would be safe then. And though she would continue loving him from afar, he would never be able to hurt her again.

All she had to do was open the door.

Philip listened to the sound of Charlotte's footsteps as they gradually receded down the hall. If he'd ever thought there was the slightest chance Charlotte would forgive him and one day return to him, it was gone now.

He hadn't expected her to say she loved him. But for her to suggest that he could so easily replace her by finding a new wife, to reject his love for her—

He simply couldn't bear to be in the same room with her any longer.

The worst of it was that he continued to hold her image before him, the opposite wall a canvas for her beauty.

She'd been sad, as Mr. Lesser reported. He'd seen that immediately when her gaze first met his. And worried. A crease lay between her brows, and her mouth was drawn downward just the tiniest bit at the corners.

Yet still she was beautiful, her sadness and her worry making her appear tragic rather than haggard, as most women would have. Philip had stepped toward her, his first thought to comfort her. But then her eyes flashed with a warning, and he remembered she did not want his comfort.

Once again, she'd made it all too clear that she didn't want him.

How he wished he'd have loved her three years ago, wished he could take back those god-awful words when he revealed that he'd married her only to exact revenge against Ethan, that he had lied to her. How he wished he hadn't been so caught up in himself—in his pride and his self-righteous anger.

Philip closed his eyes, swallowed against the pain.

And that's when he heard it.

The sound of her footsteps down the hall, tapping out a rhythm unique to her, one he'd long ago memorized.

She was returning.

Philip's eyes opened wide as the rhythm changed; she'd begun to run.

He whirled toward the doorway just as she stumbled to a halt, her arm reaching out to brace herself against the door frame.

She stared at him, gasping for air. Her cheeks were flushed, her eyes bright. Locks of her hair had tumbled down at the sides, below her bonnet, and he could see a pin hanging precariously at the end of one dark strand.

"I love you," she declared, her chest heaving.

He couldn't speak. He didn't trust the words; he'd hoped for too long. She'd said she loved him before, but she hadn't stayed.

"Did you hear me, Philip?" she asked, moving toward him. She stopped an arm's length away. "I said I—" Her voice broke, and her eyes glistened with unshed tears.

And once again, Philip had to fight not to reach for her. His hands clenched, his fingers digging into his palms.

"I love you," she repeated steadily. The slender column of her throat worked as she swallowed.

He took a hesitant step toward her. "Charlotte—"

She held out her hand. "Don't. Not yet. I need to say . . . I need to tell you. After our wedding night, I tried to make myself hate you. I've spent the last few years convincing myself I hated you. You betrayed me, and—"

"I deserved it," he said quietly.

She nodded, then dashed a tear away from her cheek.

"Go on."

"I tried so hard to protect myself from you. And I thought I'd succeeded. I thought you could never hurt me like that again. But then you said you loved me—"

"I do love you," he interjected, stepping toward her again. This time, he wiped away the tear for her. "God, Charlotte, I love you so much. I wish I could tell you—"

She lifted a finger to his lips, then shivered when he pressed a kiss to it. "Then you lied to me again. I should never have let myself believe you, but I wanted to. I wanted to believe you'd changed."

Philip's chest tightened. That, also, had come too late.

"I've been fighting with myself over coming to you," she whispered. "I needed to prove I was strong, that you couldn't affect me anymore." The tears began to stream down, too fast for him to catch each one. And she laughed—a soft, nervous laugh that tore at his heart. "But none of it matters. I belong with you—not at Sheffield House, not at Ruthven Manor, but here, where you are. I'm miserable without you. I hurt more without you than anything you ever did. I know I didn't say that right, but I hope you can understand—"

"Shh." He wrapped his arms around her then, enfolding her in his embrace. And at once he felt whole again, no longer just a man with an empty title.

"I love you," he murmured in her ear, at her temple, against her cheek. His lips traced over the path where her tears had fallen. "I'm sorry, my darling. Charlotte. I'm sorry for everything. You will never know—"

He covered her mouth with his own, then groaned as she responded with the same urgency. Her hands caught in his hair and she pressed herself against him.

He tried to tell her with the kiss everything he wasn't able to say. The words he couldn't write down in a poem, the romantic phrases she deserved to hear, the full extent of his love for her which he would never be able to adequately express. There was no rhyme or meter, but only softness and heat and the rich, addictive taste of her.

At last he broke away. "Thank you," he murmured against her mouth.

"For what?"

"For loving me. For giving me one more chance." He kissed her again; he couldn't help it. "I promise it will be the last one I need."

"It better be," she said, staring into his eyes. After a minute, she withdrew from his embrace and pushed him aside to shut the door behind them.

"I will contact my solicitor tomorrow to cancel the petition."

She paused, her hand still on the handle. "I never asked you to cancel the petition."

Philip stopped breathing. "I thought—"

"*Tsk, tsk*, Your Grace." She shoved away from the door. "I would have thought you'd have learned by now. There you are again, trying to control everything."

She drew a finger down the center of her throat, past her collarbone to the valley between her breasts. Philip's heart lurched in his chest, and suddenly he was breathing again—much, much faster than before.

She lifted her other hand and began to draw off her gloves. Slowly, the fabric lingering at the vulnerable flesh of her wrists.

Charlotte glanced up at him through her lashes. "You have much to make up for before I decide I don't want a divorce, after all. I might need some convincing." Dangling the pair of gloves in the air, her lips curved seductively. "Do you think you can convince me, Philip?"

The gloves dropped to the floor. He watched them land on the rug between them, then looked up to meet her gaze. Her eyes sparkled with laughter, desire—and love. Finally, love.

"I will certainly try my best," he said, and strode toward her.

The alley below was filthy and smelled rank, and if he fell off the ledge, Lord Alexander St. James was fairly certain he would land on a good-sized rat. Since squashing scurrying rodents was not on his list of favorite pastimes, he tightened his grip and gauged the distance to the next roof. It looked to be roughly the distance between London and Edinburgh, but in reality was probably only a few feet.

"What the devil is the matter with you?" a voice hissed out of the darkness. "Hop on over here. This was your idea."

"I do not *hop*," he shot back, unwilling to confess that heights bothered him. They had since the night he'd breached the towering wall of the citadel at Badajoz with forlorn hope. He still remembered the pounding rain, the ladders swarming with men, and that great black drop below....

"I know perfectly well this was my idea," he muttered.

"Then I'm sure, unless you have an inclination for a personal tour of Newgate Prison, which, by the by, I do not, you'll agree we need to proceed. It gets closer to dawn by the minute."

Newgate Prison. Alex didn't like confined spaces any more than he liked heights. The story his grandmother had told him just a few days ago made him wish his imagination was a little less vivid. Incarceration in a squalid cell was the last thing he wanted. But for the ones you love, he thought philosophically as he eyed the gap, and he had to admit that he adored his grandmother, risks have to be taken.

That thought proved inspiration enough for him to leap the distance, landing with a dull thud but, thankfully, keeping his balance on the sooty shingles. His companion beckoned with a wave of his hand and in a crouched position began to make a slow pilgrimage toward the next house.

The moon was a wafer obscured by clouds. Good for stealth, but not quite so wonderful for visibility. Two more alleys and harrowing jumps and they were there, easing down onto a balcony that overlooked a small walled garden.

Michael Hepburn, Marquess of Longhaven, dropped down first, light on his feet, balanced like a dancer. Alex wondered, not for the first time, just what his friend did for the War Office. He landed next to him, and said, "What did your operative tell you about the layout of the town house?"

Michael peered through the glass of the French doors into the darkened room. "I could be at our club at this very moment, enjoying a stiff brandy."

"Stop grumbling," Alex muttered. "You live for this kind of intrigue. Lucky for us, the lock is simple. I'll have this open in no time."

True to his word, a moment later one of the doors creaked open, the sound loud to Alex's ears. He led the way, slipping into the darkened bedroom, taking in with a quick glance the shrouded forms of a large canopied bed and armoire. Something white was laid out on the bed, and on closer inspection he saw that it was a nightdress edged with delicate lace, and that the coverlet was already turned back. The virginal gown made him feel very much an interloper— which, bloody hell, he was. But all for a good cause, he told himself firmly.

Michael spoke succinctly. "This is Lord Hathaway's daughter's bedroom. We'll need to search his study and his suite across the hall. Since his lordship's rooms face the street and his study is downstairs, this is a much more discreet method of entry. It is likely enough they'll be gone for several more hours, giving us time to search for your precious item. At this hour, the servants should all be abed."

"I'll take the study. It's more likely to be there."

"Alex, you do realize you are going to have to finally tell me just what we are looking for if I am going to ransack his lordship's bedroom on your behalf."

"I hope you plan on being more subtle than that."

"He'll never know I was there," Michael said with convincing confidence. "But what the devil am I looking for?"

"A key. Ornate, made of silver, so it'll be tarnished to black, I suspect. About so long." Alex spread open his hand, indicating the distance between the tip of his smallest finger and his thumb. "It'll be in a small case, also silver. There should be an engraved *S* on the cover."

"A key to *what*, dare I ask, since I am risking my neck to find it?"

Alex paused, reluctant to reveal more. But Michael had a point, and moreover, could keep a secret better than anyone of Alex's acquaintance. "I'm not sure," he admitted, quietly.

Michael's hazel eyes gleamed with interest even in the dim light. "Yet here we are, breaking into a man's house."

"It's . . . complicated."

"Things with you usually are."

"I'm not at liberty to explain to anyone, even you, my reasons for being here. Therefore my request for your assistance. In the past you have proven not only to think fast on your feet and stay cool under fire, but you also have the unique ability to keep your mouth firmly shut, which is a very valuable trait in a friend. In short, I trust you."

Michael gave a noncommittal grunt. "All right, fine."

"If it makes you feel better, I'm not going to steal anything," Alex informed him in a whisper, as he cracked open the bedroom door and peered down the hall. "What I want doesn't belong to Lord Hathaway, if he has it. Where's his study?"

"Second hallway past the bottom of the stairs. Third door on the right."

The house smelled vaguely of beeswax and smoke from the fires that kept the place warm in the late-spring weather. Alex crept—there was no other word for it—down the hall, sending a silent prayer upward to enlist heavenly aid for their little adventure to be both successful and undetected. Though he wasn't sure, with his somewhat dissolute past—or Michael's, for that matter—if he was at all in a position to ask for benevolence.

The hallway was deserted but damned dark. Michael clearly knew the exact location of Hathaway's personal set of rooms, for he went directly to the left door and cracked it open, and disappeared inside.

Alex stood at a vantage point where he could see the top of the staircase rising from the main floor, feeling an amused disbelief that he was a deliberate intruder in some-one else's house, and had enlisted Michael's aid to help him with the infiltration. He'd known Michael since Eton, and when it came down to it, no one was more reliable or loyal. He'd go with him to hell and back, and quite frankly, they *had* accompanied each other to hell in Spain.

They'd survived the fires of Hades, but had not come back to England unscathed.

Time passed in silence, and Alex relaxed a little as he made his way down the stairs into the darkened hallway, barking his shin only once on a piece of furniture that seemed to materialize out of nowhere. He stifled a very colorful curse and moved on, making a mental note not to take up burglary as a profession.

The study was redolent of old tobacco and the ghosts of a thousand glasses of brandy. Alex moved slowly, pulling the borrowed set of picklocks again from his pocket, rum-maging through the drawers he could open first, and then setting to work on the two locked ones.

Nothing. No silver case. No blasted key.

*Damn.*

The first sound of trouble was a low, sharp, excited bark.
Then he heard a woman speaking in modulated tones—
audible in the silent house—and alarm flooded through
him. The voice sounded close, but that might have been a
trick of the acoustics of the town house. At least it didn't
sound like a big dog, he told himself, feeling in a drawer
for a false back before replacing the contents and quietly
sliding it shut.

A servant? Perhaps, but it was unlikely, for it was truly
the dead of night, with dawn a few good hours away. As
early as most of the staff rose, he doubted one of them would
be up and about unless summoned by her employer.

The voice spoke again, a low murmur, and the lack of a
reply probably meant she was talking to the dog. He eased
into the hallway to peer out and saw that at the foot of
the stairs a female figure was bent over, scratching the ears
of what appeared to be a small bundle of active fur, just a
puppy, hence the lack of alarm over their presence in the
house.

She was blond, slender, and, more significantly, clad in a
fashionable gown of a light color. . . .

Several more hours, my arse. One of Lord Hathaway's
family had returned early.

It was a stroke of luck when she set down her lamp and
lifted the squirming bundle of fur in her arms, and instead
of heading upstairs, carried her delighted burden through
a door on the opposite side of the main hall, probably back
toward the kitchen.

Alex stole across the room, and went quickly up the
stairs to where Michael had disappeared, trying to be as
light-footed as possible. He opened the door a crack and
whispered, "Someone just came home. A young woman,
though I couldn't see her clearly."

"Damnation." Michael could move quietly as a cat, and
he was there instantly. "I'm only half done. We might need
to leave and come back a second time."

Alex pictured launching himself again across more ques-
tionable, stinking, yawning crevasses of London's rooftop
landscape. "I'd rather we finished it now."

"If Lady Amelia has returned alone, it should be fine," Michael murmured. "She's unlikely to come into her father's bedroom, and I just need a few more minutes. I'd ask you to help me, but you don't know where I've already searched, and the two of us whispering to each other and moving about is more of a risk. Go out the way we came in. Wait for her to go to bed, and keep an eye on her. If she looks to leave her room because she might have heard something, you're going to have to come up with a distraction. Otherwise, I'll take my chances going out this way and meet you on the roof."

With that, he was gone again and the door closed softly.

Alex uttered a stifled curse. He'd fought battles, crawled through ditches, endured soaking rains and freezing nights, marched for miles on end with his battalion, but he wasn't a damned spy. But a moment of indecision could be disastrous with Miss Patton no doubt heading for her bedroom. And what if she also woke her maid?

As a soldier, he'd learned to make swift judgments, and in this case, he trusted Michael knew what the hell he was doing and quickly slipped back into the lady's bedroom and headed for the balcony. They'd chosen that entry into the house for the discreet venue of the quiet private garden, and the assurance that no one on the street would see them and possibly recognize them in this fashionable neighborhood.

No sooner had Alex managed to close the French doors behind him than the door to the bedroom opened. He froze, hoping the shadows hid his presence, worried movement might attract the attention of the young woman who had entered the room. If she raised an alarm, Michael could be in a bad spot, even if Alex got away. She carried the small lamp, which she set on the polished table by the bed. He assumed his presence on the dark balcony would be hard to detect.

It was at that moment he realized how very beautiful she was.

Lord Hathaway's daughter. Had he met her? No, he

hadn't, but when he thought about it, he'd heard her name mentioned quite often lately. Now he knew why.

Hair a shimmering gold caught the light as she reached up and loosened the pins, dropping them one by one by the lamp and letting the cascade of curls tumble down her back. In profile her face was defined and feminine, with a dainty nose and delicate chin. And though he couldn't see the color of her eyes, they were framed by lashes long enough they cast slight shadows across her elegant cheekbones as she bent over to lift her skirts, kick off her slippers, and begin to unfasten her garters. He caught the pale gleam of slender calves and smooth thighs, and the graceful curve of her bottom.

There was something innately sensual about watching a woman undress, though usually when it was done in his presence, it was as a prelude to one of his favorite pastimes. Slim fingers worked the fastenings of her gown, and in a whisper of silk, it slid off her pale shoulders. She stepped free of the pooled fabric, wearing only a thin, lacy chemise, all gold and ivory in the flickering illumination.

*As a gentleman*, he reminded himself, *I should look away.*

The ball had been more nightmare than entertainment, and Lady Amelia Patton had ducked out as soon as possible, using her usual—and not deceptive—excuse. She picked up her silk gown, shook it out, and draped it over a carved chair by the fireplace. When her carriage had dropped her home, she'd declined to wake her maid, instead enjoying a few rare moments of privacy before bed. No one would think it amiss, as she had done the same before.

It was a crime, was it not, to kill one's father?

Not that she *really* wanted to strangle him in any way but a metaphorical one, but this evening, when he had thrust her almost literally into the arms of the Earl of Westhope, she had nearly done the unthinkable and refused to dance with his lordship in public, thereby humiliating the man and defying her father in front of all of society.

Instead, she had gritted her teeth and waltzed with the most handsome, rich, incredibly *boring* eligible bachelor of the *haut ton*.

It had encouraged him, and that was the last thing she had wanted to happen.

The earl had even had the nerve—or maybe it was just stupidity—to misquote Rabelais when he brought her a glass of champagne, saying with a flourish as he handed over the flute, "Thirst comes with eating ... but the appetite goes away with drinking."

It had really been all she could do not to correct him, since he'd got it completely backward. She had a sinking feeling that he didn't mean to be boorish; he just wasn't very bright. Still, there was nothing on earth that could have prevented her from asking him, in her most proper voice, if that meant he was bringing her champagne because he felt, perhaps, she was too plump. Her response had so flustered him that he'd excused himself hurriedly—so perhaps the entire evening hadn't been a loss after all.

Clad only in her chemise, she went to the balcony doors and opened them, glad of the fresh air, even if it was a bit cool. Loosening the ribbon on her shift, she let the material drift partway down her shoulders, her nipples tightening against the chill. The ballroom had been unbearably close and she'd had some problems breathing, an affliction that had plagued her since childhood. Being able to fill her lungs felt like heaven, and she stood there, letting her eyes close. The light wheezing had stopped, and the anxiety that came with it had lessened, as well, but she was still a little dizzy. Her father was insistent that she kept this particular flaw a secret. He seemed convinced no man would wish to marry a female who might now and again become inexplicably out of breath.

Slowly she inhaled and then let it out. Yes, it was passing. . . .

It wasn't a movement or noise that sent a flicker of unease through her, but a sudden, instinctive sense of being watched. Then a strong, masculine hand cupped her elbow. "Are you quite all right?"

Her eyes flew open and she saw a tall figure looming over her. With a gasp she jerked her chemise back up to cover her partially bared breasts. To her surprise, the shadowy figure spoke again in a cultured, modulated voice. "I'm sorry to startle you, my lady. I beg a thousand pardons, but I thought you might faint."

Amelia stared upward, as taken aback by his polite speech and appearance as she was by finding a man lurking on her balcony. The stranger had ebony hair, glossy even in the inadequate moonlight, and his face was shadowed into hollows and fine planes, eyes dark as midnight staring down at her. "I ... I ..." she stammered. *You should scream*, an inner voice suggested, but she was so paralyzed by alarm and surprise, she wasn't sure she was capable of it.

"You swayed," her mysterious visitor pointed out, as if that explained everything, a small frown drawing dark arched brows together. "Are you ill?"

Finally, she found her voice, albeit not at all her regular one, but a high, thin whisper. "No, just a bit dizzy. Sir, what are you doing here?"

"Maybe you should lie down."

To her utter shock, he lifted her into his arms as easily as if she were a child, and actually carried her inside to deposit her carefully on the bed.

*Perhaps this is a bizarre dream. . . .*

"What are you doing here? Who are you?" she demanded. It wasn't very effective, since she still couldn't manage more than a half mumble, though fright was rapidly being replaced by outraged curiosity. Even in the insubstantial light she could tell he was well dressed, and before he straightened, she caught the subtle drift of expensive cologne. Though he wore no cravat, his dark coat was fashionably cut, and his fitted breeches and Hessians not something she imagined an ordinary footpad would wear. His face was classically handsome, with a nice, straight nose and lean jaw, and she'd never seen eyes so dark.

Was he really that tall, or did he just seem so because she was sprawled on the bed and he was standing?

"I mean you no harm. Do not worry."

Easy for him to say. For heaven's sake, he was in her bedroom, no less. "You are trespassing."

"Indeed," he agreed, inclining his head.

Was he a thief? He didn't look like one. Confused, Amelia sat up, feeling very vulnerable lying there in dishabille with her tumbled hair. "My father keeps very little money in his strongbox here in the house."

"A wise man. I follow that same rule myself. If it puts your mind at ease, I do not need his money." The stranger's teeth flashed white in a quick smile.

She recognized him, she realized suddenly, the situation taking on an even greater sense of the surreal. Not a close acquaintance, no. Not one of the many gentlemen she'd danced with since the beginning of her season, but she'd seen him, nevertheless.

And he certainly had seen *her*. She was sitting there gawping at him in only her thin, lacy chemise with the bodice held together in her trembling hand. The flush of embarrassment swept upward, making her neck and cheeks hot. She could feel the rush of blood warm her knuckles when they pressed against her chest. "I . . . I'm undressed," she said unnecessarily.

"Most delightfully so," he responded with an unmistakable note of sophisticated amusement in his soft tone. "But I am not here to ravish you any more than to rob you. Though," he added with a truly wicked smile, "perhaps, in the spirit of being an effective burglar, I should steal *something*. A kiss comes to mind, for at least then I would not leave empty-handed."

*A kiss?* Was the man insane?

"You . . . wouldn't," she managed to object in disbelief. He still stood by the side of the bed, so close that if she reached out a hand, she could touch him.

"I might." His dark brows lifted a fraction, and his gaze flickered over her inadequately clad body before returning to her face. He added softly, "I have a weakness for lovely, half-dressed ladies, I'm afraid."

And no doubt they had the same weakness for him, for

he exuded a flagrant masculinity and confidence that was even more compelling than his good looks.

Her breath fluttered in her throat and it had nothing to do with her affliction. She might have been an ingenue, but she understood in an instant the power of that devastating, entirely masculine, husky tone. Like a bird stunned by smoke, she didn't move, even when he leaned down and his long fingers caught her chin, tipping her face up just a fraction. He lowered his head, brushed his mouth against hers for a moment, a mere tantalizing touch of his lips. Then, instead of kissing her, his hand slid into her hair and he gently licked the hollow of her throat. Through her dazed astonishment at his audacity, the feel of his warm lips and the teasing caress caused an odd sensation in the pit of her stomach.

This was where she should have imperiously ordered him to stop, or at least pushed him away.

But she didn't. She'd never been kissed, and though, admittedly, her girlish fantasies about this moment in her life hadn't included a mysterious stranger stealing uninvited into her bedroom, she *was* curious.

The trail of his breath made her quiver, moving upward along her jaw, the curve of her cheek, until he finally claimed her mouth, shocking her to her very core as he brushed his tongue against hers in small, sinful strokes.

She trembled, and though it wasn't a conscious act, somehow one of her hands settled on his shoulder.

It was intimate.

It was beguiling.

Then it was over.

God help her, to her *disappointment* it was over.

He straightened and looked more amused than ever at whatever expression had appeared on her face. "A virgin kiss. A coup indeed."

He obviously knew that had been her first. It wasn't so surprising, for like most unmarried young ladies, she was constantly chaperoned. She summoned some affront, though, strangely, she really wasn't affronted. "You, sir, are no gentleman."

"Oh, I am, if a somewhat jaded one. If I wasn't, I wouldn't be taking my leave lest your reputation be tarnished by our meeting, because it would be, believe me. My advice is to keep my presence here this evening to yourself."

True to his word, in a moment he was through the balcony doors, climbing up on the balustrade, and bracing himself for balance on the side of the house. Then he caught the edge of the roof, swung up in one graceful athletic motion, and was gone into the darkness.